"Deception runs through everything."

Jewel's expression was bleak as she looked at her aunt. "I don't think I can bear this, Judith. I had an identity. Who am I now? I don't even think I want to continue with the law firm. They represent Copeland Connellan. From the way Keefe Connellan spoke, he wants me out."

"Does he, now? How could he blame *you* for anything?" Judith demanded hotly. "You had no control over your own birth."

"Hard to argue with that, but he seems to think I'm manipulating the present situation." She managed a discordant laugh. "And it's all based on assumptions—on jumping to conclusions."

"He may have discovered the truth, Jewel—a truth that's as new to me as it is to you. But it all adds up. Travis Copeland used to visit the station on behalf of his father. Your mother was a very pretty girl." Judith shook her head. "And she always did have a talent for keeping secrets."

Dear Reader,

At some time we all have to grapple with the difficulties of family—as well as drawing strength and pleasure from its great joys. This story is about how one young woman tries to deal with her life when she discovers, at the age of twenty-five, that her true parentage has been kept secret from her. A monumental discovery and one that creates many new problems, invading every aspect of life. Think how those problems would be compounded if the "new" family considers itself under threat. Human beings aren't always understanding and tolerant, let alone ready to accept an "outsider" without suspicion. The best one can do is find the courage to reach out, find a way to link the past with the present.

I hope you enjoy Jewel's story. I enjoyed writing it. It has been a great pleasure and an exciting challenge for me to join the ranks of Harlequin Superromance. As always, I want to convey to my "new" audience my great love for my unique homeland, Australia. Who knows, it might lure you to come Down Under!

Margaret Way

Books by Margaret Way

HARLEQUIN SUPERROMANCE
762—THE AUSTRALIAN HEIRESS
966—THE CATTLE BARON

HARLEQUIN ROMANCE
3595—A WIFE AT KIMBARA
3607—THE BRIDESMAID'S WEDDING
3619—THE ENGLISH BRIDE
3671—MASTER OF MARAMBA

Secrets of the Outback
Margaret Way

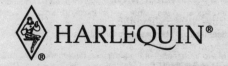

HARLEQUIN®

TORONTO • NEW YORK • LONDON
AMSTERDAM • PARIS • SYDNEY • HAMBURG
STOCKHOLM • ATHENS • TOKYO • MILAN • MADRID
PRAGUE • WARSAW • BUDAPEST • AUCKLAND

ISBN 0-373-71039-9

SECRETS OF THE OUTBACK

This edition published by arrangement with Harlequin Books S.A.

® and TM are trademarks of the publisher. Trademarks indicated with
® are registered in the United States Patent and Trademark Office, the
Canadian Trade Marks Office and in other countries.

Visit us at www.eHarlequin.com

Printed in U.S.A.

This book is dedicated to Diana Palmer,
who once told me, "If I can do it, so can you!"
Thanks, Diana.

PROLOGUE

February, 1981

STEVE BISHOP, overseer of a remote Outback cattle station, sat in one of the back pews of the Anglican cathedral in the Queensland State capital, thinking he'd never had an experience like this. In fact, it had to be the most extraordinary occasion he had attended in his thirty-one years. Living the way he did in the vast, sparsely populated Outback, he was in awe of the crowd. Used to counting head of cattle, he estimated there had to be at least three thousand people packed into the church, all sitting bolt upright in the crush. Outside on the street, mourners who couldn't make it through the door stood twenty deep, prepared to smile if a camera came near. Inner-city traffic had ground to a halt. So had business.

Today was the funeral of one of the most powerful and influential men in the nation: Sir Julius Copeland, mining magnate, land baron, executive chairman of the giant mining firm Copeland Connellan Carpentaria. Self-confessed Titan.

Important as Sir Julius had been, Steve had had no idea the funeral would be so huge. Or so glittering. Most people, himself included—and it had set him back—had suited themselves in funeral black. But the women treated their somber gear as some sort of blessing in disguise. They wore jewelry. None of your costume jewelry stuff. Lots of extravagant yellow gold. Ropes of pearls and diamond brooches that sparkled brilliantly as they caught the light. He had the notion that just one of those brooches could feed an Outback family for a year. The hats were spectacular, too. Fit for the Melbourne Cup.

The cathedral with its miles of red carpet was redolent with not only the vaguely sickening scent of flowers, great banks of them, but the smell of *money*. Big money. Power. The milieu in which Sir Julius had lived and become a monolith of industry.

As expected, the dignitaries sat up front, striving to look lofty—the governor of the state, along with the roly-poly premier who was working hard to suppress his usual big vote-winning smile. The dour leader of the Opposition sat a pew behind, holding a snowy white handkerchief to his face as though he had a nosebleed or was grieving for the deceased. Steve recognized the federal senator sent to represent the prime minister. This was the same guy he and his cattleman friends had shouted down when the senator last came Outback to deliver more empty promises. Behind them sat the representatives of the legal and business communities, their expressions masked. Then there were the cattle barons, land owners and lesser mortals, all of whom had braved the scorching heat—heck, it was hotter in the capital than in his desert home!—to pay their respects to a giant among men. At least, that was how the press had described Sir Julius in his obituary.

Steve had read it that morning with a sense of mounting wonder and irony. Sir Julius had been all sorts of things, but no one in his right mind could've called him a nice guy. Julius Copeland had been an ogre. Six foot four, built like an armored tank. Voice like the rumble of thunder. Pale ice-blue eyes sharp enough to drill holes in cement. He might have been larger than life, cleverer, more determined, more ruthless than most, but he hadn't been liked, let alone revered. Maybe *loathed* would describe it. Steve had been surprised by his boss's sudden death of a massive heart attack, but he honestly couldn't say he felt any sorrow. With no provocation, Julius Copeland had made life difficult for many, many people, including him.

Now it was time for Sir Julius to meet up with his own Boss. Yet as villains went, Steve supposed Copeland had to be a long way down the list. After all, there was Hitler, Stalin, Nero, Genghis Khan...

Across the aisle, in the front pew, sat the widow, Lady Davina Copeland, a woman much respected for her dedication to public affairs. Fighting for equality for minority groups, that kind of thing. One could say she had set herself in direct conflict with her husband. God knows why she'd ever married the man. They couldn't have hit it off. Steve could only glimpse her from the back. She looked like a woman half her age. Of course, he'd seen grainy photographs of her in the newspapers over the years, but he'd never seen her in the flesh. She was supposed to be beautiful. Very glamorous. He was determined to get a good look at her before he went home. Her godawful son Travis sat beside her. Tall, dark, saturnine, a real personage in his own opinion. Some women might find him attractive, Steve reasoned, rubbing his chin, but Travis Copeland had always made him feel downright queasy. Though Travis always acted like a power to be reckoned with, he was in no way competent to step into his father's shoes. He wasn't a total dolt, either, Steve supposed. The business community would've figured *that* out. Travis's upper-crust wife sat beside him, spine straight, allowing his body to touch hers at the shoulder. She was good-looking, sure, but skinny enough to make a man weep. It couldn't be all sunshine for Travis. Steve had heard, too, that the wife was a bit of an ogress. Must've rubbed off from her father-in-law. Steve knew they had a child, Amelia, a few years older than his own little darling. Amelia wasn't in attendance. Probably she'd been judged to be too young. Funerals weren't very pleasant at the best of times, but especially if you were a friend of the family. Now, little Amelia's grandfather, the man who'd been so very important to the state and to so many lives, would shortly be laid to rest.

If they ever got through the eulogies, Steve thought, loosening his tie. Too many. Too long. Some of them *had* to be tongue-in-cheek. Especially the archbishop's. He had to have some knowledge of Copeland's true nature. The Sir Julius that Steve knew, his boss, owner of Mingaree Station, and a string of other pastoral properties adding up to some five million hectares, was a bastard in anyone's language, and you'd better believe it.

Forgive me, Lord. Steve momentarily bent his head, ashamed of his irreverence. Not that the good Lord wouldn't agree after He'd talked to the man, however briefly. Julius Copeland had been intimidating beyond belief, so rough of tongue he made the crudest station hand blush. A complete contrast to his partner of the old days, Sir Stafford Connellan. Steve had had the greatest respect for Sir Stafford, knighted, like Cope-

land for service to his country. The big difference was
that Sir Stafford had been a great man, a bred-in-the-
bone gentleman. A real thoroughbred, now sadly deceased. Sir Stafford's son, Earle, had succeeded his father in the firm. Steve could just see where Earle
Connellan sat, his lean handsome face solemn, with his
dark-haired wife, Rebecca and their only child, a son
of around thirteen, Keefe. The boy was the image of
his father which was to say strikingly handsome, but
there was more to it. Like his father and grandfather
before him, he had that aura of integrity and high intelligence. That special look of breeding. Industrial giant though he'd been, Sir Julius had never had that. No
doubt, in time the boy Keefe would become a force in
the firm. The Connellans were still major shareholders,
despite Sir Julius's best efforts to outwit them after Sir
Stafford's death. No sense of decency there.

The Connellans, too, were possessed of great wealth,
but they'd always had virtually the opposite approach
to it. Earle Connellan stood head and shoulders above
the likes of Travis, whom Steve detested for a number
of reasons. Earle was a great guy, a man you could talk
with, no side to him for all his privileged background.
Travis, though, was an arrogant son of a bitch. Pretty
much thought himself a god. As did his old man. Not
that Steve and Thea had to suffer Travis much these
days. At one time, Travis had flown into the station
regularly in his Beech Baron, but not for ages now.
Come to that, Steve hadn't visited the city in years.
Today he was part of a contingent of cattlemen who'd
traveled a thousand miles and more to attend the great
man's funeral. Damn near mandatory. It was easy to
tell who the cattlemen were. Though suitably dark-
suited, all of them to a man balanced their trademark

akubras on their knees. As did Steve. He'd nodded to most of them as they made their bowlegged way in. Horsemen. And it showed.

Landowners were up front, as befitting the guys who owned the whole caboodle. Employees were at the back. Steve didn't mind. He wasn't part of this world of wealth and privilege. He didn't want to be. Steve considered himself blessed. He had a job he enjoyed. Plenty of back-breaking work, of course, but he was well-paid and he had security of tenure if only because he knew his job and had a good business head. He had the sweetest wife, too, his loyal Thea. She had given him such happiness since the moment he put his ring on her pretty finger. Above all, he had Jewel. God, he adored that child! She was his life. Six going on seven. The most adorable, the spunkiest, smartest, most affectionate daughter a father could want. Hair of spun gold. In total contrast, her delicate winged eyebrows were many shades darker than her hair, almost black. She had blue eyes of such radiance that he had bypassed the name she'd been christened, Eugenia after Thea's mother, to settle on the only name possible when one looked into those sparkling eyes—Jewel. Jewel Bishop. Nowadays no one on the station called her anything else. His little Jewel. His sweetheart. His treasure. He couldn't wait to get back to his "girls." He already knew what he was going to bring them as gifts. Every trip away, even a trip like this, Steve bought his girls surprises. He loved the moment they opened them, the way their eyes lit up with love for him. His girls. His life.

The service droned on to the point that he actually considered getting up and stretching his legs. About time things got moving. He couldn't bear being trussed up in this city gear. And the heat! Some guy choked up and had to be led off. Must've been an act. Still, this was no place for such an unChristian thought, Steve decided. He lowered his curly dark head to his hymn book, joining a choir of uniformed kids from one of the posh schools. Probably Sir Julius's alma mater. He tried to visualize Julius Copeland as a small boy. Couldn't. He'd always figured Sir Julius had sprung into this world fully grown—and had believed the old boy could never die. Now Sir Julius's final destination was waiting. Steve didn't know exactly where that would be, but he wouldn't be a bit surprised if Sir Julius was going straight to hell.

TEN MINUTES LATER, Steve got his first good view of Lady Copeland as she made her dignified way down the aisle. No one to support her. She probably felt as though a great weight had been lifted from her shoulders. She didn't look from side to side. She didn't look at anyone. Steve had to keep reminding himself of her age. She was Travis's mother, which had to put her well into her fifties, but behind the short black veil she wore over her face—he thought only royalty did that—she looked as youthful as her daughter-in-law.

Steve found the opportunity to study her again outside. He was tempted to go up and say hello to her. Explain he was overseer of one of the Copeland cattle stations. Of course he didn't. He hung around watching the VIPs go, instead. Her elegant beringed hand came up to push back the short veil. Now, for the first time, Steve saw her face exposed to the brilliant sunlight.

Lord God! He gulped as a terrible malevolent humming started up in his head. The clarity of shock and the pain almost felled him. In one soul-destroying moment of revelation, Steve knew his whole life had been stolen from him. He reeled with the impact. Slammed into something hard. A stone pillar. He knew beyond any doubt that he could never be happy again.

The face of this woman, Davina Copeland, was the same magical face as his own daughter's. The resemblance was startling. Here was the mould for the face of the child who had given him all the joy in the world. His daughter, Jewel. There was the hair, dressed differently, of course—maybe the woman's owed a little these days to artifice—but it was the same thick, gleaming gold. There were the distinctive winged black brows, the heavily fringed blue eyes that shone like jewels.

Now all those hazy questions he'd sealed away in his mind broke out of the vault. He turned in blind anguish, his feelings of betrayal so powerful that they were beyond words. He looked for and found Travis Copeland. The destroyer was standing by himself. Without hesitation Steve moved in. He would have liked to shout "Adulterer!" but his throat closed up. Travis was sweating and shaking, just standing there staring at him. Knowing what was coming.

Before anyone could stop him, Steve Bishop, superbly fit, launched himself at the man who had dishonored his wife, ruined his life. He grabbed him powerfully by the shoulder, then—as mourners turned, both aghast and agog—punched Travis so hard in the face that he was knocked clear off his feet. Copeland's patrician nose was most assuredly broken. Steve had felt the crunch, but without any satisfaction.

A woman in a chic black suit began to wail. Not the widow. Not the wife. Perhaps they realized this sort of display was bound to happen sooner or later. While

Travis Copeland sprawled on the stone steps, his nose gushing blood, police descended on Steve Bishop. They overpowered him swiftly although he offered no resistance. He rocked back and forth on his feet, his face ashen, not a shadow of regret in his eyes. Steve Bishop was in an altered state from which he would never give himself time to recover.

It was impossible to hide things. In the end they always came out.

CHAPTER ONE

The present

MONDAY MORNING. Traffic was heavier than normal. Jewel swung a U-turn, not exactly sure if it was legal, and took a different route, only to find some of the lights were out on Station Road, which put her farther behind. Another couple of delays would precipitate a minor crisis. She would be late for her Monday morning "chat"—a quaint tradition—with her boss, Blair Skinner, a man she found extremely abrasive. Few in the prestigious law firm of Barton Skinner Beaumont didn't, but they all wanted to hang on to a career. Instead they made jokes about him behind his back.

A vacant parking space in the small basement of her office building almost caught her unaware. She drove into it nearly dizzy with relief. The only real way to secure basement parking was to arrive early. Which she always did. Except today.... Someone, bless him or her, had obviously called in sick.

Jewel grabbed her handbag, so expensive she really should insure it, then locked her car by remote. She made directly for the lifts, feeling reassured, despite her workouts at the gym, that there were a few fellow workers about. Must've been stalled by the same set of lights. A few weeks back, another young woman who worked in the building had had a bad scare when a man approached her, pulling a gun from an inside pocket. As it later turned out after a comparatively easy citizen's arrest—the young woman's rescuer was a prominent footballer—the gun was a fake and the man had a long history of psychiatric problems. Still, no one needed an experience like that. There really should be security, she thought for perhaps the hundredth time, knowing full well it wasn't going to happen.

In the handsomely appointed ladies' rest room—thank God Barton Skinner Beaumont hadn't gone unisex like they did on *Ally McBeal*—Jewel checked herself in the mirror. Skinner demanded that the three female associates of the prestigious law firm that bore his name—well, his grandfather's—be groomed to perfection. Impeccable himself in all matters of dress, manners and taste, Skinner was very severe about it. Up until recently, Barton Skinner Beaumont hadn't even allowed bright young women through their hallowed portals. All vacancies had been filled by bright young men. But Jewel, who held firmly to the belief that women could achieve anything, had become a prime target for Skinner's "wit." Not that the male associates were entirely spared. They, too, received a fair sprinkling of Skinner's sarcastic comments without a one of them game enough to tell him to mind his own business. Extraordinarily enough, Jewel had. That was what came of being born in the bush.

Skinner wasn't going to catch her out today, even if he tried an average of three times a week. Today she'd dressed in a brand-new suit, which had substantially set her back, fine-quality midnight-blue wool, austere but beautifully cut. Under it, to add flair, she wore a brilliant silk blouse, turquoise striped with fuchsia, matched exactly by her lipstick. Incredibly, Skinner noticed things like that. The turquoise intensified the blue of her eyes. She'd had her hair cut recently to just past chin length. It fell thick and heavy in a side-parted classic pageboy. She used to wear it much longer, the way the ex–man in her life liked it, but this was a fresh start. Why did women always cut their hair on such occasions? Perhaps she could find out with a few sessions on a psychiatrist's couch. Not that she trusted psychiatrists. Not after the way they'd sorted out her mother's problems—from depression to grand psychosis.

Just thinking about it was an agony, even though it had been going on for years and years. Determinedly Jewel redirected her attention to the mirror. With her suit she wore good daytime jewelry. Nothing tacky. So what if she could only afford 9-carat gold? It was tasteful, understated. Anyone might think she'd been hired as a clotheshorse instead of a pretty good corporate lawyer, she thought with a grin. No, not *pretty* good. She was underrating herself. She was darn good, and moving up the ladder. A welcome raise after the Stanbroke deal had allowed her to indulge her weakness for beautiful shoes—which might've had something to do with the fact that she'd had to go barefoot for much of her childhood.

OUTSIDE SKINNER'S DOOR, Jewel knocked, then stood back, certain Skinner would permit himself the pleasure of making her wait. She didn't think it was worth brooding about it; it made her laugh. Finally came his peremptory "enter," as though he could ill afford the time to see her. Jewel opened the door and walked into Skinner's plush inner sanctum. It was furnished with an array of handsome Georgian bookcases holding weighty legal tomes, several favorite paintings by maritime artists and too few chairs, clearly signaling that anyone who wanted to visit him might have to stand up.

As expected, Skinner had his head down, perusing some file he seemed to want to keep secret; he held one arm around it, presumably to prevent Jewel from catching sight of the client's name. Blair Skinner, in Jewel's opinion, was the sort of man who could sour a woman on the entire male sex, but she had to concede that at forty-five he could be rated handsome by the casual observer. He oozed wealth. He loved fashion. He dressed in expensive Italian suits that she knew for a fact cost the best part of two thousand dollars; she'd checked when she'd visited an exclusive men's store with her ex. Skinner had never been known to make a single mistake with his shirts, ties, shoes and socks. He had good regular features that were always darkly tanned, thanks to his yachting expeditions, and a fine head of hair, but the close observer would have rejected those eyes, small and set too close together. Then again, other factors weighed in. He was a brilliant lawyer with a career that went swimmingly and he was, of course, grandson of one of the firm's founders. Nevertheless, Jewel always thought he could have posed for a shot of an upmarket Dirty Rotten Scoundrel. She never stood forlornly in Skinner's office waiting for his attention. She amused herself with thoughts such as this.

Finally Skinner looked up, favoring her with an all-over glance that took in her appearance to the last detail. Not offensive. Not overtly sexual. Just a quick rundown of her appearance and grooming. "My, aren't we glamorous today?'' he said with a languid wave of a well-manicured hand.

"Delighted you think so, Blair." Jewel didn't make the mistake of taking a seat before being invited to do so. That was exactly what Skinner wanted.

Skinner leaned back in his wonderfully comfortable-looking leather. "Yes, you've come on well under my tutelage," he said. "I nearly wept when I first saw you come through my door—what, all of three years ago."

Jewel nodded, not believing he was going to bring up her outfit again—white shirt, designer jeans, navy blazer. A bit on the informal side, but classy.

He was. "I know daggy dress is all the rage in the sticks, but I was frankly horrified to see someone so *scruffy* standing in my office."

As usual, he was exaggerating wildly, and on the strength of her recent achievements, Jewel tried a little taunt. "A good thing for the firm I wasn't marched off in shame."

"The only thing that saved you was your résumé," he reminded her.

"And the fact that I topped my law class, along with winning the University Medal." She would never have been so self-congratulatory with anyone else, but it was part of the routine with Skinner.

"Such revelations! And so many people to speak for you! Wonderful recommendations." He shook his head. "Generally speaking, our young males are the outright winners."

"Were," Jewel emphasized. "But if you look at the results, Blair, they've finally been overtaken."

"Not exactly," he said silkily, "but no sooner do we train them than they mooch off and get married. I hope you're not going to do that, Eugenie,'' he said as though contemplating a crime.

"Not for a good while,'' Jewel assured him. "I'm a touch nervous about marriage. I have a friend who was married for an hour.''

Skinner, divorced himself, almost giggled. "I take that to mean they were doing it for a stunt. I just love our Monday mornings, Eugenie. Even the run-ins. You seem to be one of the few courageous enough to speak your mind.'' Skinner leaned back. "Sit down, Eugenie.'' He paused, his expression reflective. "I simply can't bring myself to call you Jewel like the rest of the office. It's an over-decoration and you don't need it.''

"That's okay. Eugenie is fine. And I get a kick out of your French pronunciation. Besides, I haven't heard it in a long, long time.''

"So who started calling you Jewel?'' Skinner actually looked interested.

"My father,'' Jewel announced casually, although any mention of her father made her feel lonely and sick inside.

"I understand he was killed?'' Skinner stared at her.

Slammed his car into a power pole. "You've already read my file, Blair,'' Jewel pointed out too sharply.

"My dear, please don't take offense.'' Unexpectedly he backed off. "I have indeed studied your file. Smart and ambitious as you are, with an ability to write excellent briefs, you're still extremely lucky to be here. I have to hand it to you, Eugenie. For a little girl from the bush with absolutely no connections, you've turned yourself into a real achiever. A young lawyer with a future. Not easy.''

"But I have you on my side, Blair, rooting for me, showing me the way to professionalism, self-improvement, correct dress and behavior. As only someone born to life among the gentry can.''

He laughed. ''Watch it!'' His smooth cosmopolitan voice was mellow. ''Snob, aren't I?''

''Sincerely, yes.''

''For which you must be grateful.'' Skinner began to hunt through the files on his splendid partner's desk. ''Don't imagine for one minute that my influence hasn't helped you impress the clients. No one who works here can afford to look like a loser—'' He broke off. ''Ah, here it is.'' He withdrew a thick file from the pack. ''Remember the Quinn Corp. thing? We handled their takeover of Omega Enterprises?''

''The Copeland Connellan subsidiary?'' Jewel asked. ''I should. I put a lot of research into that. Around two-hundred pages.''

''I wouldn't have let you do it if I didn't have confidence in you,'' Skinner said a little testily. ''However…things don't appear to be working out. In fact, they're going bad.''

''Really?'' Jewel was surprised. ''I would've thought it was airtight.''

''Except some of Omega's top people didn't fully appreciate that their jobs were on the line. They're suing.''

''You mean Copeland Connellan canned them after the buyout?'' Jewel sat back, frowning.

Skinner nodded. ''Exactly. Their argument was that Omega's top guns turned out to be duds.''

''With their salaries, the Omega people can't have been pleased.''

''Don't worry about them,'' Skinner, never a man to dwell on the misfortunes of others, said equably. ''They're all millionaires. Copeland Connellan has a way of clearing out duds. Anyway, it looks like litigation—which, as we represent Copeland Connellan, we will win. Not saying it won't be tricky. So let's get started. Can't have our biggest client saying they're not getting our immediate attention. Then we've got Kussler Consolidated versus the ATA Group. Pull your chair up here. I'll be shoveling a lot of work onto your desk, so don't go making too many outside plans." He glanced up at her. "By the way, Keefe Connellan will be coming in this afternoon on an unrelated matter. He's accompanying Lady Copeland, which is somewhat surprising given the situation with Travis. I'd like to be able to tell him we're already onto the Omega thing at the same time— Haven't met Keefe, have you?" Skinner asked out of the blue.

"I haven't had that great honor," Jewel said, wondering if Skinner was doing his usual job of trying to confuse her.

"Of course you haven't." Skinner stared at her thoughtfully.

"Then, why ask?"

Skinner suddenly turned on a charming smile. "A clever young lady like you might find a way to contrive it."

Jewel had no idea what he was getting at, and merely shook her head.

"I thought every woman wanted to marry a millionaire," he murmured.

"Finding a millionaire would be the easy part. Marrying him and living happily ever after would be a lot harder," Jewel answered dryly.

"*You* could do it, I'm sure." Skinner narrowed his eyes as though thinking deeply. "Anyway, Keefe rarely comes in. He's a very busy man. Quite brilliant. Extraordinarily responsible.''

''So they say.'' Jewel nodded her head with mock solemnity. According to everyone in the know, Keefe Connellan was guaranteed to become the future executive chairman of Copeland Connellan.

''It's in the genes, of course,'' Skinner said, as though no one in *his* family had ever been accused of being an idiot. ''My family's always mixed with theirs, socially and in business. There was no finer man than Keefe's grandfather, Sir Stafford Connellan. Compared to him, Julius Copeland was a very dodgy character.''

''Who knew how to forge an empire,'' Jewel pointed out. Everyone had heard the saga of Julius Copeland and his great achievements, despite the dodgy bits.

Skinner widened his gray-blue eyes. ''You don't hold any brief for the Copelands, do you.''

''Blair, I don't *know* any of them. As you've frequently pointed out, I was a girl from the Deep North, and before that the bush. I don't mix in your... distinguished circles.''

''Nooo...but you could,'' he said thoughtfully. ''You've got what it takes. I'm absolutely sure there's an interesting story in your background. Something very unusual.''

He made it sound as though she'd been switched at birth. ''Sorry, Blair. Nothing to discover. I had a very ordinary childhood. My father was an overseer on one of the Copeland cattle stations, if you want to make something of that.''

Skinner looked like a man who'd missed out on important information. ''*Really?* This is news.''

''Considering that Sir Julius left a legacy of nearly five-hundred thousand hectares in Outback Queensland, it's not so unusual. My father died when I was six, going on seven. My mother and I went to live with my aunt almost immediately after. My father's early death left my mother a very sad woman. There wasn't much money and she wasn't always able to work. My aunt half-supported me until I could support myself. As you know, I won a scholarship to a very good girls' school. And I worked my way through university.''

"From whence you graduated with top honors.'' He inclined his head in a gesture of exaggerated respect. "I have to say I'm surprised to hear there was any connection to the Copelands. You kept that from me.''

"I didn't know you well enough then. You're not onto something here, Blair. Don't get excited. My father was an employee. A fairly lowly one at that. No real connection at all.''

"So where did you get your brains?'' Skinner asked, his tone suggesting her family had to be a bunch of morons.

"My father and mother helped out,'' she countered, her voice dry. "In addition, my aunt isn't exactly stupid.''

"Which leaves me with one question—who do you *look* like?'' Skinner asked. "Is your mother beautiful?''

"She is to me,'' Jewel said quietly, remembering her mother before grief and depression overtook her.

"Does she have that golden hair, the black brows and sapphire eyes?''

"Blair, this interest is bizarre,'' Jewel said. "Not to mention inappropriate. No, my mother doesn't have my coloring. I believe I resemble my grandmother, Eugenie.'' Though she'd never actually seen a photograph of her grandmother.

Skinner brooded a while. "I know you're considered a warm, attractive young woman, an excellent mixer, everyone seems to like you—and that's not always the case, believe me—but you tend to keep things to yourself."

"Perhaps I picked that up from you," Jewel said smoothly, making him laugh.

"It might seem strange, but when I met you I wondered where I'd seen you before."

"Maybe we met in another life?" Jewel suggested flippantly. "Otherwise our paths would never have crossed. I lived and worked over a thousand miles away."

"True," Skinner said, almost wryly. "All the same, something about you seems familiar. Anyway, if you're very good and handle all the work I give you—for which you know I'll get the credit—I'll take you along to a function or two. Lady Copeland doesn't do as much entertaining as she used to, but Travis loves to splash out. Since his divorce, his beautiful daughter, Amelia, acts as hostess for him. Leaves Travis free to pursue…other interests. He loves the ladies, does Travis. Makes no secret of it. The Connellans are far more private. So much tragedy there."

Jewel looked up, liking Skinner a little better for the soft note in his voice. "Keefe Connellan's father was killed in a mining accident, wasn't he?"

"He wouldn't have been," Skinner answered somber, "except that he was a hero. He went back to save some of the men trapped underground. Freed quite a few, but in the end he was trapped himself. It was a tragedy. None of us really got over it."

"How terrible." Jewel bowed her head, thinking events like that could never be forgotten.

"Rebecca—that's Earle's widow—was very nearly destroyed, but she had her son to think of. She and Lady Connellan, Keefe's grandmother, held the fort until Keefe came of age. Splendid young man. It's an open secret that he has his troubles with Travis—just as everyone knows Travis is trying to land Keefe for a son-in-law. A marriage of dynasties, so to speak."

"It usually works that way." Jewel shrugged. "It's a tough life. I've seen photographs of Amelia Copeland and Keefe Connellan in the papers. Both very glamorous people." Connellan was every woman's dream. A young Sean Connery.

"My dear, you could brush her aside," Skinner surprised her by saying. "She *is* beautiful, as you say, but there's not a lot of sparkle. I like sparkle in a woman. So, I fancy, does Keefe. There's nothing doing so far, despite Travis's best efforts. When I take you to one of their parties, I'll go with you to pick out your dress. Or I'll send you off to a friend of mine. She'll know exactly what's required."

Jewel stared at him, a little dazed. "Blair, I'm overcome."

"That's nice." He smirked. "There *are* perks to being one of my protégées, my dear. Of course, it's not my intention to marry again," he reassured her, quite unnecessarily. Christy, one of her colleagues, had always thought Blair was borderline gay. "It's *glorious* to be free. Now, enough of the chitchat. We must get down to business. I'm expecting Keefe at three, although if something important crops up, he might have to cancel. He has a law degree, did you know? Brilliant legal skills he puts to good use, as well as being a mining engineer. At thirty-two he has more presence than most of the big names in the state. And I believe he intends to take over the whole group eventually. He's developed a reputation as a man with a mission. That mission, so far as I can see, is to get rid of Travis Copeland."

"Sounds like you're a bit in awe of him, Blair," Jewel slipped in gently. Blair Skinner rarely spoke so highly of anyone.

"I consider it an honor to call Keefe my friend," Skinner admitted with a modest smile. "I like to think my maturity and experience has left its mark. I hope so. By the same token I often partner Travis at golf. He's an excellent player. So's Amelia. She could give most of the men a run for their money. Do you play yourself?"

"Nope." Jewel smiled. "Never had the time. Nor the money for expensive clubs. Tennis is my game."

"Don't be ashamed of tennis. If you're good enough, I'll give you a game. I can see you now!"

"Another Anna Kournikova?" Jewel asked blithely.

"Women's tennis was in the doldrums before her," Skinner said in a brisk voice. "I'm with Cash and McEnroe. The best woman player can't match a man. Couldn't come close. Now, you've got your legal pad, haven't you?"

"Open, ready and waiting," Jewel said and held up her pen. She didn't bother to tell him about her cupboard full of tennis trophies. That could wait.

ALMOST TWO HOURS LATER, Jewel made it back to her office, so small that some days she thought she'd faint from claustrophobia. She was about to enter, when Anthea, one of the receptionists, all but bolted down the corridor to speak to her.

"Jewel!"

"Hi, Anthea, anything up?" Jewel turned.

"I wanted to catch you." Anthea spoke a little breathlessly. "They don't have an appointment or anything, but two teenage boys are out front asking for you."

"Are they respectable?" Jewel grinned. "No shaved heads or outrageous tattoos?"

Anthea laughed. "No, they're just kids. Nice-looking, actually. They say they know you."

"Names please, Anthea," Jewel said patiently, desperately wanting to get on with her workload.

"Harry and Josh Hungerford."

"Good Lord," Jewel said. " I have to keep reminding myself that kids grow up. Show them through, Anthea. I grew up in Hungerford country. I can spare them a few minutes, though we'll all be knocking heads just trying to fit in my office."

A few minutes later she was shaking hands with two young men she could easily identify, even if they'd both outgrown her by many inches. "This is a wonderful surprise." She smiled at them warmly, as pleased to see them as they apparently were to see her. "Take a seat. Tell me what's going on in your lives. How's your mother? I hope you've got some good news."

"Well, no, Jewel," Harry, the older boy said, his deep voice cracking. "We couldn't think of anyone else to come to. We know you're a big-time lawyer now. We need help."

"Is something wrong?" Jewel looked from one to the other. "I don't know if I can do anything myself—" She indicated with her arm the stack of files: franchising, floats, syndicates, whatever. "But I can certainly point you in the right direction."

"No," said Josh, staring at her with his bright blue eyes. "We want *you*. You know about our life, Jewel. You know the people in it. You're one of us. From our town. We trust you."

"Well, that's sweet of you, Josh." Jewel was touched by his words. "Suppose you tell me what this is all about. I take it you're here independent of your mother and stepfather?" George Everett, never an attractive man. Jewel had always felt uncomfortable with him.

Both nodded. "Mum has betrayed us, Jewel," Harry said, turning his face away. "Ever since she married Everett, our lives have changed."

Jewel acknowledged that with a sympathetic grimace. "He hasn't been unkind to you, has he?" she demanded with sharp concern. "Abusive in any way?" It didn't seem possible with Sheila, their mother, around. Sheila adored her boys.

"He's never hit us or anything," Harry said, thrusting a hand through his short chestnut-colored hair. "He wouldn't dare. Not these days." Both boys topped six feet and had strapping country physiques.

"It's still abuse, the way he talks," Josh insisted. "He's still the same smart-mouthed, oily character, and he's getting colder and colder." He paused uncertainly. "It's financial, the reason we're here."

"Tell me," Jewel invited, instinctively pulling a legal pad forward. "I know your maternal grandfather Fletcher left you both a great deal of land just outside town. River frontage. I know it was held in trust by your mother. I know it was very valuable land then, which means it's far more valuable now. I know that after your mother remarried, she and your stepfather bought several thousand hectares of adjoining land."

"Nowhere near as valuable." Harry's voice was so tight it was distorted. "Ours has the river frontage."

Josh picked up the story. "Some time after you left town to come down to Brisbane, Mum gave herself and Everett a lease on our land."

"And listen to this—" Harry burst out loudly. "It was for fifty years. A dollar a year. Everett began working it, then they started borrowing big money using our property as security."

"Finally they mortgaged our property when they got into debt," Josh said.

"I don't believe it!" Jewel had seen a lot of fraud and deceit in her business, but she was shocked. "Your mother would never allow such a thing."

Harry shrugged, his expression unhappy. "Mum's not the same person you knew, Jewel. She's changed."

"She's like a puppet." Josh closed his eyes tight, then opened them. "Everett pulls the strings."

"So, where are you two living?" Jewel asked, beginning to feel protective. She had known the Hungerford boys since they were toddlers.

"Not in the house. We've left. We've fixed up the workers' cottage. We live there now."

"And you came all this way to see me?"

Josh folded his arms, suggesting he wasn't leaving until she helped them. "Yeah."

"But there are good solicitors in Cairns and Townsville." Jewel named two of the major cities in the far north of the state.

"Sorry, we trust you, Jewel," Harry said. "Not them. We talked it over. We rang your mum. You'd never betray us. Everett knows all the legal guys up north. He can get around anyone, he's so smarmy, the asshole. He got the bank to lend him nearly a million dollars, remember? The thing is, Jewel, we don't have a future anymore,'' Harry said, his eyes holding hers. ''Grandpa left us that land to work. The Hungerfords have always been on the land. It's our life. His legacy was our future.''

''That's always the way I saw it,'' Jewel said. ''You realize your mother has committed a breach of trust? She held that land in trust for you, her two sons. She had no legal right to mortgage the property. In doing so, she and your stepfather could be said to have squandered your inheritance, which must be worth several million. You're in a position to start legal proceedings. When do you gain direct control, or is that some way off?'' She addressed Harry, but Josh spoke.

''Just over a year. When I turn eighteen and Harry turns twenty. Our birthdays are only a month apart.'' Josh sounded as if they could barely survive until then.

''For that matter, the bank has acted improperly. They knew perfectly well the land was held in trust for you boys. We *all* knew. The whole district. Your grandfather was a highly respected and influential man.''

''One of Copeland Connellan's top mining engineers in the north,'' Josh said proudly, his eyes wandering to Jewel's wall of plaques, tributes, degrees. ''I saw on the board outside that this firm handles Copeland Connellan's legal affairs.''

''That's right, Josh.'' Jewel nodded.

Josh leaned toward her. ''Mum always said you were really going to make something of yourself. You're a corporate lawyer, right?''

Jewel nodded again. ''Corporate and commercial. I had to work hard to earn it. What about you? I take it

you finished your schooling Josh?'' Both boys were
very bright.

"End of last year,'' Josh confirmed.

"And you, Harry? What are you doing?''

"Nothing,'' Harry said glumly.

"But surely your mother wants you to go on to university or agricultural college?''

Both boys sat silent for a moment, looking exceedingly upset. "We're not talking to Mum,'' Josh said
eventually. "We *can't* talk to Mum. It's impossible to
see her without Everett. He doesn't let her out of his
sight. That's his tactic.''

"That's hard!'' Jewel frowned. "You were all so
close. How are you supporting yourselves? Where's the
money coming from?'' she asked.

"Grandpa left us some money, as well,'' Harry said.
"I got mine when I turned eighteen. I'm taking care
of Josh. We're in this together.''

"It sounds like you've been worrying yourselves
sick.'' Both boys looked as if they'd been carrying a
weight of grief on their shoulders.

"It's terrible to know we've lost Mum.'' Harry swallowed. "It's...it's like she's joined some sect. And it's
terrible to know what she's done to us. Are you going
to help us, Jewel?''

Jewel settled back in her chair, pondering the fact
that she was already loaded down with work. "I should
speak to your mother,'' she said.

"You'll never get to her.'' Josh punched one hand
into the other. "It's always the two of them. Everett's
always alongside. I suppose a legal battle would cost
a lot of money?''

"I'm afraid so, Josh. And from what you tell me, it
would be very bitter. Are you absolutely certain you'd

want to work the land if you won the case? Your stepfather and mother own and work the adjoining land.''

"It's not as though we could even sell." Harry let
loose with his anger and frustration. "It's not ours.
We're in limbo. Going nowhere. Everett thinks he has
it all over us. A couple of hick kids. You *have* to help
us, Jewel. We can't deal with all these problems. You
don't know how it feels."

"Oh, I think I do, Harry, and my heart aches for
you. Let me talk to my boss about it." Jewel started
to drum her fingers on the desk.

"What does that mean?" Josh clenched his jaw, obviously anticipating obstacles.

"I'm free to take on cases, Josh, but my boss is the
senior partner in the firm. I'd have to discuss it with
him."

"But you can help us?"

"You can be helped. Understand that. I'd like to be
the one. Where are you staying?"

"With a friend," Josh replied. "You wouldn't know
him. We boarded with him at school. He's a good
bloke. His parents are graziers on the Darling Downs.
They have an apartment for when they come to town.
Dex lives there—it's close to the university. Dex is a
real bright guy. He's studying medicine."

"Listen, why don't I take you both out tonight?"
Jewel suggested. "I'll have spoken to my boss by then.
We can really catch up. You like Italian? Thai? Indian?
Chinese? Don't for the love of God say McDonald's."

"Italian is great." Harry grinned, looking as though
he wanted to embrace her. "That's very nice of you,
Jewel."

"Hey, aren't you guys forgetting how nice your
mother always was to me?" Jewel answered quickly,

shaking her head as she considered what the boys had told her.

"You wouldn't know her now, Jewel," Josh said again, bitterness in his tanned face. "Everett has taken her over. She's his now, the stinkin' fraud."

AFTER THE BOYS HAD GONE, Jewel got feverishly down to work, refreshing her memory of the Omega deal by speed-reading through the file. At the end, she still came to the conclusion, as had Skinner, that the deal was airtight. Omega ex-executives would be ill-advised to go to litigation, but it seemed that was their intent. Bad advice from their lawyers, who would nevertheless line their pockets. It wasn't until after lunch that she had the opportunity to speak to Skinner about the Hungerford boys' situation. She expected—and received— an irritated-sounding response.

"I would've thought you had one hell of a job on your hands already," he said when she was finished.

"I can't walk away from this, Blair. I feel indebted to these boys. To their mother. She was very kind to me when I was a girl. She was directly responsible for a number of fund-raisers to send me off to university. Mr. Hungerford was alive at the time, and the boys were just kids. Really nice kids."

"Then, she's well and truly let them down, hasn't she. If what you tell me is true," Skinner said, his eyes narrowed. "Have you taken the time to check?"

"Of course. I'm thorough, Blair. You know that. Besides, there's money in it for the firm." Which, of course, was Skinner's bottom line. "The land I've been told would fetch around six million in today's market. The boys have a solid case. Their mother, apparently under the influence of her second husband, George Everett, was in breach of trust. She acted wrongly, and so did the bank.''

''How could she be so stupid as to get in so deep?'' Skinner asked. ''It was just a time bomb waiting to go off.''

''I intend to speak to her, with your permission, Blair.''

''Ah, no.'' He shook his head. ''You're not haring off to North Queensland.''

''I can do it on my own time. This weekend. Maybe you'd be good enough to grant me Monday, as well. I'll be on the job. And it'll be wonderful to see my mother.''

Skinner eyes sharpened. ''Of course. She's still up there with your aunt?''

Jewel nodded, keeping her expression cool and calm. ''I wanted her to live with me, but she doesn't like change.''

''Oh, all right, then,'' Skinner lifted his shoulders in a nonchalant shrug. ''It's a helluva distraction, but it has the smell of easy bucks.''

''Thank you, Blair.'' Jewel stood up, preparing to leave.

''I noticed a small error in your preparation of the Mayne Goddard brief.'' Skinner fixed her with such a steely glance that she sat down again.

''Really? A misplaced comma, perhaps?''

''Don't be too clever, my dear. No, it's…'' Skinner slipped his gold-rimmed glasses onto his nose. ''Ah, here it is. Good thing I picked it up. It might have cost us. You said Shipton Technologies funded the initial deal.''

Jewel breathed an inner sigh of relief. ''They did.''

"But surely it was Goddard on their own?" Skinner gave her a steady frown.

"Let me refresh your memory." Jewel spoke pleasantly. "It was supposed to be, but things changed. A man called Elliot stepped in to handle the negotiation, remember?"

Light dawned in Skinner's eyes. "Ah yes, now I do. You're off the hook, Eugenie, when I was so looking forward to catching you out. Shipton Technologies, of course." He gazed across at her, considered a minute. "By the way, if you were to pop in with some papers at around three-twenty this afternoon, I could introduce you to Lady Copeland and Keefe Connellan. They'll be here."

"My goodness. I assure you I'm appreciative of the honor."

"It's a gesture of my confidence in you, dear girl. So for God's sake, be on your best behavior. That sardonic tone might go over well enough with me, but these people are used to a lot of respect."

"I'll be so respectful they'll never know what hit them," she promised with a straight face.

"You might keep in mind that Keefe is a past master at gobbling up small fry," Skinner said acidly.

Like you hung heavily in the air.

CHAPTER TWO

BLAIR SKINNER WAS ALL SMILES, as he shook hands with his favorite clients, then waited until they'd seated themselves—he had special chairs brought in for such occasions—before he returned to his revolving leather armchair behind the desk. Lady Copeland had asked for this meeting, bringing along not her son, Travis, as might under normal circumstances have been expected, but Keefe Connellan. Keefe would provide company, support and advice. And few better, Skinner thought, scanning Connellan's handsome familiar face. Keefe had hair that was almost jet-black, and his eyes were equally dark. They were remarkable eyes, ablaze with intelligence and a shrewd intensity that a lot of people, including Skinner, found daunting, but they also had a marvelous capacity to light up with humor and an ir-resistible charm. Men as well as women felt it. Skinner, the clotheshorse, approved of Connellan's unmistak-able sense of style—the dark-gray suit, beautifully tai-lored to fit his tall, athletic body, the very pale lilac shirt worn with an olive silk tie patterned with lilac, silver and midnight blue. Keefe Connellan looked what he was: a rich, highly successful young man from a powerful and influential family.

Lady Copeland, as usual, was lovely, but getting very fragile. Skinner knew she was seventy-five but she didn't look anywhere near that age. She always dressed beautifully, today in one of her exclusive little suits, in a shade of indigo that was particularly effective with her wonderful eyes. She wore glorious triple-stranded South Sea Island pearls around her neck, chin-length pearl-white hair classically framing a face whose bone structure would probably look good forever. Her skin was extraordinarily unlined. Granted, she had the money for the most expensive skin treatments in the world, but so did other clients of the same age and none of them looked as good. Davina Copeland was and remained a genuine beauty.

She was smiling at Keefe now. Skinner could see the ease and depth of affection that lay between them. They seemed to be seasoned confidants—even co-conspirators. Certainly this kind of bond didn't appear to exist between mother and son, which was possibly one of the reasons Lady Davina Copeland still held the reins of power in Copeland Connellan.

"So?" Keefe asked with his slow smile, deliberately breaking into Skinner's thoughts. "Perhaps we could get started, Blair. I have an appointment in just over an hour. Lady Copeland has filled me in thus far, but perhaps you can tell me more. On the face of it, I don't think we can rule out industrial espionage."

Skinner inclined his head in acknowledgment. "But we want proof."

"Of course." Keefe leaned forward, assuming like lightning a different guise—official, authoritative, keeping his brilliant black gaze on the lawyer. "And I'm quite sure we can obtain it. Inside the law. Just one question."

Skinner hoped he was prepared for it....

WHEN THE KNOCK CAME some twenty-five minutes later, Skinner was so intent on the discussion, he wondered for a moment who would have the temerity to interrupt him when he was with such important clients. Anger flared in his eyes, and he swung around in his revolving chair, remembering at the last moment that he'd instructed Eugenie Bishop to make a calculated appearance around that time.

"Enter," he called curtly, his expression fixed. All exchanges with Keefe Connellan raised him to this level of intensity. Keefe was more than his equal when it came to strategy and points of law. It didn't make him dislike Connellan; rather, Skinner strove constantly to be well regarded by the younger man.

As they all glanced toward the door, Jewel opened it and walked gracefully into the room, her demeanor poised and confident. Before Skinner could open his mouth to introduce her, Lady Copeland, suddenly looking years older, simply slid from her chair onto the carpeted floor.

"My God!" Skinner leapt up in agitation, wondering if he'd imagined the icy hostility that swept Keefe Connellan's face. Clearly they were both shocked. Connellan was already down on his knees, demanding a glass of water. Lady Copeland was already stirring, her face white as a sheet.

"Keefe," she said almost desperately, clutching at his jacketed arm. "Keefe."

"It's all right," he assured her in a strangely harsh tone. "We can handle this, whatever it is. Let me get you up." He put his strong arms beneath her and lifted her into the chair, keeping a steadying hand on her shoulder.

"Is there anything else I can do for you, Lady Copeland?'' Jewel was back within seconds, carrying a glass of cold water, which she offered to the woman.

"Who are you?" Lady Copeland asked in a quavering voice. She clearly wanted some sort of answer, but Jewel felt it was beyond her.

"I should've explained," Skinner said hastily. "This is one of our associates. Eugenie Bishop, Lady Copeland."

"Bishop?" Connellan turned to stare at Jewel.

"I don't understand." It was impossible to ignore the hostility that emanated from him, the half-horrified, half-fascinated expression on Lady Copeland's face.

"Here, let me help you." Jewel moved quickly, seeing Lady Copeland's hand shake badly. She didn't even pause to consider that Lady Copeland might reject her help. As it happened she didn't, allowing Jewel to assist her in bringing the glass to her mouth.

"I'm so sorry. Are you feeling better?" Jewel asked, bending to peer into the older woman's face.

"I'm fine." Lady Copeland gave a faint little smile that struck Jewel oddly as very brave after that sudden, shocking collapse.

"And why is Ms. Bishop here, precisely?" Keefe Connellan looked at Skinner with unconcealed contempt.

"Mr. Skinner was after a particular file," Jewel fired back levelly. She'd never met a man like Connellan. Who the devil did he think he was? She felt a wave of answering aggression. More to the point, what had she missed? She'd surely missed *something*. He was looking at her as though she was playing some high-stakes game. Or as if she had secrets to hide. What on earth was going on? Whatever reaction she'd been expecting, it wasn't this.

Connellan now held out his hand like a man used to a great deal of authority. "Show me."

"I'm sorry, Mr. Connellan, it's confidential." She kept her expression neutral.

"I thought it might be," he said. "I'd like to see it, all the same."

Skinner interrupted uneasily. "Look here, Keefe, Ms. Bishop is one of our finest young lawyers and my protégée. She did a lot of research for the Quinn Corp.-Omega takeover. I thought it was time you met her."

"So you arranged it." Connellan's tone was hard.

Skinner shrugged helplessly. "I don't know what you're getting at, Keefe. Or why you're upset."

Connellan took a step closer to Lady Copeland, his manner both protective and daunting. "Are you feeling better, Davina?"

"Perhaps a cup of sweetened tea?" Jewel suggested, already turning to go.

"Thank you, my dear, but no." Lady Copeland spoke quietly and gently. "I'm sorry if Mr. Connellan and I seem distracted."

"We can scarcely fail to be," Connellan said, his voice clipped. "I'm curious, Ms. Bishop. How long have you been with the firm?"

"Three years." Jewel returned his challenging gaze with one of her own.

"Ms. Bishop came to us with wonderful references," Skinner submitted, sounding quite confused.

"And where did you work before that?" Connellan asked.

Such unfettered arrogance, Jewel thought. She named the highly respected law firm in the north.

"But you wanted to come to Brisbane?"

She nodded a shade too curtly. "It's not too terrible

to be ambitious, is it, Mr. Connellan? I needed more demanding work."

"Eugenia graduated top of her class," Skinner pointed out. "Indeed, she won the University Medal. Across all disciplines on all campuses, as I believe you did yourself, Keefe."

Connellan ignored him. "Go ahead, Ms. Bishop. As you might imagine, we're particularly interested."

"Really?" Jewel couldn't mask her surprise. "You only met me a minute ago."

Lady Copeland, who had listened without interrupting, now spoke. "What is your background, my dear?"

Jewel felt astonished by her interest. "I could show you my file, Lady Copeland, but shouldn't I be getting you a cup of tea?" She sought to keep her tone respectful.

"I'll ring for it." Skinner moved quickly to the phone, betraying an uncharacteristic agitation, not without a hint of excitement.

"I find it hard to believe you're a country girl," Keefe Connellan said, his black eyes moving so disturbingly over Jewel that she felt herself flush. She was developing a profound dislike of this too-handsome, too-arrogant, too-rich and powerful man.

"But I am, Mr. Connellan. Take it or leave it. In fact, I was born on an Outback cattle station."

Incredibly he laughed. "I hope you know what you're doing," he said strangely. Facing her, he was disconcertingly close.

"Doing?" Her vivid blue eyes sparkled with anger. Jewel was confident in herself and her own abilities. She refused to let this man belittle or insult her, no matter who he was.

But he smiled at her. A curiously unnerving smile,

for all that it lit his lean, darkly tanned face. "You'd better be good."

Lady Copeland spoke in a voice so strained it seemed almost theatrical. "It's all falling into place. Your father was a Steven Bishop? Overseer on one of our properties, Mingaree Station, some twenty years ago."

Skinner looked over at Jewel quizzically. He had always sensed this girl had some mystery to her. Was that what it was all about? Her father? What had Bishop done?

Jewel inclined her gleaming blond head, one side sweeping forward to shield her face. "He was. Perhaps you could tell me, Lady Copeland, why you and Mr. Connellan are so interested. My father died tragically, as you must know—or perhaps you don't. He wasn't important in your scheme of things."

"I didn't know him, my dear," Lady Copeland confirmed gently. "I saw him only once in my life, at my late husband's funeral."

"I was six at the time," Jewel answered, just as quietly. "I don't really remember Dad going, but my mother told me he attended the funeral with a party of cattlemen."

"What else do you remember?" Keefe Connellan asked.

Jewel turned on him with magnificent disdain. "He never came home."

In the midst of the bitterness, he suddenly sounded sincere. "I'm sorry."

"Blair, I wonder if you'd mind leaving us for a few minutes?" Lady Copeland unexpectedly took the initiative. "I would appreciate it."

Keefe Connellan intervened. "Davina, I don't think

this is the right time. You just fainted and you're still very pale. I should take you home.''

"Ten minutes, no more." Lady Copeland threw him a trusting smile.

"Take as long as you want, Lady Copeland," Blair Skinner said, not meeting Jewel's eyes. "I have things I can attend to."

He went to the door, practically colliding with a secretary carrying a silver tea tray. The secretary smiled at Jewel, who went to her and said thank you, then put the tray down on a side table. As Skinner shut the door, Jewel poured Lady Copeland a cup of tea, asking over her shoulder if she took milk.

"No, my dear. No sugar, either, but perhaps today…''

Jewel ladled in two teaspoons and passed the elegant cup and saucer to Lady Copeland, who took it with a steadier hand. "Tell me about yourself," Lady Copeland invited, gesturing to the armchair Keefe Connellan had vacated. He stood, arms folded, and leaned against Skinner's desk.

"You're dying to tell someone, aren't you," he said.

"Pardon me, but are you insane?" Jewel let her own hostility spill over.

He stared at her for a few moments, his handsome face drawn into somber lines. "I'm so very sorry, Ms. Bishop, if I'm Goddamn offending you."

"Keefe!" Lady Copeland endeavored to soothe him. "Maybe she doesn't—"

"Doesn't what?" Jewel asked, finding the whole situation bizarre. Yet was it? Now that she was really looking at Lady Copeland, she was swept by a strange sense of familiarity.

"Does your mother live with you?" Lady Copeland asked, sipping her tea, then putting it down.

"My mother lives in Hungerford, North Queensland, where I was raised. Perhaps you can give me a clue, Lady Copeland. I have no idea what you're getting at."

"You haven't looked in the mirror for a while?" Keefe Connellan asked in a dark voice.

Jewel sat back wearily. "Could this possibly be the nature of your enquiry, Mr. Connellan? My appearance?"

Though she spoke sardonically, inside her was growing panic, confusion, even fear.

"So it's come to you at last. My, my, my!" he drawled, eyes snapping.

In desperation, Jewel turned to Lady Copeland, who was now excessively pale. "Please tell me! I swear I don't know what this is all about." Lady Copeland was gazing at her with such a strange expression but for the moment seemed quite unable to reply.

"We didn't get much notice, either," Keefe Connellan said, his handsome features drawn tight. "Tell me, are there many golden-haired, black-browed, sapphire-eyed women in your family?" he asked. "Don't look so stunned. You're a beautiful woman with very distinctive features."

"So?" Jewel spread her hands. "Please continue."

"But, Ms. Bishop, you've even got your hair cut the same way. Tell me, are you and Skinner enjoying this? I assure you your enjoyment won't last long."

Jewel stood up, her mind racing. This meeting had implications that were deeply disturbing. They could also cost her her job. "There's no way I can continue to sit here and listen to this," she said. "Either you come out with the information you appear to have, or

I'll break all the rules by walking out on you." Arrogant son of a bitch. He could get her fired, but she no longer cared.

Behind her Lady Copeland sighed heavily. "My dear, I may be almost three times your age and I, too, am breaking all the rules by saying this, but you're the living image of me when I was in my twenties."

"The question is, why haven't *you* noticed?" Keefe Connellan demanded before Jewel could hope to speak.

He moved suddenly, taking her by the arm and guiding her toward a gilded mirror that hung between two ceiling-high Georgian bookcases.

"Please let go of me," Jewel said from between clenched teeth. Her confusion was growing.

He removed his hand immediately but continued to watch her with careful eyes, their two heads reflected in the mirror. "Are you going to tell us what's going on, Ms. Bishop?" he asked.

She felt as though she was hardly breathing. "Fine, there's a resemblance," she conceded. "I see it now, but I was never looking for it. Hardly! All I can say is that it's a coincidence. And for the record, Blair Skinner has never remarked on any such resemblance."

"He must have known," Connellan said.

"Known what?" She swung on him. Tall herself, she had to look up at him. "What sense is there in keeping me in the dark? I'm not a fool. You seem to be implying that Blair Skinner and I have devised some strategy to bring me to Lady Copeland's attention."

"Haven't you?" he challenged.

"Please, Keefe." Lady Copeland spoke quietly.

Jewel ignored him and walked back to where Lady Copeland was sitting. She noticed that a fraction of color had come back into the woman's face. Jewel sat down so her own face would be level with the older woman's, staring into eyes she now saw with shocking clarity were indeed like her own. "I wouldn't for the world be party to any plan to upset you, Lady Copeland. Neither would Blair Skinner. He respects you greatly. It was exactly as he said. I've done quite a bit of work on the Quinn Corp.–Omega takeover. I'm well thought of in this firm. He felt it was time I met some of our more important clients."

"Surely you could up with something better than that?" Connellan stood tall, his expression cool and cutting. An imposing figure who clearly didn't believe her.

"I don't think I could come up with anything better than the truth. In any case, this isn't a courtroom, Mr. Connellan," she reminded him.

"But you're playing a dangerous game."

"Nonsense!" she said emphatically.

"Perhaps, my dear, we've all been taken by surprise?" Lady Copeland suggested, still looking as if she'd seen a ghost.

"Or you and Mr. Connellan have leapt to a conclusion," Jewel countered. "I don't allow myself to be used by anybody. That includes my boss."

"Maybe you could visit me so I could find out more about you." Lady Copeland for all her power and influence seemed to be pleading.

Jewel stared back at her, perturbed. "There *can't* be any connection between us, Lady Copeland, no matter how strong the resemblance. Isn't it said we all have a double somewhere?"

"Perhaps not so close to hand. I have to admit you play the game well," Keefe Connellan said dryly.

Jewel faced him, terribly unnerved but determined

not to be thrown off balance. "Game, what game?" she asked. "Why do you seem to think it's your place to confront me, Mr. Connellan? Why this hostility? My God, it fills the room! I don't feel the same antagonism coming from Lady Copeland." It was perfectly true. Lady Copeland's demeanor was curiously nonthreatening.

Connellan merely shrugged. "To answer your question, I've known Lady Copeland all my life. I care about her. We're part of a tight circle. Whoever disturbs her, disturbs me. I wonder if you fully appreciate that."

"I'm not afraid of you, Mr. Connellan." Jewel met his gaze unflinchingly.

"Perhaps you should be." A faint smile curved his mouth. "What was the plan? First the meeting, then the blackmail?"

It was an insult too great to be borne. Before she knew it, Jewel's hand flew up spontaneously and she struck Keefe Connellan across his arrogant face.

The silence in the room was profound. Jewel felt her heart flutter.

"Oh God, I didn't mean that," she said.

"Yes, you did." Connellan rubbed his cheek thoughtfully. "It's a first, anyway. I'm sure you'll tell me next that you're the proud possessor of a black belt."

"I apologize," Jewel said, feeling his whole aura intensely. "But you have to admit you deserved it."

"What else have you got up your sleeve?" he enquired with mock politeness.

Jewel was utterly exasperated. "I want to hold onto my job. I deeply regret this upset, but I feel I'm the innocent victim here." She turned to Lady Copeland, who appeared to be hanging on her every word. "This is the first time I've ever laid eyes on you, Lady Copeland. I'm sorry if—for whatever reason—that makes you sad." And sorrow was the expression printed on Davina Copeland's face.

"Oh, it does, my dear." Lady Copeland flung a narrow hand to her heart. "Forgive me, but…you're not hiding anything from us?"

This would be ridiculous if it weren't so disturbing. "I'm sorry, Lady Copeland. I've already told you no. If we've finished our conversation, I should get back to work."

Again Keefe Connellan intervened. "So how did you get this job? Who offered it?" He glanced at his watch.

"I'm not sure this is any of your business, Mr. Connellan."

"Oh, it is," he muttered grimly.

"I was recommended to Mr. Skinner by Professor Goldner from the university," she said, knowing he would check.

"So Skinner is definitely mixed up in it?"

Jewel sighed in disbelief. "I haven't the vaguest idea what you mean. I came with very good references and recommendations. Let's get that straight."

"By all means," he said tersely.

"I hope you're discreet, Ms. Bishop?" Lady Copeland suddenly appealed to her.

Jewel frowned. "Lady Copeland, what do I have to be discreet about? Do you think people will gossip if they notice our strong resemblance?"

Keefe Connellan exhaled loudly. "You bet your life they will. It's impossible to miss."

"Do you think so? They'd have to be looking for a

hidden mystery then," Jewel said. "However, it hardly matters, since I don't move in Lady Copeland's circles."

"No doubt Skinner hoped to change that?" He spoke so sharply his words gave Jewel a twinge of fear.

They stared at each other like combatants, neither yielding, both tense. "No need to investigate Blair Skinner," Jewel said firmly. "He never puts a foot wrong."

"You mean *so far*," Connellan returned curtly. "Playing us for fools would guarantee disaster." He moved then, touching Lady Copeland's delicate shoulder. "I think we should go, Davina. Jacob will take you home and drop me on the way. I have an appointment with Drew Westaway uptown. I'd break it, but it's critical." He glanced at Jewel, brilliant black eyes narrowed. "You can inform your boss we're leaving," he said, his face taut.

"If that's what you want. Let me say again that I deeply regret any upset I may unwittingly have caused you, Lady Copeland. I'll speak of it to no one."

Connellan laughed—an attractive if discordant sound. "That's a bit rich. Skinner can't wait to discuss this."

"What do you expect, given your attack on me? Naturally I have to say *something*."

"Of course. Is your mother in on this, too?"

Nothing so far had prepared Jewel for that. She went white. "My mother is a very sick woman, so watch it, Mr. Connellan. I'd just love to slap you again."

"Only this time, I'll deal with it," he promised, gently propelling Lady Copeland to the door.

Nearing it, Lady Copeland paused. "If I asked you to come and visit me, would you consider it, Eugenie?'' Her still-beautiful face revealed a strange longing.

Jewel found herself nodding, lured somehow by the use of her Christian name. ''I think I want that, too, Lady Copeland, just so long as Mr. Connellan is nowhere nearby.''

''Are you sure about that, Davina?'' Connellan shot a questioning look at her.

''Quite sure, my dear.'' She smiled at him and patted his arm. ''I need to learn more about Eugenie. You see that, don't you?''

He turned, studying Jewel's resolute stance. ''I do, in a strange sort of way,'' he admitted. ''Just bear in mind that Ms. Bishop, for all her beauty and avowed brightness, could pry us all apart.''

Shaking inside but using her characteristic self-confidence as camouflage, Jewel went in search of Blair Skinner, finding him in the boardroom frowning over a coffee.

''Well?'' He looked distressed, and was without his usual bold quip. ''Can I go back into my office?''

''They're gone, Blair.'' Jewel resisted a groan. ''Connellan had an appointment.''

''*Mr.* Connellan to you,'' Skinner reminded her stonily and stood up. ''I don't understand this. They left without speaking to me?''

''I'm sure Mr. Connellan will be remedying that,'' Jewel answered abruptly, bringing a chill to Skinner's eyes.

''What exactly is that supposed to mean?''

''Beats the hell out of me, Blair.'' She gave a brittle laugh. ''It'll be mentioned, so I'm not betraying a confidence. It seems that both of them—Lady Copeland

and Mr. Connellan—figure we're playing some kind of game with them. I'm quoting Mr. Connellan himself.''

Skinner actually blanched. ''My God, Eugenia, you can't be serious.''

''I'm deadly serious,'' she said.

He looked at her with a grim expression. ''You're hiding something from me, aren't you,'' he accused. ''I suspected it right from the beginning.''

''Nevertheless you hired me. Why?'' The *why* was starting to worry her.

''Because I thought there was something special about you,'' he answered testily. ''Don't act like a dolt. It doesn't suit you. What caused Lady Copeland to faint? Keefe looked at me quite murderously. It was all about you, wasn't it. And your father. What on earth did he do? If you tell me he made off with Copeland money, I promise I won't scream. God knows, old Sir Julius broke a few laws. But then, he had us legal eagles to get him out of trouble. What does hurt is the fact that you've never seen fit to confide in me, Eugenie.''

''I never thought I had much to confide.''

''Sit down,'' Skinner advised briskly. ''I know you well enough to realize beneath that brazen exterior you're falling to pieces.''

Jewel took a seat. ''I think you're right. What about getting me a cup of coffee—to show you care?''

This was received with a scowl. ''You're really something. You know that?'' He disappeared, then returned a moment later with two steaming china mugs. ''Give it to me straight. Any lies, and I promise you'll be out of here just like that!'' He snapped his fingers.

''You and me both.'' Jewel took a tentative sip. Too hot. At least the coffee was good. ''Blair, I'm going to ask you something." She switched her eyes from the mug to him. "And I'd appreciate the truth. Have you been aware of the resemblance between Lady Copeland and me?"

Skinner's jaw dropped in amazement. Either he was a wonderful actor or he had just suffered a severe shock. "What are you saying, Eugenie?"

"Have—you—ever—noticed?" She leaned closer to him, deliberately spacing her words.

"Sweet, sweet Lord! What a fool I am."

"Welcome to the club. I take it you haven't. However, the cat is out of the bag. Whatever cat it might happen to be." Jewel had just enough left in her to speak flippantly. It was her way of overcoming her own tremendous shock. "Lady Copeland told me she thought I was the image of herself when young."

Skinner put his knuckles in his mouth. He rose to his feet shouting, "That's right!" then fell back, lowering his head and holding it in his hands. "And they think the two of us set up a meeting!" he muttered despairingly.

"I think they saw themselves as two blackmail victims."

"If I've made enemies of those two, I'll have to move abroad. Oh, my God!" he cried. "I could weep."

"Ordinarily I'd enjoy that, but bear with me," Jewel said, taking another gulp of the strong coffee. "I told them you'd never, ever remarked on even a passing resemblance. You are a man of great integrity. I kept assuring them of that. I told them you respected Lady Copeland far too much to ever want to upset her. I explained that I'd never laid eyes on her in my entire life. The whole thing was one monumental coincidence."

"My dear, my mother taught me to be very suspicious of monumental coincidences," Skinner said. "This is not the end," he predicted. "So, how can we make sense of this? Now that the scales have fallen from my eyes, I can see you're a dead ringer for Davina. I knew there was something familiar about you, right from the beginning. I even ran through a few film stars. The young Lana Turner with blue, blue eyes. That kind of look. Soft, sexy yet challenging."

Jewel gazed at him in astonishment. "You thought all this, Blair? Shame on you. I've always seen you as a good, solid father figure." A dreadful lie.

He shook his head. "Just an objective judgment. I have eyes. Or so I believed." He stared at her directly. "What would you advise?"

"You mean, you're going to listen?" This all felt like a strange dream, except that she was actually hurting.

"What I'm saying is you were there the whole time. How did it all end?"

"In Lady Copeland inviting me to visit her."

Skinner made a whistling sound through his mouth. It could have been admiration. "And Keefe?"

"What a gorgon!" Jewel said with a shudder.

"A gorgon, my dear, was one of three snake-haired sisters in Greek mythology. Of course, you didn't have a classical education."

"All right, make that a bastard."

Skinner snorted. "Don't get on the wrong side of Keefe Connellan," he warned her. "He loves Davina. They love each other. I could almost feel sorry for Travis. At one time, his father was threatening to disinherit him. Damn, I'm talking too much. Should I ring him?"

"Who, Connellan? I wouldn't give him that satisfaction," Jewel said disgustedly. "But expect a phone call…"

IT WAS IMPOSSIBLE to concentrate on anything for the rest of the afternoon. There seemed no rational explanation for what had happened in Blair Skinner's office, but it all had to do with the striking resemblance between her and Lady Copeland and the fact that her father had once worked for the family. Jewel was outraged by the way Keefe Connellan had treated her. Outraged by everything about the man. Being with him was like being in an emotional and intellectual combat zone. He acted as though she was cruelly impersonating someone closely linked to Lady Copeland's life. Someone Lady Copeland really needed or cared about. A daughter, a granddaughter who'd died? Jewel couldn't figure it out.

More than anything, she wanted to call her mother to see if Thea could offer an explanation. A couple of times she'd even picked up the phone but knew there was little point in it. Her mother, even if she came to the phone, would be made highly anxious by any kind of questioning. Thea experienced bouts of severe anxiety, and talking to her would do no good at all. In fact, it might make a difficult situation worse. Her mother lived in a permanent state of depression, a kind of helplessness, even worthlessness, that Jewel often found overwhelming.

"Thank God you never took after your mother. I'd go crazy."

That was what Aunt Judith always said. A single woman with a crackling persona, sometimes cyclonic, far from unattractive—she'd once had a fiancé who had simply "vanished," a calamity at the time. It had been two weeks before the wedding and the theory was that he'd been taken by a crocodile on one of his nighttime fishing trips. Judith was thin, terribly thin, but always on the go, impatient, trying to do her best but totally unequipped by nature to deal with a sister who had "emotional problems." In all fairness Aunt Judith had tried to cope with Thea's physical and mental inertia, but her initial sympathy had passed quickly, mainly because she, like Jewel, was a person who was anything but stationary.

Her aunt Judith. Jewel owed her a great deal.

They'd gone to live with Judith after her father's death. Her mother had little money, but she still retained a half-share in the family home, a marvelous spooky old colonial Queenslander some miles out of town. Jewel would never forget her first sight of it. She was an imaginative child, and it had seemed to her the house of a witch. Set in a great blossoming forest with gem-colored birds and enormous blue butterflies circling the riotous overgrown gardens, it was filled with towering palms and soaring ferns and great mango trees whose fruit littered the ground. And there was Aunt Judith confirming her childish suspicions, standing on the deep shadowy front veranda overhung by a scarlet bougainvillea that had woven itself through the length of the white wrought-iron banisters and threatened to bring down the huge pillars that supported the luminous green roof. She stood there, thin arms outstretched, a wild mane of curly dark hair cascading down her back, her clothes like clothes Jewel had never seen before. Long and loose and floating with big stars all over them, like a magician's. She soon learned that outfit was called a caftan and Aunt Judith had painted the stars herself. After the harshness and the terra-cotta colors of her Outback home, it was like being invited into the Garden of Eden—where there were plenty of snakes. It was and remained a magical house, the place her mother and Aunt Judith had been born and where her mother now hid.

Aunt Judith had welcomed them, glad of their company. The day they arrived, the ceiling of the huge living room dripped colored streamers and bunches of balloons hanging from the lovely Chinese lanterns with painted wooden panels that shielded the lightbulbs. But Aunt Judith had quickly come to the realization that Thea wasn't going to be any company, let alone help. To herself, her little daughter or indeed anyone else. And Judith came to realize, not without shock, that her pretty sister, who'd run off to get married when she was barely nineteen, no longer cared if she lived or died. There was only the child to be salvaged.

Me, Jewel thought.

So they'd all settled into their strange new life— Jewel confronting lots of hair-raising experiences in what was virtually a wilderness. Aunt Judith ran a small, successful business in the town. It was a sort of treasure shop selling the handiwork of the artists of the district—a dizzying array of wonderfully dressed dolls and stuffed toys to patchwork quilts, imaginative clothing, exotic cushions, watercolors, oils, pottery, handmade jewelry, clocks, so-called sacred objects, you name it. As a child Jewel had always enjoyed helping Aunt Judith in the shop. Her mother had tried, frowning with concentration over the least little thing, but she couldn't manage it. Thea Bishop's slump into depression had not been gradual. It had been dramatic, dating from the very day her father was killed. Before that, her mother had seemed a different person. Sweet, loving, fun to be with. Then the terrible descent into a kind of quiet madness when only glimpses of her former self showed through. Jewel had lived all her childhood with the knowledge that her mother wasn't like other mothers, but a heartbreakingly sad person, a woman who could never be relied on to help Aunt Judith, to turn up at speech days or concerts or fetes or to fetch her from school in the afternoons. This she had accepted as testament to her mother's grief. A thinking child who had adored her father, Jewel could remember her own terrible pain and sadness when she was told her daddy had gone to heaven. How much worse for her mother to lose her beloved husband, her life's companion, at such a young age. The trauma held her mother in thrall. It refused to let go.

"For God's sake, Thea, other people suffer terrible losses and go on!" Aunt Judith, voice imploring, would urge her sister to try to keep her physical and mental integrity intact. "The child needs you!"

Her mother would stare back at them, lost in some subterranean labyrinth. She had started crying the day she learned of her loss and she had never stopped, falling deeper and deeper into an inertia that was agonizing to watch. Jewel, who loved her mother and was fiercely protective of her, never put her own confused and frightened thoughts into words, even during her mother's worst periods. Aunt Judith did that for her, coming home every night to a sister "off on another planet," under the influence of all the pills that were prescribed by her doctors. At the age of ten, Jewel had taken charge of her mother, reversing their roles, while Aunt Judith strove to keep all three afloat. This arrangement had endured until Jewel won a full scholarship to a leading girls' school, which she'd entered as a boarder with her aunt's full approval and support.

"One of us has got to spring the trap," was the way Aunt Judith had put it. Outwardly sharp and increasingly without sympathy for her sister's "self-inflicted" condition, Aunt Judith nonetheless refused to cast Thea aside. The two of them would "survive, but it won't be much fun!"

So many of the things Aunt Judith had said over the years stuck in Jewel's mind. Her aunt had not been a witch, thank goodness; she was a courageous and unusual woman, with a sharp tongue. The last time Jewel had visited her mother and aunt, just over a month before, they seemed to have eased into an arrangement that worked. Aunt Judith ran the shop, ordered in all the provisions and she'd hired a handyman to halfway tame the spectacular abandoned jungle they lived in, while her mother tried to keep the house in order and have a meal ready for Judith when she arrived home from work. For some years now, Jewel had been able to help out financially, easing the burden on her aunt who, to her great credit, had never complained about all the "extras." As well, Jewel bought her mother's clothes and enjoyed finding unconventional outfits for her aunt. Her aunt Judith had become something of a local celebrity, just as her mother had become the local misfit, the outcast, even if word was she still looked fetching.

Jewel tried hard to organize her chaotic thoughts. The best she could do was speak to her aunt over the weekend. In the early days, Aunt Judith had spent countless hours listening to her sister's mournful outpourings. Maybe Judith knew something that would shed some light on the bewildering situation that had confronted her. Briskly Jewel picked up the phone to book an early-morning flight to the "far north." North of Capricorn. Another world. After that, she would ring her aunt at the shop. It was the usual routine designed by both of them to shield Thea.

CHAPTER THREE

IT WAS AFTER SIX before she left the office, intending to take the bus the couple of blocks to her club, the Caxton. Named after an early female activist, it had been formed a few years back for young, professional women, mostly from legal circles. She enjoyed being part of it and meeting other young women whose interests matched her own. At the club she could relax and freshen up before going on to meet the Hungerford boys at the restaurant. They had assured her they could find it.

It was much too late to go home, home being a small townhouse in a trendy suburb near the river. She was paying it off, but not as quickly as she would've liked. There were too many other considerations, not the least of them keeping up the appearance her job required, especially since Blair Skinner had taken her under his wing. After such a strange and frustrating afternoon, the boys' unhappy home and financial situation had somehow paled into insignificance beside her own affairs. She would have to get herself back on track. Going up north to visit her mother would address two issues at once. Her own family mystery and how Sheila Hungerford, now Sheila Everett, had come to betray her adored sons.

Lost in thought, Jewel didn't immediately notice the big silver-gray limousine that was purring alongside her as she strolled along. Finally it caught her attention, and she swung her head. Shock was like a live wire sparking inside her. The face that looked out at her belonged to Keefe Connellan. She couldn't believe it. Was he following her? He was seated in the rear of the chauffeur-driven vehicle, the window wound down. He called to her, his tone of voice quietly authoritative.

"Ms. Bishop." The limousine slid into a loading zone a short distance ahead, and he emerged from the back seat, leaving the door open and looking toward her. "Could you spare a moment?"

Her pulse picked up and the blood tingled through her veins. She hated the way he was looking at her. "I don't think so, Mr. Connellan. I have an evening appointment." She spoke doubtfully, as if it were a regretful statement of fact. She was careful not to reveal her unease.

"Are you going home?" He, too, kept his tone polite—but managed to sound somehow derisive.

"As it happens, I'm off to my club."

"The Caxton?"

It seemed he approved. Not that she cared. She dropped her pretense, realizing she was under careful scrutiny. "Now, how did you discover that?"

He smiled, a white flash that attracted her in spite of herself.

"Would you believe I have a marvelous networking system?" he said. "Please get in. You're not five minutes away, if we drive you."

Jewel took a decisive step to one side, head up, shoulders straight. "That's quite all right. I like to walk."

"Obviously, since you're in the best of shape." His glance licked over her. "But indulge me."

"What, after today?" Those black eyes made her think of the Medicis and hidden daggers.

"I'm interested in talking to you further," he said mildly, his expression giving nothing away.

"Really? There's nothing to learn."

"We both know there is." He stared down into her face, then he put out a hand and gently grasped her arm.

Jewel's knees turned to mush.

"You're forcing me into your car?" She lifted her brows, feeling an unwelcome thrill she sought to banish.

"I never forget my manners."

"You forgot them this afternoon." Knowing she had little chance of getting away, short of screaming, Jewel slid into the back seat of the Rolls. A smartly uniformed chauffeur sat behind the wheel awaiting instructions. He didn't turn his head.

"The Caxton, Jacob," Keefe Connellan said. He got in beside Jewel, shutting the door.

"Yes, sir. I know it."

Keefe Connellan focused his attention on Jewel, while the chauffeur activated a device to bring up a glass partition between front and back seats.

"This is a lot like getting kidnapped."

He looked at her in mock amazement. "Please don't feel threatened. There's nothing wrong with privacy."

"So you're a private investigator now." Jewel leaned back slightly, her nostrils beguiled by the scent of the plush leather.

"Lady Copeland is someone I care about," he said curtly, revealing the anger beneath the smooth surface.

"She has a *son*," Jewel said pointedly.

"Obviously." He watched her in a way she couldn't fathom. "She has a granddaughter, too."

"Amelia. Yes, I know." Jewel glanced out the window at the homebound crowds. "I've often seen her photograph in the social pages. She's very beautiful. Do you care about her, too?" She tossed her head defiantly, pleased that she'd rattled him.

"Why? Is it any of your business?"

"In my view, yes. If you think it's within your rights to investigate me, why should you object to my right to investigate you? Unless you think being very wealthy gives you some authority over the rest of us."

He turned his lean body so he was confronting her. "What is it, Ms. Bishop, that you hope to achieve? To get close to Lady Copeland? To make yourself a member of the family? You don't know Travis." He shook his head. "He won't be very pleased to welcome you. Neither will Amelia. You're already the cause of intense emotional anguish."

"How?" Jewel demanded, holding his eyes. "No speaking in tongues this time. How exactly?"

His answer, when it came, took her completely by surprise. "You're pretty damn amazing, you know that?"

"I don't care for you, either." She was barely able to remain seated beside him. Large as the interior of the Rolls was, she had never felt so claustrophobic. "In fact, I've never met a man I find so hateful."

"Words. Mere words, Ms. Bishop. What you are is somewhat wary of me. As you should be."

"Particularly as you appear to be stalking me."

His laugh was unexpected and profoundly attractive. "I prefer to say 'running a few checks.'"

"Well, I hope you've dropped Blair Skinner from

your investigation,'' Jewel said. ''He's as straightforward as anyone you could meet.''

He pondered that a while. ''I wouldn't have thought
him the sort of man to pull something like this.''

''Something like what?'' Her eyes opened wide in
indignation. ''This colossal *con?* Is that what it's supposed to be?''

He smiled slightly, no humor in it. ''Perhaps if I
keep you off balance, you'll crack.''

''To hell with that!'' Jewel muttered, one arm extended toward the door. ''There is where I get off.''

''Of course.'' He nodded his coal-black head. ''Perhaps you'll invite me inside for a drink. I haven't seen
the place since they renovated. One of our subsidiary
companies did the job. Leave the door,'' he advised.
''You can depend on Jacob to open it.''

Jewel took a deep breath, glancing at him slowly.
''Oh, what it is to be rich!'' she said in a bitter voice.
''Attendants on every side—and the power to inspire
fear.''

''When did you decide you wanted that, too?'' he
asked tautly.

''I have enough money to live on.'' She shot him a
disgusted look.

''You've got *no* money,'' he corrected, rather in-
dolently.

''I beg your pardon.'' She thought she'd been holding her own but that got to her. He had taken the time
to find out everything, it seemed. A massive invasion
of her privacy.

''A very nice town house,'' he continued in a deceptively pleasant tone. ''You're paying it off. And
look at your beautiful clothes!'' He shifted slightly to

gaze at her, making her very conscious of her body. "Buying clothes must take a lot of your pay."

Jewel stared back for a few moments, her cheeks burning. "God, you're offensive."

"I just keep thinking about what *you're* trying to do," he countered quietly.

"What? Join the Copeland family?" She spoke crisply. "Come on, give me a clue. Instead of looking down your arrogant nose at me. Why don't you share your suspicions? That would be a good start. Obviously, your thoughts differ appreciably from mine."

He wondered how much longer she'd be able to keep up the act, drawn and repelled at the same time. Then he said what he had never intended. Judgment clouded by a beautiful woman? "I'm prepared to talk over a quick drink."

She blinked hard and looked away. "Otherwise, say goodbye to my career, my reputation?"

"That's a take-it-or-leave-it offer," he answered.

EVERYONE LOOKED AT THEM when they walked into the quiet elegance of the Caxton's lounge. There were a few male guests mixed in with the women. All were seated in comfortable leather armchairs ranged around circular tables, nursing drinks and talking in a relaxed fashion. Most of them Jewel knew. She smiled, waved and nodded her way across the room with its attractive contemporary carpet, while most of the eyes widened and the smiles grew.

"It's Jewel—and just see who she's with!"

What they couldn't know was that she wasn't enjoying it. She felt like a fictional character, aware of the little eddies of excitement that ran through the room.

Keefe Connellan knew quite a few people, too, because he lifted his hand, that beautiful white smile flashing.

No sooner were they seated at a quiet table for two overlooking the small rear garden than a waiter appeared, bending over deferentially. ''Good evening, Mr. Connellan. Miss Bishop.''

Jewel nodded, doing her best to smile. ''Good evening, Archie.''

''That's it—*Archie*.'' Connellan took a long look at the waiter. ''You worked at the Polo Club for a while?''

''Yes, sir.''

''And the Queensland. You get around, Archie.''

Archie nodded, grinning delightedly. ''I like a change. Could I take your order, sir?''

Keefe Connellan looked at the quietly seething Jewel, with her golden hair. ''No one drinks much anymore. Not when they're going on to an evening appointment,'' he said, a little sarcastically.

''A martini,'' she said. ''A very, very dry martini. One olive.''

''Fabulous!'' Connellan said. ''I'll join you.''

''When can we stop all this?'' Jewel asked, after Archie had gone, his expression conveying his absolute fascination at seeing them together. ''I think we've moved beyond the conspiracy theory.''

''All right.'' He leaned forward, stared into her deeply blue, black-lashed eyes, aware that every man in the room was staring at her. Why not? Physically she was an inspiration. It was her character that worried him. ''One doesn't have to be a super-sleuth to realize you're somehow related to Lady Copeland. Either that or you've had plastic surgery.''

She forcibly shut down her mounting panic. "What do *you* think?"

"I can't even see the tiniest wrinkle. You have beautiful skin. This, of course, we already know."

Despite the mocking banter, Jewel felt chilled. "I swear I have no idea what you're talking about. I know of no connection. I've lived my life a thousand miles from her. I've already told you that. It would save a lot of time if you answered my questions honestly instead of shrouding everything in mystery."

"You didn't happen to discuss all this with your mother?" he asked, eyes piercing. "I'm prepared to believe she didn't tell you until very recently."

"Tell me what? That I was snatched from the cradle? There was a mix-up at the hospital?" She looked highly skeptical. "That I'm someone's *love child?*"

"Hadn't you already suspected it?" he asked quietly.

Jewel felt the pain attack her temples. "I'm going to get up and go now. What you're saying is impossible. Unforgivable, really."

"Please don't." He reached out, putting his hand over hers, an action she knew would be totally misinterpreted by everyone watching them. "God only knows what people here would make of it," he murmured.

Her cheeks were flushed, and not only with anger. "I don't understand any of this. I only met Lady Copeland today."

"And it was a wonderful performance," he informed her, releasing her hand. "She took to you immediately. It must give you hope."

Jewel turned her head to gaze out the window. Outside in the small Italianate courtyard, a fountain was playing peacefully. No peace inside. "You've allowed yourself to see some kind of conspiracy where there is none. My appearance and the fact that I met Lady Copeland are nothing more than coincidences."

Little brackets appeared at the sides of his mouth. At another time she would have found them sexy. Not now. "I don't think you're going to get many people to accept that," he said. "Feature by feature, the similarity is extraordinary. Skinner had to be blind not to notice it right from the start."

"Why should he?" Jewel met his eyes. "He wasn't expecting any such thing. Lady Copeland must be well into her seventies. I know she still looks wonderful, but one would have to know us both very well for the resemblance to register."

"Exactly," he said, his voice dry. "Hasn't it ever worried you that you resembled no one in your family?"

Jewel attempted to speak; for a moment she couldn't. Why should she tell him her most private confusions? "I could be the very image of my father, for all you know," she said angrily although she still had enough control to keep her voice down. "And this has something to do with my father, doesn't it?"

"It has everything to do with your father," he answered, grim-faced.

"And who is my father?" She was beginning to feel dizzy. "Come on, say it. There has to be some justification for this torture."

"I can't believe you don't know. You're a very clever woman. Fact-finding is part of your daily life. You've seen many photographs of Lady Copeland—who hasn't? She's always inhabited the world of glamour and power. Not only that, she's always been a beauty with a needle-sharp brain.''

''No ornament like her granddaughter?'' Jewel was stung into asking. Everyone knew that Amelia Copeland, the heiress, had claimed immunity from daily toil.

''I'm sure you made it your business to check out Amelia, as well.'' His eyes were black as jet.

''Are you sure she *is* Lady Copeland's granddaughter?'' Jewel asked facetiously, raising her brows. ''She doesn't resemble her in the least. Not in coloring or bone structure. Perhaps I'm the real granddaughter and your girlfriend's an impostor?'' It was a deliberate thrust, and he didn't like it.

''Even if you *were* Lady Copeland's granddaughter, Eugenie, it wouldn't get you far.''

''Really? I thought it would transport me overnight to the family home,'' she retorted.

''Perhaps that's what I mean,'' he said. ''The Copeland household is a dysfunctional one, to say the least.''

''Perhaps you yourself create some of that tension,'' she accused him, herself on the attack.

''The fact that Travis Copeland and I are often at loggerheads has nothing to do with you. As you seem destined to find out. It's no secret. For almost fifty years, Lady Copeland has carried with her a photograph of her little daughter. Her name was Angela. Her golden child.''

Jewel stared down at her hand. It trembled. ''I had no idea Lady Copeland had a daughter.''

His eyes contested that. ''I'm amazed. A fact you missed? It's a matter of public record. The little girl died of bacterial meningitis when she was six.''

''How sad!'' Even her voice trembled slightly.

"Indeed it was. Although Lady Copeland has led a very full and active life, I suspect she's been weeping inside ever since. Angela was, from all accounts, a lovely little girl. A Botticelli angel. Sparkling with life. She looked pretty much the way you would have as a child."

Jewel fought hard to master her emotions. "My God!" she breathed. "You're very cruel."

He gripped the arm of the chair, his knuckles showing white. "And you're very—" He broke off immediately at Archie's approach with their drinks.

"Could I get you anything else?" Archie put down the drinks on the club coasters, then glanced from one to the other, obviously picking up on their tension.

"No, no, thank you." With a flick of his wrist Keefe Connellan produced a wallet, selecting a note that more than covered the price of the martinis. "Thanks, Archie."

"A pleasure, Mr. Connellan. Good evening, Ms. Bishop." Archie accepted the money and all but skipped off.

"I don't want this drink," Jewel said, feeling as nerve-ridden as if there were ghosts at the table.

"Just sip it," he replied. "I'd like to continue this…unique conversation."

"Why? I'm beginning to wonder if you're slightly unhinged," she suggested shortly.

The comment caused him to smile. "I don't think so. Whoever you are, Eugenie Bishop, you're not presenting your case—if you have one—in the right way."

"I have no case," she said angrily. "It's all in your mind. In any event, I'm flying home this weekend. I'll speak to my mother then."

"So she can come up with an explanation? Or perhaps tell you what you should do next?"

She returned his stare coolly. "My mother isn't a well woman."

"I'm sorry. What's wrong with her?"

Her blue eyes flashed. "She suffers from chronic depression. She's done so for many years."

"But surely she can be treated?" he asked, unexpectedly showing concern.

"There doesn't seem to be anything the doctors can do—and they've tried."

"Who's looking after her?"

She stiffened, although this time his tone was anything but confrontational. "I wanted her to come and live with me. But she dislikes change. She lives with my aunt Judith, her sister, in the family home."

"So there are only the three of you? No one else?"

"Unless *you've* come up with someone," she said with more than a touch of bitterness. "My father's death brought about great changes in our lives. My mother has been in deep mourning all these years."

"I'm sorry. That's tragic." He drank a little of his martini, set it down. "It must have affected your whole world."

"Of course." Jewel didn't touch her drink.

"So you sought to correct the past?"

Jewel suddenly reached flash point. She rose from her seat like the jet from the sparkling fountain. "My father was killed. It was a tragedy. Forgive me if I can't speak about it."

She left him sitting at the table, indifferent to the fascinated eyes that watched her progress across the room and into the lobby.

CHAPTER FOUR

IT WAS A LONG TRIP HOME. Two hours in the plane, another hour before she reached Hungerford by minibus, then the town taxi out to the house. The heat did not help her mood. She had almost forgotten how hot it was North of Capricorn, how humid. The driver left her at the gate. She picked up her overnight bag and began the trek through the garden, and its extraordinary lush beauty began the ritual soothing.

The place was drowned in golden-green light, heavy scents and birdsong. Dozens of brilliant rainbow lorikeets were dive-bombing the fruit trees, chattering and screeching. Everything grew in the utmost profusion here. Mangoes, bananas, custard apples, papaws, loquats and guavas; all manner of citrus trees—lemon, grapefruit, mandarin, lime; a whole grove of avocados and, lining the side fence, a row of long-established Queensland nut trees spreading their branches so they interlocked. These wonderful nut trees, native to the state, were *bauples* to the aborigines who had dined on them probably since the dawn of time, macadamias to the rest of the world. Some enterprising Hawaiian businessman had had the foresight to take them back home to found a profitable industry. But the *bauples* belonged to Queensland. Every child in the state knew the frustration of trying to crack the hard shells with a brick before exposing the most delicious of nuts.

Jewel walked on. Perspiration beaded her neck and her temples, trickling down her back. She approached two tall tank stands near the house; Aunt Judith always washed her hair in tank water, encouraging Jewel to do the same. Passionfruit vines climbed all over the stands. At this time of the year they were covered in the bronze-purple fruit. She had never tasted passionfruit as good as the ones that grew at home. Aunt Judith usually made up a beautiful tropical fruit salad fresh from the garden whenever she came to visit.

Someone had recently cut the grass, she noticed. Not a professional job, by any means, but a brave attempt to keep sections of the acreage clear and discourage the snakes. Such a fragrance rose from the earth. Intoxicating, really. Like incense. Jewel paused a few moments beneath a magnificent poinciana just past its flowering; she set down her overnight bag so she could breathe in all the exotic scents. Waxy gardenias massed themselves in the shaded areas; the frangipanis and oleanders flaunted their beauty out in the brilliant sunshine, where the honeysuckle and ginger blossoms gave up their nostalgic perfume. When she'd first come to live here, Aunt Judith had warned her never to touch the oleanders, never to break off the pretty sweet-smelling flowers. Every part of the shrub was toxic. And Judith, being Judith, had gone on to tell her that a woman in the district had tried—mercifully without success—to murder her husband by adding some brewed oleander leaves to his coffee. Jewel had never forgotten that story.

She continued on her way, eyes focusing on the house as it finally emerged out of the semi-jungle. The intervening years had done nothing to lessen her belief that this place was magical. Haunted. Lost in time. The vivid red bougainvillea scrambled over the walls, giving every appearance that it was holding up the house now. She began to whistle the way she used to as a child copying the birdcalls, only this time it was an old song her mother had always loved. "Danny Boy." Her mother was easily startled by strange noises but she would recognize the tune and the whistler.

Before she'd even climbed the steps, her mother was there, rushing toward her with outstretched arms, a tiny creature, slight as a waif despite the oversize muslin dress, with big luminous green eyes and a wild cascade of dark hair.

"Darling, darling, girl."

Incredible, the love and pain that passed between them.

"Mama." Jewel gathered her mother to her, hugging her as if she were a child. Taller by several inches, Jewel felt infinitely stronger, infinitely older. How fragile her mother was. How delicate her bones! Her hair smelled lovely. She must have washed it. "Here, let me look at you." Jewel drew back, holding her mother's shoulders. "You never age."

It was almost true. Her mother, unlike other people, never seemed to grow older. In her late forties, Thea Bishop could have passed for a woman ten years her junior. At a distance, a teenager. She wore no makeup and really didn't need it. Her expression was open, yet her fragile mental state showed itself in every line of her body. "How are you, Mama?" Jewel asked, wondering how her mother could ever face up to the unpleasant questions she needed to ask.

"Terrific. I feel terrific. Never better, darling." The mildness of her voice was at odds with her words.

"What a wonderful surprise! I heard the whistling but I thought I was dreaming."

"But Aunt Judith told you I was coming?"

Her mother frowned in concentration. "Did she?"

"I'm sure she did, Mama, but no worries. I'm here now."

"And it's marvelous!" Her mother laughed aloud, then instantly sobered. "I pray and pray every day that the good Lord will protect you."

"And He does, too, Mama," Jewel said quickly. "Oh, it's good to be home. Let's go in, shall we?"

Aunt Judith came home not long after, thin to the bone, wearing a tiered cotton voile skirt in shades of orange, green and violet, with colored flowers sewn all over it and a rakish little V-neck sleeveless green top that echoed her clear eyes.

"You look great, Jewel!" They both moved to kiss.

"You look wonderful!" "I love the outfit!" They spoke together, stopped, laughed.

"Part of my summer collection!" Judith twirled. "I shut the shop," she told Jewel cheerfully. "I don't want to miss a minute of you while you're home."

"And you're going to love what I've brought you. Both of you." Jewel reached out to put her arm around her mother's waist.

"You spoil us," Thea said, resting against her daughter.

"Sure I do. Because I love you."

"I've been no use to you most of your life," her mother said in a completely different voice. Dull and self-flagellating. "I never took proper care of you. I never did the right thing."

"How about lunch?" Aunt Judith intervened briskly,

turning the conversation. "I haven't had a bite since six o'clock."

"No wonder you never put on a pound." Jewel joined ranks with her aunt, continuing to stroke her mother's trembling back. "I'll help. Give Mama a rest. What's it to be?"

"Ham salad?" Judith suggested blithely, obviously determined to be happy. "There's a beautiful ham in the fridge. Saves Thea worrying about cooking."

"I'm going to do the cooking while I'm here," Jewel announced, striving, as was Judith, to keep the mood light. "I'm a whiz with salads. All sorts of salads. You should try my Indonesian bird's nest salad with peanut sauce. Takes a bit of time, so we'll have to settle for avocado and grapefruit. All those lovely fresh ingredients. It'll go well with the ham."

"Or we've got some smoked salmon, if you prefer," Judith tossed over her shoulder on the way to her bedroom. "Over lunch you can tell us what else has been happening to the Hungerford boys. It wasn't right for Sheila to marry that Everett. I can't ever understand how it happened. He must have laid a spell on her."

Thea turned to her daughter, fear and despair in her look. She whispered, "It does happen. One mistake can change lives."

"Hush, Mama." Jewel spoke gently, very gently, unwilling to stir up the demons. "I can help the boys. I may even be able to help Sheila."

"And *me*, Jewel. God help me," her mother said.

THEY ATE ON THE VERANDA. Judith polished off her lunch, which included a fresh baguette from town, disproving a lot of people's theories that she never ate; Thea merely pushed the ham and greens around her plate but forked a few segments of the ruby grapefruit into her mouth.

Jewel filled them in on her discussion with the Hungerford boys, not sure if her mother was listening; she described their visit to the office and the pleasant catch-up meal they'd shared the night before. She didn't have it in her heart to raise the subject of Lady Copeland, much less her meeting with Keefe Connellan and his veiled accusations. Strangely enough, it was Judith who brought up the fact that the boys' grandfather had been a longtime employee of Copeland Connellan Carpentaria at their copper mine, Mount Esmeralda, some thirty miles inland.

"Frank Fletcher was their top engineer for many years, don't you remember, Thea? Sheila's father?" Judith spoke as though her sister were deaf.

"Why would we want to hear that name here?" Thea shuddered, her eyes filling with tears.

"*What* name?" Judith asked in astonishment. "Fletcher was a grand old man. He'd turn in his grave to know what was going on now."

"Who are you talking about, Mama?" Jewel risked asking, finding her mother's reaction ominous. "Copeland Connellan?" If so, Aunt Judith had really started something.

Thea's green eyes were burning, burning, blazing with intensity. "That name ruined our lives. I never want to hear it in this house."

"Well, it hasn't been used for the past twenty years," Judith said dismissively.

"Why does it make you so unhappy, Mama?" Jewel persisted, trying to keep the urgency out of her voice.

"The way they dealt with me and your father." Thea spoke tightly.

"Thea, does it do any good to go over this?" Judith implored. "Steve's accident could hardly be laid at their door."

"They destroyed him." Thea lifted a bread-and-butter plate and threw it. Then she bent right over, rocking her body.

"*How,* Mama?" Jewel ignored the shattered plate, placing her hand on her mother's neck. She desperately wanted to keep her mother talking, knowing that otherwise all information would be lost to her. "You've never mentioned one word of this all these years."

Her mother straightened, giving a great cry of anguish. "My only wish was to protect you."

"From what?" Jewel caught her mother's wrist and held it.

Thea's eyes filled again. "You've been happy, baby, haven't you?" she whimpered.

Judith exploded. "How the hell could she be happy? You've given up on life, Thea. You let go of the reins. Jewel had to turn into a woman by the time she was ten. You could've saved her from that."

"Judith, please," Jewel begged of her aunt. "Let Mama talk. Something's eating her away inside."

"Well, it sure as hell isn't hormones. Thea went into a decline twenty years ago. Don't tell me the Hungerford kids have stirred up some big mystery."

Mystery? Jewel felt her world begin to crash around her. "All along," she whispered, "I've been aware that so much has been kept from me."

Judith shook her head strenuously. "Not by me, love. I've kept nothing from you because I *know* nothin'. I've lived the good life and followed the commandments. Whatever is eating away at your mother, she's kept it all to her tiny self, the poor poop. In the early days, when you first came to live here, I did everything in my power to get her to open up. It was obvious she was in one hell of a mess. Not even losing Steve could account for it all. Hell, I lost Andy. The bloody crocs took him. But there was no one around to hold my hand or wipe my tears.'' She shook her head. ''We've had more than our fair share of misfortune. Losing Mum and Dad the way we did. They *would* drive into town in a bloody cyclone—'' Judith broke off sounding anguished and angry. She must have been remembering how a tree had come crashing down in their parents' path, crushing car and occupants.

''We're cursed, Judi,'' Thea said, holding her frail body taut. ''I've accepted my punishment.''

''Gawd, here we go again!'' Judith snapped. ''Tell me, whose life is perfect? Personally I find it incredible that you've kept this up so long. Accusing yourself of every kind of weakness. Anyone would think you'd *murdered* poor old Steve.''

Thea sprang from her chair, wheeling so sharply that her dress floated out. ''I did worse, far worse! Better he'd married any other girl.''

''Only he was hooked on you.'' Judith gave a broken laugh. ''You'll never figure your mother out, Jewel,'' she said, watching her niece with pity. ''I've known her longer than you have and I haven't got a clue.''

But Jewel had decided to try. ''So what does this have to do with the Copelands, Mama?'' she continued, although Thea shook her dark head quickly. ''You say *they* destroyed Dad? *How?''*

Her mother's eyes were a deep shining green. ''It was a tragedy. An unbearable tragedy. I can't speak of it. Love killed him.''

"Love?" Jewel's voice rose. "He loved you. He loved me."

"He *adored* you," Thea emphasized. "You were his golden child."

As little Angela had been Davina Copeland's? Jewel was struck by the same description.

"Then, why wasn't *my* love worth living for, Mama?" she asked, reliving for a moment the endless hurts and disappointments.

"That's right, kiddo." Judith applauded her, staring across at her sister in challenge. "Give it to her. Your daughter loves you, Thea. And you let her down."

"I didn't mean to!" Thea started to weep, falling back against the vine covered pillar, oblivious of the thorns.

"Yes, you did!" Judith began to shout, the usual ritual. "And quit the hysterics. Why, in God's name? I never thought Mum and Dad raised a couple of wimps. What happened to you? Anyone would think you carried the sins of the world on your shoulders. What bloody sin did you commit that you can't speak of it?" By now Judith's voice revealed a great weary anger mixed up with pity.

"What do the Copelands have to do with it, Mama?" Jewel, too, hammered away. "Do you realize my law firm represents Copeland Connellan?"

Thea's olive skin blanched and her head shot up. "You've never said." She sounded truly frightened. She even raised her hands to her eyes as though a ghost stood before her.

"Probably realized it was going to be a big problem." Judith flung her mane of dark curly hair, witchlike, over her shoulders.

"Mama, I'll take a plane out of here by nightfall if

you don't speak,'' Jewel threatened, feeling close to tears herself.

"She'll never set foot in this house again,'' Judith added for good measure. "What have you got against the Copelands, Thea? We all know Steve worked for them Outback. Hell, I thought you were happy there. You always said so in your letters. I've still got all the photographs you sent me. Do you want me to get them?'' Judith half-rose, causing her sister to break out in moans.

"Nooo, nooo. For God's sake, have some mercy, Judi.''

"Ah, cool it, Thea,'' Judith said disgustedly. "You're giving me the creeps. All this time, Jewel and I have been showing you mercy at the cost of *ourselves.* I think now we've been doing the wrong thing. What happened at Mingaree Station? What went on? Was there some...unpleasantness? Did Steve get himself into some disgrace? I've often wondered. What did Steve *really* look like? You only brought him home once and there's no good photo of him. I remember he was dark-haired, a nice guy. But who does Jewel look like? Look at her. *Look* at her like you've never bothered to look before. She's a beauty. Okay, so we were pretty when we were young, but neither of us could hold a candle to Jewel. She could be on the cover of some Goddamn magazine. Who the hell does she look like? It sure isn't you and I'm fairly certain it wasn't Steve. Where did she get the golden hair? The black brows and lashes? The violet eyes?''

"From Steve's mother, of course,'' Thea said, wiping her mouth with the back of her hand.

"That's bunkum!'' Judith answered with a hiss. "Blondes like that can marry millionaires. You've said yourself, Steve's family didn't have a cracker. Might as well pack your bags, Jewel.'' She addressed her niece, pointing dramatically to the door. ''Your mother is never going to come clean.''

Jewel felt her heart begin a long painful tattoo. ''Yesterday for the first time, I met Lady Copeland,'' she announced, afraid, so afraid of what was coming. ''She visited the office with Keefe Connellan. That's—''

''I know who he is.'' The words shot out of Thea as wildly as a bolting brumby.

''Keep going, Jewel,'' Judith all but shrieked her encouragement.

''Lady Copeland took one look at me and fainted,'' Jewel told them, stunned she was saying this. ''She simply slid from the chair to the floor.''

It was as though no one breathed.

''Do you know what caused it, Jewel?'' Judith finally asked, the attack draining out of her.

''Do *you* know, Mama?'' As much as she loved her mother, Jewel was determined to back her into a corner.

''Know? How should I know?'' Thea, although she looked heartbreakingly frightened, had a furtive air.

''Then, I'll tell you.'' Jewel pulled her mother into a chair, a little roughly. ''She said, and I could *see* it clearly, Mama, that I was the image of her at the same age. Keefe Connellan also told me he saw a striking resemblance. Even my boss admitted he must've been blind. It could be sheer coincidence, of course, but I don't think so. What does it mean? You're the only one who can tell us.''

Thea stared back at her, pale. ''Darling, darling, take my hand.''

Jewel did so, tightening her two hands around her mother's. "Whatever it is, Mama, remember I love you. Nothing will change that."

"But it *is* nothing, my darling," Thea wailed. She looked honestly shocked. "You're my daughter. Steven was your father. I know nothing about Lady Copeland. She never ever came to the station. Sir Julius himself came infrequently."

"God, Thea. I kinda hoped you'd make an effort," Judith burst out. "So who *did* come, Thea? Came a lot. Was it that bloody son of hers—what's his name, that nasty Trevor?"

"Travis. Travis Copeland." Jewel gave her aunt a stricken look. She felt ill. Somehow soiled.

"Did *he* visit the station, Mama?" Jewel shook her mother's frail shoulders.

"He did come at times," Thea breathed. "I never liked him. He was the most arrogant man. He thought there was nothing in this world he couldn't have."

"The question is, did he have *you?*" Judith leapt up. "The filthy, cowardly blaggard. Is that what this is all about? This long nightmare. Some bloody pathetic affair? When Steve was away on muster, did you let Copeland into your bed?"

"Judi!" Thea said in a small protesting voice. Her eyes rolled back and she slumped to the floor. Jewel jumped up to grab her. She settled her mother in the chair, supporting her with one hand.

"Mama. Mama," she moaned in dismay before turning on her aunt. "Lord, Judith, did we have to do this to her? She's so pitiful."

"She's strong as a bloody horse!" Judith raged, suddenly bursting into tears. "These weak ones, these weak ones, how they pull the rest of us down! We've pandered to Thea forever. Holding her hand. Drying her tears. Coping with her faints. They've always struck me as a bit convenient—like faints on demand. She has the doctors feeling sorry for her. Pretty little thing. She wouldn't have gotten half the pills or the sympathy if she'd looked like a horse. Maybe someone should've given her a good kick in the backside.''

Deceptively violent words, when her aunt was so obviously upset.

''I know, Judith, I know.'' Jewel shook her head. ''Maybe everything's been a big mistake. But it's so painful to look at her.'' She sighed in relief as her mother came around or, as Judith suggested, simply stopped her fake faint. Jewel went down on her knees, staring into her mother's face. ''It's all right, Mama,'' she said soothingly, unable to break long years of habit. ''Everything's okay. Would you like to lie down for a while?''

''Why not? More avoidance.'' Judith laughed iron-ically, coming to assist Jewel as they helped Thea out of the chair and into the house.

''Your mother's mind isn't as scrambled as you think, my darlin','' Judith said after they'd deposited Thea on the bed and closed the door. ''My advice to you is to keep hammering away at her. She's been hiding from her ghosts all these years. Now they're beginning to catch up with her.''

JEWEL DROVE JUDITH'S SMALL CAR over to the old Hungerford farm, traveling through the great sweep of river valley that lay beneath the cloudless peacock-blue sky. The beauty of this tropical landscape had always affected her—the marvelous lushness, the clarity and brilliance of the air. Farther west, beyond the ragged larkspur ranges, lay sun-bleached cattle country, the vast stations that carried the nation's great herds. But here on the verdant coastal strip, luminous green sugar lands ran for hundreds of square miles, as far as the eye could see, the deep red soil of the ploughed paddocks contrasting vividly with the green cane, the rich ochres of the earth touching early memories of her childhood desert home. Where the eternal cane stopped, the mango plantations took over, the tropical fruit farms growing all the exotic new fruits, many of which not even she could name. Beyond them the prosperous tea and coffee plantations on the tablelands were expanding now that the tobacco industry had foundered.

Thirty miles west, almost in dense scrub, lay the rich Copeland Connellan copper mine, Esmeralda, where the boys' grandfather, Fletcher, had been employed for most of his working life. Employed and grown wealthy. The Hungerford farm she remembered used to grow sorghum, maize, safflower and winter feed for cattle, but apparently with the unlawful acquisition of the boys' inheritance, the farm had become a much bigger operation. Her visit today was in the nature of a private visit to an old friend. Once any proceedings started—and she hoped that could be averted—she'd have to restrict all contact to Sheila and George Everett's solicitor. The boys had already told her Everett had removed the family's affairs from one of the biggest law firms in the north, putting them in the hands of some new guy who'd managed to rack up a fairly significant clientele.

All along her route, the bougainvillea broke out in open country, crimson, white, mauve, climbing in spectacular fashion over everything in sight—fences, trees, spindly old rotted shacks and abandoned rainwater tanks that must once have served tenants long gone. The impressive white timber gates that marked the entry to the farm were closed. Jewel got out, opened them, then drove through and closed them behind her. The long drive up to the house was lined by the ubiquitous coconut palms. It took her past the stoneworker's cottage; she could see it through the great shade trees, some of them still carrying small bouquets of scarlet flowers. A wide area around the cottage had been cleared, the grass neatly mown. Two wooden planter's chairs, a freshly painted yellow, had been placed in the shade of the front veranda.

How had it come to this? The boys in the cottage. Sheila and Everett up at the house. Obviously it only took one person to wreck a happy home. She didn't know much about George Everett. As yet, she hadn't had time to run her own checks, but what she recalled of him she hadn't liked. It was more an intuitive reaction than anything else. Before the marriage, he'd tried very hard to ingratiate himself with the people of the district, who collectively had thought him a very poor successor to the much-respected Stewart Hungerford, Sheila's late husband and the boys' father. Jewel's own trauma of the morning, the seriousness of this present situation and what she herself intended to do about it, put her in a sober frame of mind.

The house came into view, allowing her to see the changes that had been wrought over the intervening years. Not all of them for the better, she thought with a stab of dismay. The huge homestead was a Queenslander par excellence, entirely surrounded by wide verandas. It had a steeply sloping iron roof and a small hip that had been repainted. No longer the pristine white it had always been, with a green roof and dark green glossy shutters offsetting the pairs of French doors, it had been refurbished in Federation colors inappropriate to the building. The once-luxuriant flower beds along the house frontage had been dug up and replaced by turf, the central fountain taken away. A clean sweep of green lawn remained with nary a flower or shrub. In the hectically blossoming tropics it was a relatively leafless environment.

Not Sheila's work, she thought. The old Sheila had taken great pride in her garden. This had to be Everett's decision. If so, it was a wonder he hadn't had the great fig trees cut down, as well. Perhaps too much work or Sheila had rebelled. As Jewel parked at the base of the curved flight of steps, she saw one of the filmy curtains in the old drawing room stir. A woman's outline was visible. *Sheila.* Thank God she was home. A further blessing might be in store; George Everett might be out in the fields.

Jewel took the steps lightly, trying to convey by her demeanor that this was just a pleasant visit from a friend. The front door with its lovely leaded side lights had always stood open in the early days, so the cooling breeze could waft down the wide central hallway; today it was firmly closed. Jewel rang the bell, listening to its familiar peal through the quiet, rather dim interior.

No one came. Nerves badly frayed by the events of the morning, Jewel stood back, biting her lip. Surely Sheila wasn't going to ignore her. It made her wonder seriously what this marriage had done to the woman. My God, these weren't Victorian times! George Everett would have to be very, very stupid to ill-treat this particular woman. Jewel put her finger on the bell yet again. More moments passed. She had no intention of returning to the car. She was starting to feel so worried about Sheila, she was even prepared to walk around the veranda to the rear of the house. She started to do so, glancing discreetly inside. The decor of the living room appeared to be changed. Where was the magnificent landscape painting that had always hung over the white marble mantel?

"Yoo-hoo, Sheila!" she called. "It's me, Jewel, home for a visit!"

The front door opened forcibly. Jewel whirled around to see George Everett staring at her, a deep furrow between his eyes, his stance aggressive.

"Why, Mr. Everett!" She turned on the charm. Usually it worked wonders, but George Everett, a powerfully built man with slicked-back graying hair and stony, searching, almost colorless eyes, wasn't responding. Undeterred, Jewel advanced, smiling and holding out her hand. "It's so good to see you!" She should choke on that lie. "Do you remember me? Jewel Bishop?"

The grim aspect lifted to a patronizing near sneer. "Of course I remember you, Miss Bishop." He took her outstretched hand, crushed it. "What are you doing back in these parts?"

Jewel would've loved to say "I'm after you." Instead, she kept up the smile. "Why, visiting Mama and my aunt. Just for the weekend. I couldn't let today go past without popping in to see Sheila. She was always so kind to me."

For a minute, Jewel thought he was about to slam the door shut. "Not today, Miss Bishop. Sheila suffers from bad headaches."

They locked stares. "I might cheer her up. I get to

see so little of her. Why don't you just ask her if she could spare me ten minutes to say hello?'' Jewel half turned and waved a hand in pretended admiration. ''I see you've made a great many improvements since I was here last.''

He glared at her, obviously trying to see if she was having him on. He must have decided she was sincere. ''Got rid of all those damn flower beds, at least,'' he finally muttered. ''I had to, just so Sheila wouldn't work herself to death. Come in if you like, Miss Bishop.''

''Oh, please, it's *Jewel!*'' she cooed, knowing George Everett was the sort of man who detested clever women.

''And that's no exaggeration,'' he amazed her by saying. ''You're even more beautiful than you used to be.''

''Why, how nice of you to say so.'' Jewel grasped the opportunity to make a full sweep of the entrance hall, with glimpses of the main reception rooms that led off it. The Hungerfords had always been wealthy. But it appeared that quite a few of the treasures she remembered had either departed or been put in storage.

''If you'll take a seat for a moment, I'll go see if Sheila's fit to talk.''

''That's really sweet of you.''

''I'd appreciate it, however, if you could keep your visit short. I like to protect my wife as much as possible.''

Really? From *what?* Having a few friends in? Jewel positioned herself sweetly, hands on lap, legs crossed at the ankle, on an elaborately carved mahogany bench with rampant lions for arms—at least *it* was still there—and waited. She could've sworn there used to

be a small side table right inside the door, genuine
Thomas Chippendale. A Tang dynasty horse, hundreds
of years old, used to sit atop it. She recalled the exquisite painting that had hung above the table, a wa-
tercolor by a classical Chinese master. Two white her-
ons with lotus leaves and pink lilies and a Chinese
poem written in calligraphy down the right-hand side.
Nothing had been put in the place of those three objects, which wasn't a smart move. One could see where
they'd been. The color scheme had been changed here,
as well. Too dull and too heavy with all the dark tim-
berwork. George would never make a successful interior decorator. He didn't have the taste to carry it off.
Sheila was a warm, outgoing woman who'd always
lived the gracious life, and Jewel couldn't imagine how
she'd allowed this man to walk over her, let alone ren-
der her fraudulent. So perplexed did she feel on every
front, Jewel felt like smacking her forehead with the
palm of her hand. The only thing that stopped her was
catching sight of herself in the hall mirror.

She was the skeleton in the closet! Generally speaking, every family had one. That didn't make her feel
any better. The very idea of having a double sent a
cold shiver down her spine. Of course, there were
twins, mirror images, even stand-ins for film stars. According to popular wisdom, everyone had a double
somewhere in the world. The thing was, she didn't believe it. Nor, despite what she'd insisted to Keefe Connellan, did she believe in coincidence. So what did that
make her? Travis Copeland's illegitimate love child?
She frowned for a minute, considering rape. That
would be too dreadful. At this point, she didn't think
she could even cope with the idea of her mother having
had an affair. Yet the person looking back at her with

those blue, blue eyes might not be Jewel Bishop at all.
Literally overnight, she could be demoted to the status
of a Copeland bastard. There were still a few people
around who called the innocent that.

Her mother was hurting, had been hurting all these
years. Now *she* was hurting, too. She had to face the
fact that her mother might've been living a lie all these
years. She could have lied to her husband, the man
Jewel had called "Daddy" as a child. She couldn't
visualize his face anymore but the memory of him was
warm. She knew he'd loved her. Kept her safe. He had
loved her mother, too. His "girls."

For a moment Jewel almost hated her mother for
what she might have done to Steve Bishop.

Damn Everett! Where did he have Sheila stashed
away? One of the outbuildings? They were taking a
devil of a time. She stood up, suddenly tired of waiting,
and then she heard footsteps.

Oh God!

George Everett had finally untied Sheila. He was
leading her into the room the way a beefy, overbearing
caregiver might lead in a psychiatric patient. Here was
a shadow of the woman Sheila had been. The lovely
chestnut hair Jewel remembered as long and flowing
was cut in a thick wedge as short as a boy's, the
slightly plump curvaceous figure whittled down to almost nothing, the widely spaced hazel eyes reflecting
an inner misery Jewel could feel like a blast from the
Antarctic. But those eyes when they fell on Jewel
showed a hopeful ray of light.

"Jewel, my dear!" It came out as a soft wail. "How
kind of you to come and visit me."

George Everett had done this to her.

Jewel took no heed of his possessive stance. Well

might he look at her as if she was some sort of threat. She *was!* She swooped toward Sheila, using the advantage of surprise to prise her away from George.

"Do you think I could possibly forget your kindnesses to me?" she exclaimed. "It's so good to see you, Sheila. It's been far too long." The two women embraced, Jewel keeping an affectionate arm around Sheila's waist, even though the scowling expression on George Everett's face would have persuaded a lesser woman to let go. Who was this boorish man? How had Sheila been drawn to him? Some sort of sexual compulsion? Sheer loneliness? A need for a physically strong man to run the farm for her? Sometimes women made terrible mistakes without meaning to. She'd made a few herself. But nothing as bad as George.

"Jewel, you're a sight for sore eyes," Sheila was saying as she studied Jewel's chic informal getup. "So much polish!"

Not bad for a kid with a weird mother who forgot to buy her child shoes.

"We have lots to catch up on." Jewel turned to confront the silent, glowering George. "You won't want to be part of this, Mr. Everett. Girl talk."

"I've already told you Sheila isn't well," said George, obviously refusing to cooperate. "We can give you ten minutes."

"You don't trust me with fifteen?" Jewel joked, subduing the brief violent desire to tell him to get lost.

"Can I offer you something, Jewel? A cold drink?" Sheila asked quickly, an unbecoming flush mottling her throat.

"You wouldn't have a Coke, would you?" Jewel smiled at her. With any luck they might make it to the privacy of the kitchen.

"No, dear. I do have some homemade lemonade, though." Sheila made a little jerky movement backward, looking more and more distraught.

"That'll be fine. Why don't we go to the kitchen to get it? Would you care for some too, Mr. Everett?"

"I couldn't think of anything worse," he said.

How gracious. For one unbelievable moment, Jewel thought he was about to follow them, but he turned back, walking into the drawing room, instead.

Sheila wore a floral cotton dress that was dreadful to behold—she'd always been the trendsetter in the district with money to splurge. Once in the kitchen, she went quickly to the refrigerator, withdrawing a glass jug covered with cling wrap. "I made it this morning. I like it, if George doesn't," she added with the vaguest hint of defiance.

"I don't know that I like it when they're so *completely* honest," Jewel said flippantly. "What *does* George like—besides beer, I mean?"

"Beats the hell out of me." A glimpse of the old Sheila. "If I ever find out, you'll be the first to know."

Jewel paused, deciding she had to speak. "You don't look well, Sheila. You must have lost twenty pounds or more."

"More," Sheila told her in a wry voice. "There was a time I couldn't lose a pound, no matter which diet, but George soon cured me of that. I'm not a happy woman, Jewel."

"Can you talk about it?" Jewel said in her soothing lawyer's voice. "I'm your friend, Sheila. You have lots of friends, remember?"

"I used to have friends. Not anymore. George has cut me off, but the really sick thing, the shameful thing, is I've allowed him to do it."

"He is a very intimidating man," Jewel pointed out. "I've seen the boys," she told Sheila, quickly looking over her shoulder in case George was lurking in the doorway. "They're worried about you."

Sheila almost dropped two crystal glasses. "Saw them. Where?"

Jewel took the glasses out of Sheila's nerveless hands and set them down. "They're in Brisbane, Sheila, staying with an old school friend. They're fine. We had a very nice meal at a restaurant last night. It was great to catch up."

"They came to see you, didn't they." Sheila's hazel eyes filled with tears.

"I *am* a friend of the family," Jewel said gently. A lawyer, too.

"You always did have the knack of getting on with everybody," Sheila said, blinking hard. "If the boys are worried about me, I'm frantic about them. Without my ever wanting it, we've become estranged. They hated George right from the start."

"Maybe they didn't give George enough of a chance?" An absurd notion.

"George doesn't have your sympathetic personality, Jewel," Sheila said, quite unnecessarily. "He's a very stiff, stern man, though he wasn't too bad at the beginning. The problem is I never listened to anyone before I married him. So many people, including my own father, warned me it wouldn't work. But it was unbearable without Stewart. I had to fill the terrible void."

"You could have waited a while."

"I know." Sheila squirmed. "It seems obvious to me now. But I couldn't handle the sudden pressure in my life. Having a big farm to run. To continue to keep it successful for the boys. If nothing else, George is a good farmer."

Yet the boys had indicated the farm was on the edge of economic disaster.

"That doesn't give him the right to talk you into taking over the boys' property, Sheila." Jewel went to the heart of it. "That's illegal."

"I'm not clever like you, Jewel. I've done some really bad things."

"And the bank let you," Jewel added.

"Oh, they've always been on side. We had a name in this part of the world, Jewel."

"Absolutely correct." Jewel nodded. "Are you aware the boys aren't going to stand for it anymore?"

"You're not representing them, are you, Jewel?" Sheila burst out.

"Not today. I came to you as a friend only, Sheila. Not the boys' representative. I'm not supposed to talk legalities. But you must know you and the boys could settle all this privately. You and George don't have a leg to stand on."

"We stole their inheritance from them," Sheila said dolefully.

Jewel's voice was wry. "It's certainly the view of the town."

"Why do you think I don't go there anymore?" Sheila's eyes filled again. "I'm so ashamed. It was mostly stupidity, you know. George convinced me we'd be doing the best possible thing for the boys. We'd be trebling the income."

"And have you?" Jewel asked.

"No. But I don't know the details. George keeps such a lot from me."

"You still own this house, don't you, Sheila?" Jewel looked directly at the older woman.

"Yes."

"Then, you can tell George to get lost any time."

"Can I?" Sheila leaned closer, appearing amazed.

"You'd better believe it. You can do it if you want to. This is your house, Sheila—and your life."

"It's no life at all," Sheila said wretchedly. "I got myself into this terrible situation and I don't know how to get out."

"Find the strength for your boys," Jewel urged. "Surely seeing them robbed would put steel in your backbone?"

"That's the problem, Jewel." Sheila gave a broken laugh. "I've lost all my confidence. It went with Stewart. I adored him. Marrying George... For whatever reasons, I've become a gutless woman. The marriage would never have worked with George even if he'd taken a fatherly interest in the boys, which of course he didn't. I got a sinking feeling the minute I said, 'I do!' but I'd already made my bed."

"Crises can be resolved, Sheila." Jewel sought to reassure her. "You have people who love you. Ask for help and you'll get it. You have to reach out, not struggle alone."

A furious voice from the door shocked them. "How could she possibly be *alone?* She has me." George Everett strode into the room, his square-jawed face contorted with rage. "How dare you come into this house under false pretenses, young lady. What's your game?"

"Tennis." Jewel said after a moment's hesitation, trying to control her anger. "I used to be a good swimmer but I gave up on the training."

Sheila reached out tentatively and touched Jewel's hand. "Don't, dear," she warned.

"Don't what? Don't provoke George? You may live in fear of him, Sheila. I certainly don't. You can take that threatening expression right off your face, Mr. Everett. Lay one finger on me and you'll be slapped with an assault charge. I should add that Judge Donovan in town considers me one of his grandchildren."

"Don't play the fool with me," Everett shouted. "You young people know nothing about respect."

"Personally, I consider bellowing extremely disrespectful. I'm not getting into any argument with you, Mr. Everett. I came to see Sheila. I came on my own behalf and for the boys. They're very worried about her. As they need to be, from the look of her."

"She looks fine," Everett maintained furiously. "As for those boys, they're afraid to work for a living."

"They need an education first." Jewel stared back at him. "Their father would have wanted them to go to university or agricultural college. As it is, they've got nothing. And it's because of *you*, Mr. Everett."

At once his glowering expression changed, became wary. "Ah, so they got themselves down to Brisbane to cry on your shoulder?"

"It's obvious they couldn't look to *you* for support," Jewel shot back.

"Or me, either," Sheila said brokenly. "We've acted very wrong, George. We have to put things right."

It clearly wasn't a plan of action George intended to take. "Get out of my house, Miss Bishop," he said tautly, advancing not on Jewel but his wife.

"I'll go when Sheila tells me." Jewel stood her ground, afraid for Sheila. How did she know the man wasn't physically abusive? "It's *her* house, lest you forget."

"That's right, George." Sheila looked down pointedly at the strong fingers clamped around her arm. "Would you mind letting go?"

He stared at her balefully. "Have you lost your senses, Sheila? This girl comes in here stirring things up and—"

"Things that *need* to be stirred up, George. I have to sleep at night. I have to be able to look at myself in the mirror. Poppa would turn in his grave if he knew what I'd done."

"Don't be ridiculous!" Everett cried in his browbeating voice. "It had nothing to do with stealing. I've slaved to make this place work. It's a far bigger operation and eventually it'll all go to the boys."

"It's theirs *now,* Mr. Everett," Jewel pointed out quietly. "Or it will be, as soon as Sheila puts things right."

"Ah, the lawyer!" He looked at her with contempt. "You're a troublemaker."

"Go, Jewel," Sheila implored. "Please go. I thank you for trying to help me."

"I haven't finished yet, Sheila," Jewel said in a determined voice. "Why don't you leave with me?"

Everett was livid. "How dare you come between man and wife?" he demanded. "What is it you fancy yourself now, a marriage counsellor?"

"If I were, I'd tell you your wife is frightened of you, Mr. Everett," Jewel retorted. "That's no way to live. No way for any woman, let alone the Sheila Fletcher Hungerford I knew. You've got control of her. I perceive that as being very bad, very dangerous. She needs help."

"Not from you." He appeared genuinely menacing.

"Then, maybe the local police sergeant. No woman should be intimidated, especially not in her own home. Sheila has a perfect right to ask you to pack your belongings and go."

By now George Everett's colorless eyes were almost bulging from his head. "My God, you have a hide!" he cried, in a filthy temper. "But then, you had a very odd upbringing. You and your crazy mother and that eccentric aunt."

"You make them look like pillars of society," Jewel said sharply. "My mother does no one harm. My aunt runs a successful legitimate business, which is more than I can say for you."

"Get out!" He ground his teeth, the blood mounting alarmingly to his face.

Jewel walked past him, reaching out for Sheila. "Are you coming, Sheila? My crazy mother and eccentric aunt would love to have you." She prayed Sheila would have the strength to make a bid for release, but Sheila looked as though she was remembering slaps in the face. Or perhaps beatings. Could anything be worse?

"I want you to leave, Jewel," she begged. "I'll see you to the door."

"Very well, Sheila." Jewel didn't give Everett so much as a sideways glance. "If that's what you want."

"I said *I'll* go, George." Sheila spoke with dignity. "I've got a little too used to being chained to your side."

Yet he came after them, though keeping a small distance.

"I'm so frightened," Sheila whispered as they stood

in the open doorway, her voice so low Jewel had to bend her head to hear. "So ashamed."

"Don't give up, Sheila," Jewel said, hugging the older woman to her as if providing a protective shield. "I'll be back."

CHAPTER FIVE

SKINNER GAVE HER the extra time she needed, which turned out to be a week, without the slightest dispute. A huge relief! As long as there was money in it for Barton Skinner Beaumont and she kept up with her other legal work, it appeared schedules could be adjusted. Much had happened since she'd called on Sheila Hungerford that fateful afternoon. The most significant event was that George Everett had been turned out of the Hungerford family home. Sheila had sounded terrified when Jewel had left the farm, and Jewel, totally averse to abandoning a friend in trouble, drove straight back into town to the local police station manned by burly Gordon Matheson and his well-muscled constable. A responsible lawyer, known to them forever, she didn't have a lot of difficulty convincing them Sheila needed police protection.

As a consequence, they'd all returned to the farm, where George greeted them so warmly that the police might have been guests and Jewel a good friend. It was a charm card that Jewel, for one, had never suspected he had in the pack. Handsome in a big, dark, glowering fashion, George played the solid, highly respected citizen quite at a loss as to why this visit could actually be official and not something to do with a police fundraiser. Despite George's concern for his wife—he claimed her migraine was much worse—Sheila was

eventually summoned, displaying to their horror the be-
ginnings of a black eye, the swollen lid closing. Even
then, she was loath to say George had caused it, though
they all knew he had. Jewel was well aware that physical abuse is a demeaning experience, the victims often
feeling too humiliated or ashamed to confide in anyone.
It was an irrational response but easily understood.

In the end, Jewel persuaded Sheila to speak of
George's treatment, dreading what shocks might lie in
store...and there were quite a few. Once started, Sheila
couldn't seem to stop, so after a while they all had to
sit down. They heard of the psychological abuse, which
had caused Sheila's alienation from her sons and her
friends, the occasional physical abuse when George
felt provoked into giving his complaining wife a back-
hander.

Jewel's visit had precipitated a whole chain of
events. George, protesting violently, was allowed time
to pack a bag before being escorted into town. Sheila
spent the night with Jewel. The boys reconciled with
their mother over the phone and lost no time in catching the first available plane home. Sheila's former family solicitors were reinstated, arranging a restraining order to keep George Everett away from Sheila and her
boys, and divorce proceedings were placed on the
agenda. First thing Monday morning, Jewel started her
own lengthy search, uncovering the fact that George
Everett had siphoned off a considerable amount of the
loan he and Sheila had received to upgrade the property, using the boys' inheritance from their grandfather
as security to the bank. With mother and sons reconciled, Jewel was now in a position to act for all three.
Litigation against George Everett would proceed to win

back the boys' property. The whole scenario had worked out well for everyone. Except George.

AUNT JUDITH DROVE HER to the airport early Monday morning, ten days later, leaving the shop in the care of her assistant, Dolly, who practiced white magic and read tarot cards at the Sunday markets.

"I just can't believe what's going on around here anymore," Judith said, still in the grip of multiple shocks. "You were pretty good taking on George Everett." Judith glanced at her niece with admiration. "The whole thought of it worries me. He's one scary guy. I'm still trying to figure out what Sheila ever saw in him. Maybe he was more affectionate toward her when they first met...."

"Come on, George Everett never had a tender moment in his whole life. Anyway, he doesn't scare me." Jewel moved her hand to touch her aunt's. "Besides, as soon as he saw Gordon, he backed right off. George is the kind who only treats *women* badly."

Judith smiled wanly. "Poor old Sheila. I'd just love a man to take a swipe at me. I'd clobber him with whatever I could lay my hands on. But for the marriage to finish just like that!" Judith gave an amazed hoot.

"According to Sheila, it was finished almost as soon as it began. She made a very bad decision at a critical point in her life. But the boys are safely back home."

"Two fine strapping lads," Judith said with satisfaction, "who at last know the truth. What happens now?"

"I'll get cracking with the action against George. Sheila's solicitor will act for her on the divorce. Basically, I'm around to protect the boys. We'll win. The boys will get their property back. As for Sheila, she's probably had enough of men.''

''I honestly can't see her remaining a single woman.'' Judith frowned for a moment. ''Sheila's one of those women who always has to have a man around. She was blessed with Stewart.''

''Let's just hope she doesn't take on another George.''

''Everett must hate you.'' Judith turned her head briefly, an expression of worry on her face.

''Doesn't he hate everybody? Who cares about the Everetts of this world?'' Jewel looked out the window at the lush tropical landscape. A beautiful black horse, coat gleaming, was pounding around a paddock on delicate thoroughbred legs.

''You don't think he could be nasty?'' Judith persisted.

''It's possible. Very possible. But he's already in a very bad position and Sergeant Matheson made that very plain— None of which solves my own *huge* dilemma.''

''No.'' Judith jutted out her chin. ''We have to face it, kiddo, your mother had an affair and she's been blaming herself ever since. You are the result of that affair. The depth of her grief can now be revealed to us two suffering souls. She always felt extremely guilty, as one tends to do when one breaks the commandments.''

''But she wasn't responsible for Dad's death,'' Jewel argued emotionally. ''He had a car accident, didn't he—or is that a lie, as well?''

''No lie. He did.''

''You're certain of that, Judith?'' Jewel asked. ''Because I'm going to look it all up in the archives, going back to Sir Julius Copeland's funeral. The man I called Daddy died that day.''

Judith struggled to keep the distress out of her voice. "He slammed his car into a power pole.''

"God!" It had never been explained. "Was it raining or something? Did he lose control? Dad could drive anything. Anywhere.''

Judith shook her head, her voice grim. "I don't know, love. I only know your mother's been punishing us all ever since. Maybe your dad—Steve—was suspicious. Maybe he found out something. Maybe he met Lady Copeland? He certainly would've seen her at the funeral. That was twenty years ago. She would've been in her fifties. You say she's a beauty now.''

"She'll always be a beauty,'' Jewel said. "He may have been taken unaware by the resemblance. He may have jumped to conclusions.''

"He may have discovered the truth, girl. It all adds up. Travis Copeland used to visit the station on behalf of his father. Your mother was a very pretty girl. A dark-haired Mia Farrow. Strange how this all has happened,'' Judith mused. "The Hungerford issue fueled it.''

"Deception runs through everything,'' Jewel said, her face bleak. "I don't think I can bear this, Judith. I had an identity. Who am I now? I don't even think I want to continue with the firm. They represent Copeland Connellan. From the way Keefe Connellan spoke, he wants me out.''

"Does he now! How could he blame *you* for anything?'' Judith demanded hotly. "You had no control over your own birth.''

"Hard to argue with that, but he seems to think I'm manipulating the present situation.''

"I'd like to have a few minutes with him." Judith set her teeth.

Jewel managed a discordant laugh. "You think George Everett is scary? This man is the real thing. He can tear you up with his eyes. He doesn't have to say a word. Besides, even *I* think it looks suspicious. I could have worked my way into the firm. Put myself into the best possible place for drawing attention."

"Your boss didn't notice anything," Judith pointed out.

"He noticed *something*. He just needed a little nudge to put two and two together." She sighed. "The Copelands won't want to know me. I'd be nothing more than a terrible embarrassment. A huge problem they'd probably pay to go away. Blackmail is obviously on Keefe Connellan's mind. They're the elite, the Establishment, among the most powerful and influential people in the state."

"To hell with that!" Judith burst out in disgust. "They're no better than the rest of us. Probably a damn sight worse. To most people it would be a seven-day wonder. Anyway, I thought you told me Lady Copeland wanted you to visit her?"

"She does." Jewel gave her aunt a tight smile. "I think I've touched some chord. She wasn't at all angry. She wasn't fearful or judgmental."

"Especially when her adulterous son comes into it. Why should she judge you?" Judith challenged. "You've done nothing wrong. You're a splendid young woman—you could take your place anywhere."

"Travis Copeland has a daughter," Jewel said quietly, after a short silence. Emotions were running high inside the car.

"Amelia, isn't it?" Judith asked, adjusting the sun shield against the mirage.

"Amelia wouldn't want to know me," Jewel said, shaking her head.

"Her loss." Judith, obviously feeling tender and protective, looked ferocious. "But you don't know she feels that way, do you? She might love to have a sister. Surely to God there's enough money to go around."

Jewel nearly choked. "I don't want their money," she said violently, her words resounding in the small car's interior.

"Bless you, your mother could do with some." Judith paid no attention. "I figure your bloody father had something to do with it all. Your birth father, I mean— not Steve."

"He mightn't have known a thing about it." Jewel didn't want to consider the specter of a father's lifelong abandonment. "Mama might have kept it from everyone. She kept it from you, her own sister."

"Thea always did have a great talent for keeping secrets," Judith said wryly. "We didn't even know she had a boyfriend until she and Steve turned up at the door. Next thing, they're married. A week after that, they were a thousand miles away, working some damn cattle station. Of course at the time we thought Thea was pregnant. The big rush to the altar and all. But she didn't have you until two years later. Always knew something wasn't right, but I could never flush Thea out."

"We're still not having much success," Jewel observed, not without underlying humor.

"Makes you wonder what'll happen on Judgment Day." Judith glanced at her niece, green eyes ironic. "The good Lord asking and Thea refusing to talk."

Despite the anguish Jewel was battling, she chuckled at that, heartened by the powerful attachment between them. "You know I love you, don't you?"

"I know exactly," Judith said and smiled.

THE DOMESTIC AIR TERMINAL was full of people coming and going. This was one of the jumping-off points for the crowds of tourists going to the beautiful resorts of the Great Barrier Reef. Jewel checked her luggage and made her way to the departure lounge. The torrent of conversation had apparently affected the pressure of Judith's foot on the accelerator, so she'd made record time, which gave Jewel a full thirty minutes before boarding time. She debated having a cup of coffee, then decided against it, walking over to the small shop that sold souvenirs, paperbacks and a range of magazines.

She was almost there, when a physically large, hard-eyed man loomed in front of her. Too late for her to react, George Everett clamped her arm so tightly she couldn't shake it off, though she wrenched hard. He then proceeded to maneuver her swiftly out of the mainstream and back against a large pillar, which effectively concealed her.

"Don't think I'm finished with you," he snarled.

"What do you want, Mr. Everett?" Jewel didn't have to work up to anger. It exploded out of her. "And take your hand off my arm. You're already in big trouble."

"Unfortunately, yes." He grimaced. "Because of *you*. How quickly you messed up my life. I still can't believe it."

"Your life was messed up long before I came on the scene," Jewel said with contempt.

"You think I count for nothing, don't you." He fixed her with his gaze, as a big cat might fix its quarry.

"I try not to think about you at all." Jewel made no attempt to conceal her scorn. "Any involvement with you is over, so I'll ask you to please leave me alone."

His colorless eyes were like poisoned wells. "I love my wife, whatever you choose to think." He pressed closer, probably in case she tried to make a break.

"It's got nothing to do with me. I do remember Sheila telling us all of your physical abuse, if that's your idea of *loving*."

He raised one large hand, made a fist. "You shut up."

Jewel was stunned by the fact that this was actually happening to her. Associates of Barton Skinner Beaumont didn't get into ugly public fistfights, but this brutish man was infuriating her. "Don't threaten me, Mr. Everett," she said coldly. "You'll regret it. Fair warning. I'm a lawyer, remember? What are you doing here, anyway?"

"What do you think?" He regarded her with such enmity; if they weren't in a public place, Jewel might have panicked. It might take very little to turn this man dangerous, more dangerous even than Sheila had led them to believe.

"I'm here for my say," he exclaimed violently, thrusting his face forward. "I'm entitled to one, aren't I? You ruined my life, putting ideas into Sheila's head. Going to the police. How dare you! By the time Sheila finishes with me, I'll have nothing left."

"You started with nothing, as I recall." Jewel began her move, inwardly agitated, outwardly composed. "You could've had a good life had you shown any decency. Instead, you started on a criminal course of action. Please get out of my way now, before this all gets out of hand. I'm not impressed by your scare tactics.''

Everett's stolid frame remained rooted to the ground, blocking her path. His skin was slicked with sweat and his breath reeked of whiskey. "Then, you're not reading me right, lady," he rasped. "Don't think you're going to crucify me and get off scot-free. You're talking to a desperate man…."

"Then, make it easier on yourself by walking away," Jewel retorted with vigor, though warm dread was spreading through her body. It might help if she screamed. People were so busy with their own affairs, they weren't really looking in this direction. It didn't help that Everett's bulk was hiding her, either.

GEORGE EVERETT SPAT the word "bitch!" over and over. Something in this woman's face, her contempt for him, her inherent spirit, was tipping him over the edge. For most of his life he'd intimidated others. Women were a pushover; Sheila was the proof. Now here was this one, this blonde, the way she held her shoulders, the way she held her head, figuring she was a man's match. He'd show her, for shaming him. He wasn't just anyone. He'd led a comfortable life since marrying Sheila, the life of the local squire. Now this girl had ruined everything.

Everett recoiled, pulling back his powerful arm….

ABOUT THE SAME TIME Jewel arrived at the airport, Keefe Connellan was seeing off a small party of Japanese clients en route to Hayman Island, one of the great island luxury resorts of the world. Connellan had flown them up on the company Learjet, all talking business until the last moment, but now it was time for a little R&R. Afterward, when the Japanese businessmen had boarded the Sikorsky helicopter that would ferry them to the Great Barrier Reef island, he walked back into the terminal to find his pilot, Dan Halliwell. Dan had gone in search of a coffee, so Connellan moved in that direction, thinking he'd have one himself.

He was walking through the terminal, oblivious to all the attention directed his way—a kind of celebrity he had long since put into perspective—when he was stunned to see the young woman who had so cleverly insinuated herself into Davina's life. Eugenie Bishop. The young woman he himself was so dangerously drawn to, even as he realized she could plunge them all into turmoil.

In any company she would stand out, he thought. Her spun-gold hair seemed to draw all the light, although she'd pulled the full sweep of it back off her face and arranged it in a coil on her nape. She wore a casual white outfit with the easy glamour that seemed to be a part of her, as it was very much a part of Davina—a sleeveless tunic top over a side-split straight skirt that showed a tantalizing glimpse of one long golden-brown leg, strappy sandals on her narrow feet. In the tropical heat she put him in mind of a lily. Cool and immaculate. Her companion was a tall, broad-shouldered, heavyset man who was standing, in Connellan's opinion, far too close. Crowding her. The man had his back turned but he was obviously staring down into her beautiful face. Why not? Most men wouldn't be able to take their eyes off her. Whatever they were talking about, it wasn't relaxed or friendly. As he watched, the discussion grew more intense. She was already effectively hemmed in by the man's bulk, although she appeared to be trying to leave. Connellan immediately increased his stride in response to a gut feeling that she could be in danger. Intimidation of women was deplorable at any time; in this instance, he was ready to take physical action if he discovered that Eugenie Bishop was being threatened.

She was staring up at the man, her face smooth and composed. It was her "legal" face, but he was still set on finding out what was going on. She might look in control—he'd already found she had an authority of her own—but he had concerns about the big man's body language. It spelled anger and aggression. Emotions he was all too familiar with in the cutthroat world of big business. Yet he sensed *this* confrontation was personal.

He had almost reached them, fully intending to break in on the conversation whether she welcomed it or not, when the man's face was fully exposed to him. Anger bordering on the psychotic was imprinted there, an expression that propelled him into a dazzling burst of action.

At a run he roared, "That's enough!" Instantly all the noise and chatter stopped and everybody turned to gape at him. One woman screamed.

He saw the heavyset man fling a glance over his shoulder. Then, too far gone to stop, the man swung at Jewel. Mercifully she ducked reflexively, so the blow missed her face and landed on her shoulder. Keefe reached Everett, spun him around, pinning one arm to his side and wrenching the other up between his shoulder blades.

"What the hell is going on here?" he demanded. He was fully prepared to deliver a disabling blow to this howling bully, who was blubbering incoherently that he was being hurt.

Jewel realized she was shaking badly. "I'll tell you when I've regained my balance." All around her was relief, excitement, incredulity. What was Keefe Connellan, of all people, doing here, bringing the weight of his physical strength and impressive presence to bear? She had difficulty taking it all in.

"You bitch!" Everett's face was scarlet with impotent rage, his big body writhing.

"Be quiet," Connellan warned him, his voice revealing disgust and revulsion. "Or I might just knock your head off."

"No, please, no." Jewel placed a staying hand on Keefe Connellan's arm. "He's not worth it. Security is on the way." She turned her head to see two uniformed men come running, alerted by the commotion.

"Let me go. You're breaking my arm," George Everett, the wife beater, was yelling.

Connellan clamped his arm tighter. The first security man reached them, producing a pair of handcuffs that he swiftly clamped around Everett's wrists.

"What's happening here, Mr. Connellan?" The security man, who knew Keefe Connellan by sight, now asked, trying to absorb the situation.

Connellan nodded toward Jewel, who'd pulled herself together sufficiently to explain. "I'm a lawyer. My name is Jewel Bishop. This man here is George Everett, the husband of a client, Mrs. Sheila Hungerford Everett."

"Of course, Mrs. Hungerford…Everett!" The security man corrected himself. "A well-respected lady."

Jewel continued her explanation. "Mrs. Everett has taken out a restraining order against her husband. Di-

vorce proceedings instigated by my client will follow.
Mr. Everett, appears to blame me for his current situation.''

''It appears you'll need a restraining order, too,''
Keefe Connellan advised sharply. ''I remember you
now, Everett, from talk around the district. How many
times have you done this, throwing punches at
women?''

George Everett groaned and shuddered, apparently
without the strength to fire up again. ''She drove me
to it. I only did what any other man would do.''

''You're a bully with a twisted mind.'' Connellan
returned his gaze to the security men. ''The police will
have to deal with this. We'll have to make formal statements.''

''I've already given them a call,'' the older guard
told him. ''They should arrive in a few minutes.''

Connellan looked across at Jewel, filled with a huge
rage at what had been done to her. ''Are you all right?''

''I'm okay,'' she said, nodding. ''I don't know if I
could've gone another round if you hadn't shown up.
Thanks... I'm supposed to be on the next flight to Brisbane. It'll be boarding shortly.''

He shook his head. ''I think you'd be much more
comfortable if you flew back with me.'' Connellan
turned to acknowledge his pilot, who, on hearing of the
ruckus, had come running. ''The company jet is out on
the tarmac. We've just dropped off a party of Japanese
clients en route to Hayman.''

''I don't think...'' Shaken by the incident, Jewel
found herself weakening.

''Make it easy on yourself,'' he suggested, overcoming all her resistance. ''First, though, I want to see this
guy Everett led away.'' He reached out and took her

arm with such gentleness, it made her rethink her initial hostility. "Why don't we go and sit down while we're waiting for the police? You've had a shock."

"Much better than a broken nose," she said in a wry voice, wincing as she moved her shoulder. There would be a bruise where Everett had struck her.

IT WAS MORE THAN AN HOUR LATER that the Copeland Connellan Learjet was given clearance to take off. Once airborne, Jewel unsnapped her seat belt, embossed with the company logo in red, blue and silver, the same logo that was imprinted on the jet's tail. It was hard for her to believe she was traveling with a man who—only ten days before—had questioned her integrity, her motivations, her very identity. Now he'd established himself as her rescuer. A sobering thought. She wondered if she'd be tough enough to deal with him. He was seated in an armchair just across from her, dark head lowered as he read what looked like a balance sheet—familiar territory for Jewel. His name and position had made things easy for her with the police. He'd outlined what had happened, allowing her a necessary calming period before she had to relate her part of the story. George Everett had been led away, protesting he'd merely been having a conversation. He was to be held in the police detention center until he'd sobered up. Jewel readily informed him that she would be bringing an assault charge, which she hoped might stop him from bothering her again. But for now, she had to put the incident, upsetting as it was, behind her. It was far from the only upset of her professional life.

Jewel shifted her gaze from Keefe Connellan's glossy black head to look around the jet's interior. It was carpeted and furnished like a study, with plush armchairs in a deep champagne color and fixed timber tables polished to a mirror finish. Very attractive. This man had been born to privilege, while her life, until recent times, had been a struggle.

Jewel turned to look out the porthole, watching the shimmering sunlight glance off the silver wing. Having a company jet was certainly the way to travel.

"Feeling better?" Keefe Connellan asked with concern, shutting a file and putting it aside.

She turned her head, not forgetting to smile. "I don't need any medical treatment, but I was still thinking about George. Lucky you were there. It seems quite incredible."

"How the hand of fate guides us," he replied in a gently sardonic voice.

"Yes, indeed. I've been traveling back and forth for years now and I've never seen you at the airport."

"Not surprising," he said. "I don't usually check in our overseas clients. Travis likes to do that."

"Ah, Travis," she said. "How strange you should even bring him up."

His faint smile acknowledged the mockery. "You've had a shock. I was making small talk—giving you time to recover. Speaking of less confrontational things, I recall meeting Sheila Hungerford, as she was then, years ago when both her husband and her father were still alive. It was at an amateur race meeting she'd organized. Quite a lot of fun. I wasn't long out of university, although it wasn't my first visit to Esmeralda. Her father, Frank Fletcher, was our senior mining engineer there for many years. She was a very happy woman then. Very pretty, too."

Jewel sighed deeply. "She made a bad mistake when she married George."

"So it seems." He held her eyes. "A little patience and she might have met someone far better. I can't imagine how a woman like that, who seemed to tolerate no nonsense from anybody, could tolerate physical abuse. She had a whole town to turn to."

Jewel shrugged—a little movement that reminded her of her sore shoulder. "In the beginning she chose George. She thought she wanted him. Pure and simple."

"And you're going to handle the litigation?" he asked.

"Yes. I'm not finished with George Everett yet."

"Then, I'm sure it will all work out. Tell me, how did the trip go with your family?"

She looked at him and saw that he was dangerous to her. In so many ways. "Plenty of talk. Plenty of food. What with Sheila—she stayed with us that first night—plenty of action. How's that for an answer?"

"Sort of evasive. I'd say it would help a lot if you could lay your cards on the table."

"If I had cards. Is it blackmail you're implying?"

"Routine question. I'm acting for Lady Copeland. You're acting for yourself. Surely we can get together on this. If you are who I think you are."

"And who am I supposed to be?"

"I thought we'd established that." He met her eyes. "Travis Copeland's daughter. It would put you in a very strong bargaining position. You're a lawyer. I have a law degree. We both know how to work the system."

"Well, I'll certainly try," she said with mock bravado. "If I am Travis Copeland's daughter, don't you think he should pay?"

His gaze didn't shift. "He could certainly afford to. Is that it—revenge?"

She shook her head. "Revenge I can do without. Besides, do I look like a vengeful person?"

His smile wasn't without humor. "If you are, I can't see it. You look like a very sexy angel, if there's such a thing. But you don't know Travis Copeland. I'm not trying to upset your little applecart when I say he won't want anything to do with you. He'll refuse to recognize you even if your identity's staring him in the face."

"Really?" Jewel began tapping the side of the armchair. "There's such a thing as DNA."

"You surely don't think you'd get him to take a test?" He looked at her with acute skepticism.

"He could be *made* to," Jewel said. "If I put myself in the position of one of my own clients, I'd feel very confident."

He shook his head. His own voice hardened. "A man like that wouldn't stand for public humiliation."

"What do *you* stand for?" Jewel challenged him outright.

"The truth, Ms. Bishop. And you're not telling it." She let a few seconds pass. "Before I met you, I never had a problem with people believing me."

He leaned forward in his chair, his shoulders hunched. "How do you know I don't yearn to believe you? But we're dealing with very serious matters here. Matters that might be beyond you. When did you first hear the whole story?"

She fixed him with her gaze. "What whole story do you mean, Mr. Connellan? That I'm Travis Copeland's love child?"

He gave a slight yet daunting smile. "Look, I don't blame you if you're profoundly angry. I just don't want this to become a nightmare. I'm very fond of Lady Copeland. She's getting on in years and her health isn't as robust as it used to be. A tremendous amount of pressure was put on her as chairman of the Copeland Connellan board.''

"She must be a very clever woman."

"Indeed she is. One of the reasons I admire and respect her so much."

"But you have a problem with Travis?"

"Nothing like the problems you might cause for yourself. Travis's brutality in emotional matters is legendary."

"You don't trust me."

"Were you expecting me to?"

Jewel looked down at her linked hands. "I was expecting absolutely nothing."

He made a small disbelieving sound. "How many millions do you think the Copelands are worth?

"Oh, brilliant!" she scoffed. "I read *Business Review.* 'The Rich 200 List.' I know how much they're worth. I know how much the Connellan family is worth."

"Expecting too much might be your downfall," he warned.

Jewel glanced out the porthole, her tone deliberately flippant. "What's money?"

"Quite a lot when you haven't got it," he retorted.

"Well, *you've* got it and you seem to want more. And power, as well?"

"Why not?" he said, clearly not uncomfortable with the charge. "I won't stop until I'm the chair. In the meantime, I'd settle for CEO."

"Over Travis Copeland?" She uttered a mock gasp.

"We're both in the running. I believe I'll succeed."

"So you have considerable ambitions of your own." It was said with more than a flash of sarcasm, which he acknowledged with a brief nod.

"The press never fails to point that out. I'm also obsessed by the thought that Julius Copeland did some terrible things to my grandfather in business. Julius Copeland could be very cruel."

"Lovely relations I've apparently got." Jewel's smile was self-deprecating. "What I don't understand is how your knightly affection for Lady Copeland came about."

His brown muscular throat tensed. "On her husband's death, Lady Copeland quickly reversed his underhanded dealings. My family had reason to be grateful to her. My grandfather was a far cleverer man than Julius Copeland, but he was no match for him when it came to ruthlessness."

"So there it is." Jewel threw out her hands. "You and Travis are still around to fight the war. It would seem we've both suffered at Copeland's hands. For your information, though, I have no intention of claiming Travis Copeland for a daddy. I think he's a complete bastard. By the way, just to frustrate you, Mother swears I'm Steven Bishop's child."

He studied her for a moment, then drawled, "She must love games, too."

"Even when I beseeched her," Jewel continued, leaning back and putting both hands behind her head.

"Jewel, I don't believe you." His eyes moved lightly over her, yet they made her extravagantly conscious of her own body.

"Of course you don't." She slowly straightened, pulling the gold clasp from her hair. "And who said you could call me Jewel?"

"I couldn't call you anything else." He smiled. "It goes with your starry eyes. What does your aunt have to say?"

"You'd better take care," Jewel warned. "My aunt has a very hot temper. She can't stand to see me criticized in any way. She actually said she'd like to spend an hour with you."

"Maybe then we'd be able to work out the puzzle," he reasoned, his voice unperturbed. "Your aunt must know the story."

"What she knows is very sad." Jewel showed him her profile. "All these years later I've only just learned that Dad slammed his car into a power pole. I loved him. I still remember his love for me. If he thought I wasn't his daughter, it would have destroyed him."

Keefe Connellan looked at her with a mixture of sympathy and suspicion. "I think he knew that, don't you, Jewel?"

"Why do you say that?" Jewel was suddenly afraid.

"Oh, for God's sake!" His handsome face showed his impatience. "You must know Travis Copeland and Steve Bishop had a scuffle right outside the cathedral the day of Sir Julius's funeral. Travis was punched to the ground and suffered a broken nose. It was something I'll never forget."

Jewel felt unnerved. "You saw it?"

He gave an emphatic nod. "I attended the funeral with my parents. The incident was hushed up as much as possible, but many people witnessed it. You're asking me to believe that a clever professional woman like yourself, a lawyer, hasn't checked all this out—even if your mother frustrated your every attempt to learn the full story?"

"As I told you before, my mother suffers from depression,'' Jewel said. ''She has a terror of being asked questions, so I no longer ask them. I've spent all my life believing Steven Bishop was my father. I understood and never questioned that he was killed in a car crash. I didn't deliberately position myself at Barton Skinner Beaumont, as you seem to think. However, like you, I'm ambitious. An old professor of mine recommended me to the firm. I'd never laid eyes on Lady Copeland or you until that day in Skinner's office. At the time I thought Lady Copeland looked strangely familiar, but the fact that she recognized *me* took my breath away. Until that moment, I had an identity. You've successfully taken it away from me.''

He stared at her, frowning, carefully weighing her words. ''How could I? You couldn't possibly hope to keep the resemblance secret. Davina has had her portrait painted three times. All of them hang at the house. You could have posed for the one in the early days of her marriage.'' He paused. ''Once you took a step into Davina's world, everyone would find out—and the flurry of rumors would begin.''

''Yet she wants to see me.'' Jewel raised her eyebrows.

''Of course she wants to see you. She's had precious little love in her life. You touched her heart.''

''Quite a feat for a gold digger,'' she taunted. ''Lady Copeland has a son, a granddaughter. Surely she receives love from them.''

''My view of Travis is that he has no true feelings,'' he said, his tone more dismayed than judgmental. ''Amelia is very...well...self-absorbed. She's her father's heiress. The daughter he wants. She's good-looking. Excellent at playing hostess. She has no job, no profession, but she excels at sports. She plays golf

with her father and friends. Tennis, squash. She goes
out on the boat with him. She does everything he re-
quires and wants of a daughter.''

"I hope that's what *she* wants, too?"

"It's all about money, Jewel. Lots of it. Amelia has
lived like a princess. She's not about to give that up."

She stared at him, trying to suppress a very strong,
if edgy, sexual attraction. "Then, I'll make sure I keep
my distance from her."

"Too late to go back, Jewel," he said quietly.
"Things were set in motion as soon as you came in
contact with Davina. What's going to be the outcome?
That's the question."

CHAPTER SIX

A FEW DAYS AFTER she returned to work, Jewel received an invitation from Lady Copeland asking her to lunch at the Copeland riverside mansion on Friday at noon—an honor Blair Skinner received with delight.

"Doesn't that prove something, Eugenie?" He looked up from his jotting to chortle. "When I hired you I just knew you'd turn out to be Somebody." He smacked his lips over the "Somebody."

She held up a cautioning palm. "Don't tell Keefe Connellan that. I'm Jewel Bishop at the moment. Don't let either of us forget it."

"Not me, my dear." Skinner shuddered and slightly loosened his silk tie. "The last thing I'm about to do is fall out with such powerful people. Take as much time as you want. You're a worker, I'll say that for you. You'll catch up. Please give Lady Copeland my warmest regards. You're going to love the house. It's just splendid."

"When were you last there?" Jewel asked, raising her eyes to his smooth, polished face.

"Not for a few years now," he admitted freely. "Not since Travis and his darling daughter took over the reins. Honestly, I've never met two people so completely vain."

That amused her, coming from Blair. "Why didn't you ever see Lady Copeland's portraits?" Jewel asked, with a worried frown. "I understand they're all over the house."

Skinner looked surprised. "My dear girl, I assure you I've never seen a one. They must've moved them. Who told you this, anyway?"

"Keefe Connellan."

Skinner swallowed visibly. "He can't possibly still suspect me of anything, can he?" he asked, seeming startled.

"What if *I* decide to suspect you?" Jewel waited a few seconds, then leaned forward in her chair to whisper, "Only fooling. I would've thought they'd hang at least one in the living room."

He shook his head, at the same time tossing down his expensive Mont Blanc pen. "Maybe they're upstairs. I never did get upstairs."

"Not a peek into the bedroom?"

"I never got into the library, either."

"See what you've missed?" Jewel rose from her chair. "If I get the chance, I'll ask to see the portraits."

"Will you? I'd love to know what they're like." Skinner kissed his fingertips. "*Bellissima,* I'll bet. Such a beautiful woman. And she'll love you. It's all plain sailing there. I don't know if I can say anything so positive about Travis. Or Amelia, for that matter. That's a very pampered girl. And she's been named as heiress."

"So she's a big step ahead of me," Jewel said with dark humor. "Anyway, let's take this one thing at a time. I'm simply having lunch."

"You go out and have a wonderful day," Skinner urged. "It's not everyone who gets invited to lunch with Lady Copeland. I, for instance, have never received a call. You're honored, my dear."

"I don't feel honored, Blair," Jewel paused, speaking seriously. "I feel under a lot of pressure. It could degenerate into a big storm. Suddenly I've found I want to be sure of who I am—the way I was just a few weeks ago."

"That's easy," he said, eyes shrewd. "You're Lady Copeland's granddaughter. Travis Copeland's daughter. The most we can say for Travis is maybe he was lonely. In need of comfort. I knew his wife—thin, thin, thin, with a blade of a tongue. I think the old man, Sir Julius, pushed Travis into marrying her. She was a Watson Smythe."

"Really? I'm not familiar with the name."

He looked at her in astonishment. "My dear, they're the landed gentry. You really will have to bone up. Especially now you're moving into the big time."

"Bye, Blair," Jewel said.

"All the best," he called, laughing lightly. "Never forget I gave you your big chance."

AS THE TIME FOR HER MEETING with Lady Copeland approached, Jewel tried hard to get a grip on herself and the major issue that now confronted her—the business of her real identity. It wasn't easy contending with such a bombardment of mixed emotions, an overload that seemed too chaotic for her mind to contain. On the one hand, she felt a sense of excitement, as though she was being handed some wonderful present, swiftly followed by moments of extreme inner turmoil, a sense of rootlessness, as though she'd suddenly become a foreigner in her own country. Was she really who they all thought her to be, or was it some incredible coincidence, after all? The fact that Steven Bishop, an enduring memory in her life, wasn't her father at all seemed the saddest thing, so much so that she couldn't let it register yet. She needed time to absorb the shock and pain, the question mark over his sudden, violent end.

She thought she would never adapt to thinking of Travis Copeland as her father. She felt absolutely no sense of relatedness to him, although she'd experienced an immediate rapport with Lady Copeland. And if all that wasn't enough to confound her, there were her encounters with Keefe Connellan, who seemed to be playing a pivotal role in this whole tremendously unsettling business. The hours she'd spent with him remained shockingly vivid in her mind. She put it down to the swiftness of their involvement—that and his extraordinary aura. It distinguished him from any other man she had ever known. She'd even discovered, with some trepidation, a powerful sexual attraction to him. At twenty-six she'd come to take it for granted that she was the "controlling" one in her relationships with men. All her boyfriends had claimed she could wrap them around her little finger, and it had seemed, even to her, to be the truth. She knew that would never be the case with Keefe Connellan. This was a man who threw out challenges, and so far she was the one very much on the defensive.

She found herself puzzling long and hard over his relationship with Amelia. Both families appeared to have had expectations of a match. Amelia had lived a life of privilege, which probably meant she was used to getting everything she wanted. So where had the courtship gone wrong? Actually, if she was being honest, Jewel had to admit that the idea of a serious relationship between Keefe Connellan and Amelia dismayed her. And how would Amelia react to the sudden discovery of a half sister? The result, moreover, of an illicit relationship in her father's past. Being the Copeland heiress no doubt gave great meaning to Amelia's life. Now for something like this to surface! A scandal. Let alone Amelia's grandmother inviting a total stranger to their home, even if only to delve into the stranger's past. Travis Copeland could be counted on to continue disowning her.

Small wonder Jewel felt both excitement and fear. What happened next ultimately depended on how well she and Lady Copeland related to each other. If Davina Copeland believed she was her granddaughter, surely it had to be so. Then, Travis Copeland was the one who had abandoned her and her mother. A terrible and cowardly thing to do.

After Keefe Connellan's revelations, she'd read everything she could find on Sir Julius Copeland, going way back to the early days when he and Stafford Connellan had started out on their mineral exploration, a scant year after they'd both graduated from university. She read about the Copeland pastoral interests, which were huge. She read about Travis Copeland's wedding to Sonia Watson Smythe. The wedding of the year! The old newspapers showed a handsome, smiling young man with a surprisingly prune-faced bride on his arm. Jewel saw the birth notice of their first and only child, Amelia, and the many society page articles once Amelia was launched on the social scene. Countless photographs had been taken of her with a certain drop-dead gorgeous man.

Keefe Connellan.

Jewel studied the photographs with a curious lurch of the heart. Who had dropped whom? Or had their romance degenerated into a love-hate? She read every line of reportage on Sir Julius's funeral. She read how Travis Copeland had been accosted outside the cathedral by a young man believed to be a disgruntled employee. An employee so unimportant they hadn't even printed his name.

She knew that name. Steven Bishop. Not her birth dad, it now seemed, but the best dad in the world. She couldn't bear to think his accident might not have been an accident at all. What had been in his mind when he slammed that car into a tree? His young wife's infidelity? Travis Copeland's adultery with a young woman he would never have given the time of day, on his home ground? She'd found the tiny article reporting his death tucked away along the side of page four. It was written up like another fatal case of drunk driving. She couldn't find any reported link between Travis Copeland's assailant at the funeral and the young man whose life had ended hours later.

How the rich and powerful could arrange their cover-ups!

She and her mother had never seen Steven Bishop again. They hadn't even brought his body back. Aunt Judith alone had flown to Brisbane for the cremation that followed. Her mother had been engulfed by what she and Aunt Judith believed to be a wife's inconsolable grief at the loss of her mate, her spouse.

But Jewel had come to realize that other unresolved feelings had presided there. Guilt too acute to be grappled with. Quite simply, guilt had rendered her mother powerless. On one occasion she had become depressed enough to want to die, but the overdose of pills she had taken only made her violently ill.

In a sense she'd been orphaned at six, Jewel thought. Emotionally orphaned, anyway. Her mother was there

physically but rarely in spirit. God knows what would
have happened to her without Aunt Judith. Judith had
kept her sufficiently on track, encouraging her "clev-
erness," telling her if she worked she could break out
of the "terrible rut" that had claimed the sisters' lives.

And how she'd worked—with great energy and
spirit, a compulsive student throughout her academic
life. She knew she wanted a future, a life in complete
contrast to the depressed and negative one of her
mother. Maybe her fighting spirit, her commitment, her
daring was inherited from her grandmother, Davina
Copeland.

Her stomach tight with nerves, Jewel turned into the
broad leafy avenue—the Millionaire Row—lined with
the imposing mansions of the rich. A mixed bag of
architectural styles, she thought. There were the carefully preserved or meticulously restored grand coloni-
als, large and elegant with enveloping lacework bal-
ustrades and valances on the wide verandas so suited
to the city's subtropical climate. There were Gothic-
style "lodges," built of stone, more suited as English
country residences. The fairly recent Italianate villas
were all set in large beautiful tropical gardens with
fountains playing in the heat. Long wrought-iron fences
with massive wrought-iron gates kept out the world;
the gates hung on huge pillars, while the fences were
adorned with flowering bougainvilleas color-matched
to the houses.

The Copeland mansion was as big as a village. Lined
on either side by jacarandas, it presented itself to the
street as one of those palatial villas the senators of an-
cient Rome used to retire to when things got hot either
politically or on nature's front. This was the only res-
idence that saw the need for solid walls. To keep the

family in or keep the neighbors out? To add to the cloistered look, few windows punctuated the bold facade, at least on the first floor, yet in the third-floor tower, she saw three. Obviously no one was about to creep up on them. The tower might even be manned by security guards.

Jewel pulled into the flagstone driveway, lowering her window so she could press the button on a brass box mounted on a pedestal. There was a glass-covered hole she took to be the seeing "eye."

Hello, there!

It was all a far cry from the sprawling Queenslander she'd grown up in, with its wild but incredibly picturesque acres. This might have been a six-star hotel designed by the late Versace.

A disembodied voice said, "Yes?"

"Jewel Bishop for Lady Copeland."

The massive gates immediately opened, allowing Jewel to cruise up the drive. Moments later she was standing in front of the huge classical facade. With the river to the back, she presumed the mansion would open up along the rear, perhaps with lots of large windows to take advantage of the beautiful view of the wide, deep river. A breeze that usually came in from the bay about noon was already springing up, fanning the sun-ray pleats of her delicate silk shirtdress. It was a shimmering shade of beige that suited her coloring. Expensive it might have been, but she loved the beauty of movement of the skirt. She'd slung a wide leather belt around her hips; it matched her handbag and her tan sandals. Looking good gave her some of the confidence she needed.

Bracing herself, Jewel walked up the short flight of steps, too nervous to smile. A pleasant-faced, middle-aged woman, breathing a little heavily, dressed in what appeared to be modern-day livery, met her at the door, telling her Lady Copeland was looking forward to seeing her. The woman was trying unsuccessfully not to stare—not that Jewel blamed her. She showed Jewel through a vaulted entrance hall exhibiting busts of hawk-nosed Roman emperors, its austere effect softened by two massive bronze planters filled with white orchids. Then they moved on to an enormous living room, with another barrel-vaulted ceiling, painted this time by someone with pretensions to the Da Vinci style. Loads of antiques and paintings, very unusual glass chandeliers and baroque mirrors, a marble fireplace. Dazzled in spite of herself, Jewel followed the woman into another large room at the rear of the house with French doors leading onto a flower-filled terrace. Beyond that was a great sweep of emerald lawn set with towering palms, running down to the sun-splashed sequined river.

Lady Copeland was seated within hailing distance in a large-scale armchair that all but swallowed her. As soon as Jewel entered the room, the woman rose, a lovely smile of welcome on her face, right hand extended.

"Eugenie, I'm so glad you could come."

Jewel didn't know whether to laugh or break out in sobs. Instead, she moved forward gracefully to clasp the delicate hand, her own smile in place. "I really appreciate your asking me, Lady Copeland." *Grandma?* God, this was overwhelming.

"Well…well…." Lady Copeland continued to hold her hand, turning her head slightly to speak to the woman who'd brought Jewel through. "Thank you,

Holly. We'll talk for a little while, then you can serve lunch. Say in half an hour.''

"Very well, Lady Copeland." Holly, who'd been staring at Jewel in apparent fascination, dismissed herself slowly, as though backing away from a sovereign. Her expression was three parts respectful to one part avid speculation.

Lady Copeland ignored her. "Please, Eugenie, sit down." She indicated one of the oversize armchairs that could easily have served as a bed.

"Thank you." Jewel wondered for a frivolous moment if Lady Copeland was about to tell her of some complex genealogy, according to which the two of them were descended from the royal House of Savoy. What else could account for this sumptuous fortress furnished in such princely fashion?

As if she could read Jewel's mind, Lady Copeland threw her hands in the air. "To understand all of this, my dear, you'd have had to know my late husband, Sir Julius. Stafford Connellan built a very beautiful house—you may know it. Stafford and Margaret had exquisite taste and Julius thought he had to go one better. The result was this. A house fit for Julius Caesar. Sometimes I think my late husband convinced himself he might've been descended from that line.''

Jewel smiled at the little irony. "It's very impressive, Lady Copeland. So…you don't see yourself as the woman who married Julius Caesar?''

Davina burst out laughing. "I've made a few attempts to tone it down, but the house will pass to Travis when I'm gone. He loves it. He never got on with his father but he's passionately loyal to his memory. Astonishing, really. Later I'll show you some of the antiques Julius acquired. If you put them end to end they'd probably stretch around Australia. There's even a Renaissance portrait of a Venetian noble, fine haughty face framed by a ruff. Julius bought it because the dealer said it looked like him.''

''And does it?'' Jewel asked.

''Extraordinarily enough, it does. Julius could look very distinguished when he had to. All those years in public life. You know the saying, street angel, home devil—he was a bit of a home devil, I'm afraid.''

''But you loved him?''

Davina Copeland's still-vivid blue eyes gazed off into the past. ''He was a man of great energy, marvelously handsome. A true buccaneer. How I actually came to marry him remains a mystery to this day. I don't ever recall saying *yes*. He must have swept me off my feet.''

''It happens,'' Jewel said wryly, recalling for a moment Keefe Connellan's impact on her. Too full of nervous tension to ease into the reason for this visit, she said rather emotionally, ''I believe my own father, the man I *called* my father, was there on the day of Sir Julius's funeral? Steven Bishop.''

''He was, Eugenie.'' Davina Copeland's voice held a world of regrets.

''I treasure his memory,'' Jewel murmured. ''I remember the love he had for me and for my mother.''

''How is your mother?'' Davina asked. ''Have you spoken to her?''

Jewel inclined her head. ''This…situation has transformed my life,'' she answered evasively.

''Of course it has. What do you think our meeting has done to me? I've lived all these years believing I had only one grandchild.''

''Are you really *that* sure?''

"Come with me." Davina Copeland stood up purposefully, leading the way through more grand spaces to a small feminine study that offered sanctuary from the rest of the house. No splendid embellishments here. Restraint, refinement and, above an English gilt side table adorned with pink roses, a wonderful portrait of a beautiful young woman in evening dress. "Proof?" Lady Copeland asked, her eyes on Jewel as she stared up at it.

"It's an incredible likeness," Jewel said, her throat tight.

"Julius loved this one." Davina touched her abundant upswept hair. "It used to hang in our bedroom but I had it moved here. Too many reminders of growing old. It's not easy resembling oneself less and less." She laughed. "There are other portraits. Julius reveled in commissioning them, supposedly as a record of his love. This is the one I really wanted you to see."

"You've taken a huge step inviting me here." Jewel turned to face this elderly woman who was looking at her with such—God, was it love? If it was, Jewel wanted to capture it, hold on to it. "Do you *really* mean to acknowledge me?"

"Of course I do," Davina maintained, her tone firm. "You're my own flesh and blood. Surely you didn't expect me to turn my back on you?"

"A great many would. I couldn't blame you if you did. We could still see each other without any formal acknowledgment." Jewel wanted to make perfectly clear that she was after nothing.

"I think you *would* blame me, Eugenie," Davina said quietly. "It wouldn't work, in any case. You saw Holly's face. Why have people gossiping behind our backs? It doesn't suit me at all."

"Even if it creates a scandal?"

"At my age I'd jump at a scandal."

"You sound a bit like me." Jewel smiled. "Your sense of humor. But other members of the family mightn't be so welcoming."

Davina exhaled, sank onto a nearby sofa and gestured for Jewel to join her. "That's their problem. I would, of course, speak to them. I wanted us to talk first."

Jewel could actually hear the loud pulse of her heart. "I have to tell you, my mother denies any relationship with...your son," she said hesitantly. "In fact, she became hysterical at the very mention."

Davina nodded. "One can understand the path your mother took. Her terrible sense of grief and guilt when life caught up with her. She's lived all these years under a great burden. I'm hoping if we can straighten things out, the burden will be lifted. A simple test would prove Travis's paternity—as if we need proof. It all adds up. The protagonists were in place. Your mother was young, vulnerable, no doubt lonely with her husband away. Travis can be very charming and persuasive when it suits him. At any rate, he's had a great deal of success with women. Your mother could have been in awe of his position, too. These things happen in life. We can all make bad choices." She paused for a moment. "I have no wish to upset your mother. On the other hand, I'm not going to be denied my granddaughter. I could have loved you, helped you all these years. Both of you. You can't know what this means to me." Her lovely mellow voice was trembling with emotion.

Jewel leaned closer. "I could understand better if I knew what's missing from your life. You have your son. Your granddaughter, Amelia. Most people would see that as a blessing.''

Davina lifted a slow hand. ''My dear, I'm moving through a period of my life in which I feel very much alone. I know people think I've always had everything, but I haven't and I don't. My health isn't as good as it was. I've had to curtail most of my activities. I used to keep very busy with my charity work and support groups. I've given up hope of reaching my son. Strange thing to say, but it's true. His father was always much more important to him than I was. Travis sees himself as the head of the family, and the fact that his father left the reins to me has only alienated us further. I'm sorry,'' she said with a shrug, ''but that's the way it is. As for Amelia? Her father's attention is what she's always craved. I love her and I know she loves me in a charming childlike fashion. But her father is the dominant force in her life—as Julius was in Travis's.''

''And Keefe Connellan?'' Jewel found herself needing to know. ''I can't see him as a substitute son.''

''Good Lord, no. All that vigor and masculine intensity. Travis has high hopes for a match with Amelia, although their romance appears to have gone off the boil. Keefe is very high achiever. I know he'd be looking for a woman who could expand his horizons—intellectually, emotionally, in every other way. An equal. Amelia has allowed her father to clip her wings, to diminish her. It saddens me. Women are only ornaments to Travis. Their job is to keep *him* happy. That even applies to his own daughter. I've tried to interest Amelia in other things beyond pleasurable pursuits, but her father runs her life.''

''What about her mother?'' Sonia Watson Smythe Copeland, member of the ruling elite.

"Her mother had the same experience with her as I have," Davina said. "Amelia idolizes her father. She's spent her life striving for his approval. Both of them maneuvered Sonia out." There followed a long, rather difficult silence. "Sonia isn't an easy person," Davina continued. "A certain...stuffiness, but I've always had a lot of sympathy for her. Ultimately Travis broke her heart."

"How awful. You're being very frank with me, Lady Copeland."

"Just so," Davina smiled. "I'm not normally. But I feel very different with you, Eugenie. I feel I already know you. It's wonderful, wonderful...."

Lady Copeland sounded so poignant Jewel thought she would suddenly find herself in tears. Instead she took the woman's frail hand. "Isn't that what love's all about? You know, my dad always called me Jewel—because of my blue eyes. *Our* blue eyes. It ceased to be a nickname and became my given name. I've been Jewel all my life. I'd like you to call me that."

"I would be honored to do so," Davina said, tightening her hand.

Davina had her back to the door, so it was Jewel who saw Amelia first. Saw the horror in her dark almond eyes.

Davina caught Jewel's dismayed expression, turning her head in response. "Amelia! What are you doing at home, my dear?" she asked in some bewilderment. "I thought you were going waterskiing with your friends?"

Amelia Copeland remained frozen, her face, more handsome than beautiful, distorted by a mixture of emotions. None of them pleasant.

"I was *warned,* Davina," she said, her white teeth tightly clenched.

"Warned?" Davina Copeland stood up, all of a sudden the very figure of authority. "What on earth do you mean?"

"About this girl here." Amelia took several steps toward Jewel. "Who *are* you?"

"She's my guest." Davina Copeland stood between them, anger spilling out of her eyes. "How dare you, Amelia."

But Amelia's emotions had erupted out of control. "What's she *doing* here? Who is she? Why does she look like you?"

Davina moved toward her granddaughter, but Amelia shrank back. "I'm afraid there's no other way to say it, Amelia dear. I believe this young woman—her name is Jewel Bishop—is my granddaughter, just as you are."

Amelia's cry was almost a howl of rage. "She can't be! Where did she come from? I've never seen her before in life. Why can't she speak for herself?"

Jewel stood up resolutely, although her stomach had somersaulted twice. "I know this must be a terrible shock to you, Ms. Copeland, but the shock was no less for me. I've only very recently come into your grandmother's life."

"And what are you after?" Amelia reached out to grasp a small porcelain statue as though she was about to hurl it. "It has to be *money!*"

What had she expected from her new life but horror and suspicion? "I'd prefer to know who supposedly warned you," Jewel said, keeping her voice even. "Could it have been Keefe Connellan?"

For an instant Amelia's fine features were wiped clean. "Keefe?" she asked, almost blankly.

"He knew I was coming here. If he didn't know the exact date, he would've had a fair idea."

Amelia tossed her dark hair over a golden-brown shoulder. "Who else would it be? Keefe will do anything to protect me."

"From what?" Davina asked crisply. "Keefe didn't tell you at all. Did he? Please don't lie to me, dear."

"He did." Amelia didn't waver. "Why would he trust someone like *that?*" She threw an accusing hand in Jewel's direction. "Someone plucked out of nowhere to betray me. Someone who could've had cosmetic surgery, dyed her hair. You can't really know a thing about her except that she *claims* to be your granddaughter."

"Please sit down, Amelia," Davina begged. "I realize this is a big shock to you, but I'm confident you'll come around to seeing things my way. Jewel has never made any claims."

"I don't believe that," Amelia shot back with undisguised bitterness.

"Nevertheless, it's true. I had every intention of speaking to you and your father, but your unexpected return has changed all that. I'd like you to sit down and listen to what I have to say."

Amelia, tall and whipcord slim, remained standing. "I've never, *ever* thought you were a fool, Gran."

"Indeed, I'm very happy to hear that," Davina said, studying her granddaughter. "I would remind you that this is my home. You live here because of my love for you—and my generosity."

A high flush of pink appeared on Amelia's cheeks. "I'm sorry. I apologize."

"And I accept your apology, Amelia. It's not often you forget yourself. Please, won't you sit down?"

Amelia, dressed in a bright red camisole with hip-hugging jeans and a silver-studded belt, slid into a chair like a model fresh from the catwalk. "If I must," she said with no attempt at grace. She bore little resemblance to her grandmother, either in appearance or manner. Still, Jewel felt genuine sympathy for her. This was the heiress. The legitimate child. A member of one of the richest families in the country, with everything that entailed. Amelia was probably so pampered and protected, a thing like this could actually destroy her. She, Jewel, had been cast in the role of fortune hunter. Even her name marked her. Jewel! The long-lost claimant. As for Keefe Connellan, she'd handed him the information he needed when he was the last living person she should have trusted with anything—particularly considering his relationship with Amelia. Clearly he and Amelia were still close.

While both young women sat tensely, Davina Copeland outlined the sequence of events for Amelia. She spoke of the Copeland Outback station Mingaree, part of the Copeland pastoral empire to this day. She fixed people in place and time. Travis Copeland, Thea Bishop, her young husband, Steven Bishop, who had since died. She didn't mention how or when. Jewel could see that Amelia, like her, had never known.

"I just don't believe this, Davina," Amelia said, when her grandmother finished. "Why is this person here? Is that hair even natural? Why would she turn up now? God, is she some substitute for the daughter you lost? I mean, I don't feel I've ever belonged to you, really." She took a deep breath. "What do you think Father is going to say to all of this? He'll be furious."

"Life has a way of unlocking the secrets of the past," Davina said, her fragile shoulders a little hunched. "We have to handle this like a family. I believe your father may have suspected he fathered Thea Bishop's child, Amelia. I recall now that he was very keen on taking over the job of overseeing the station. Then it abruptly stopped. He didn't want to go there at all."

"But that doesn't mean a thing." Amelia looked as though she was about to burst into tears. "What are you trying to do to us, Davina? We have a proud name. A position. People expect—"

"We have what started with my husband. Your grandfather," Davina cut in. "Some journalist recently dubbed him a robber baron. I believe that journalist intends to write a biography, needless to say without my help. Anyway, your grandfather certainly didn't do it all by the rules. Since he died, I've tried to change that. I've chaired Copeland Connellan and I don't believe there's anybody who'll tell you I didn't do a good job. We're rich, Amelia, but the foundation of the wealth is, in some respects, questionable. Nonetheless, you've benefited from it. You grew up wanting for nothing, with the assumption that you are the heir. Jewel didn't have it anywhere near so easy. Not that it appears to have done her much harm."

"So *what* is she?" Amelia repeated forcefully, pointing across the room. "A rocket scientist?" Despite the sarcasm, it was obvious she was reeling from shock, although the full impact probably hadn't reached her yet.

"I think I can establish my credentials," Jewel said, trying to get Amelia to look at her. "I'm a lawyer. I specialize in company law. I'm with your grand-mother's firm, Barton Skinner Beaumont.''

"Lawyer?" Amelia repeated the word almost stu-pidly, then crowed in derision. "Of course you are! I suppose it was only a matter of time before you and Gran met up. Which must've been your intention all along."

"No." Jewel shook her head. "Being with her firm had nothing to do with it. Pure coincidence. I was for-tunate enough to win a University Gold Medal, which helped me along the fast track, and landed up at Barton Skinner Beaumont. As your grandmother has told you, that's where we met for the first time."

"And where's your documentation?" Amelia chal-lenged. "I assume you have some. Birth certificate, that sort of thing."

"I was reared as Steven Bishop's child," Jewel said, distressed by Amelia's violent reaction to her but trying not to show it. What had she expected, anyway—sis-terly love? "I've always believed he was my father."

"Well, he *is*. *My* father isn't." Amelia's dark eyes burned.

"You're welcome to him." Jewel stared back un-flinchingly. "If he was aware of my existence, he made no attempt to see me, let alone send along a birthday card. He made no attempt to make my life or my mother's any easier. And it *was* hard. Meeting your father all those years ago had a devastating effect on my mother. She's a very vulnerable person. Easily hurt." She paused, then added coolly, "Paternity is easy to prove these days—as I'm sure you know."

Amelia got to her feet, thrusting her hands into the pockets of her jeans. "You surely don't think Father would undergo any humiliating tests for *you?*"

"I'm not asking him to." Jewel shrugged. "I'm not asking for anything, except to know who my family really is."

"And that's all you want?" Amelia flashed her a contemptuous look.

"Be quiet for a minute, Amelia," Davina intervened sharply. "I haven't the slightest doubt Jewel is my granddaughter, just as you are. I can see by your face that you're finding the resemblance between us unnerving. If you turn your head and look at that portrait of me, you can see Jewel might have posed for it. The resemblance is that close."

"It's incredible." Amelia glanced briefly at the portrait. "It's incredible, this whole business. I won't let you bring shame to this family, whoever you are." She sat down again, staring at Jewel.

"What happened in the past isn't my fault, Amelia." Jewel tried hard to relax her own tension. "I'm the innocent party here."

"By your own admission, you're a smart lawyer," Amelia retorted. Jewel sensed that she resisted believing any of this, but much as she might want to, Amelia couldn't explain away the extraordinary resemblance. "You're just playing an old woman along."

To Jewel's ears it sounded dreadful. Where was Amelia's love and respect for her grandmother now?

"Is that how you see it, Amelia?" Davina Copeland's voice was low and dangerous in that serene and beautiful room.

Amelia recovered rapidly. "S-sorry, Gran," she stammered. "I'm just describing it the way this person here is seeing it. Apart from the bizarre resemblance, there's no *real* evidence."

"There's a mountain of it, Amelia," Davina said.

"You're just hiding your head in the sand. Like it or not, Jewel is a blood relative. Your half sister, in fact. It would make everything so much easier for us all if you could give her some understanding and compassion. Don't see Jewel as a usurper. She's your own flesh and blood."

Amelia banged her long legs together in sheer frustration. "How do you intend to go about telling Father? Or are you going to issue a press statement?"

"That will do, Amelia," Davina ordered quietly, although anger glittered from her violet-blue eyes. "The whole situation has to be thoroughly discussed, then we'll come to an agreement as a family. It might help you to know that I need no further proof. Jewel is my granddaughter, just as you are."

"You keep saying that! Oh my God!" The words died on Amelia's lips, then she rallied, her glossy head shooting up. "Have you really thought this over, Gran? All it's going to bring is a horrible scandal. God alone knows what Mother will make of it. She'll be nastier than ever. She hates Father as it is."

"Perhaps he's given her good reason, Amelia," Davina said stiffly. "And she doesn't hate him at all. Your father likes to put that mischief about. Your father, as we both know, has had many affairs. We've both come face to face with them."

"But he hasn't married anyone, has he?" Amelia said, almost gratefully. "He's a very handsome, powerful man. He can have his affairs if he wants. And he's not just going to pack up to suit you."

Davina clearly had had enough. "He might have to behave a little better if he thinks he's going to inherit this place!" she said tartly, her slim hands stirring in her lap. "You are your father's rightful heiress, Amelia. Please don't be frightened. You'll never be cheated of that.''

"Then, find out what her price is, Gran," Amelia said. "Pay her off, if that's what it takes."

Jewel stood up, unable to listen a minute more. "I don't think you understand either of us, Ms. Copeland. I'm not interested in making any claims on your family's money."

"Put it in writing," Amelia responded, glaring up at Jewel as if she blamed her for everything. "Everyone has a price. Father's always telling me that."

"Perhaps you shouldn't be so willing to listen." Jewel snatched up her handbag. "I don't give a damn about this house, luxury yachts, luxury cars, the whole social scene. I earn a good living. I like what I do. Helping people makes me feel good. I have a nice town house. Good friends. I find, however, I do want my grandmother. Forgive me for that. I'll drop any interest to being your half sister, if you'd prefer."

Amelia curled her lip. "Oh, you're clever!"

"I believe I am. Moreover, I have integrity."

"Don't go. Please don't go yet," Davina Copeland implored rather breathlessly, as Jewel showed her determination to leave.

"I must." Jewel's expression softened as she looked into Davina's eyes, glittering with unshed tears.

"And don't come back," Amelia cried. "Leave now. Get the hell out of here."

Adrenaline spurted into Jewel's veins. She didn't have to take this from anyone. She stood poised and calm. "Please be quiet," she said in a voice that carried the confidence of achievement and the expectation that she would be obeyed. "I'm here on the invitation of Lady Copeland. I'll leave when she tells me. I'm very sorry you've found all this such a shock. Nevertheless, I'm not impressed by your behavior. Where is your pity? Your sense of blood? Your reactions begin and end with yourself. I didn't start any of this, Amelia. It's just as you've been told.''

"In that case, God help us." Amelia buried her face in her hands.

CHAPTER SEVEN

JEWEL RETURNED to the office depressed, fighting mad, and minus her lunch.

"How did it go?" Blair Skinner stood framed in the doorway, his eyes bright with interest.

"Terrible. Absolutely terrible," Jewel said, the tips of her fingers on an aching temple.

"Tell me all about it." Skinner advanced into the small room, taking the chair opposite Jewel's desk. "Hmm," he murmured, looking around, "we'll have to get you a better office. So, what happened? I told my secretary I wouldn't be accepting any calls."

"You're becoming very nosy, Blair." Jewel stared at him for a minute or two.

"Dear girl, I've been nosy all my life," Skinner answered promptly. "It's the only way I ever get to know anything. But you surprise me. I thought the whole thing would go off extremely well."

"Except, Amelia showed up," Jewel said stonily. "She was supposed to be out on the river waterskiing and having a jolly time with her layabout gang, only someone tipped her off."

"That you were there?" Skinner's expression was incredulous.

"Exactly. She claims it was Keefe Connellan."

That clearly disturbed him. "But how could he possibly know?"

"I told him," Jewel confessed, her tone filled with self-disgust. "I even told him I was looking forward to the meeting. I didn't say exactly when it was, but he could've found out easily enough."

"Dear God!"

"Don't act so surprised, Blair. Wouldn't you expect her to be the *first* to know? Weren't they an item? Neither of them has found anyone else."

Skinner still looked doubtful. "I don't think Keefe would be in a hurry to upset Lady Copeland. It doesn't sound like him."

"He's...he's wicked," Jewel said wildly.

"So it wasn't the nice reunion Lady Copeland had in mind...."

She shook her head. "Amelia was shocked—and pretty damn rude. I don't know what I expected from her. I thought a well-brought-up young woman could have handled it better. I'm reasonably certain I would have."

"It didn't degenerate into a screaming match, did it?" Skinner asked, hunching forward.

"Not really. She just carried on like a maniac. I'd have had a hard time swallowing lunch, so I left."

Skinner stared at her. "You've had a bad day. I don't imagine Lady Copeland was pleased, either."

"She was very upset." Jewel's voice conveyed her concern. "If I'd been her, I would've thrown Amelia out. She showed no consideration whatsoever for her grandmother. It was all for herself. And, just between the two of us, for dear *Father*."

"What else is new? Did she threaten you with anything?"

"Not really. If she could've called down a thunderbolt from heaven, she would have. I think it's the money that's getting to her.'' Jewel pondered. "I'm sure she'd be agreeable to paying me off. I might work on it.''

"You're joking!''

"Yes, I am, but I might want to leave her guessing. I can understand her feelings—I'm still in a state of shock myself—but I could never speak to anyone the way she spoke to me. I'm charged and convicted. A gold digger. Guilty as hell.''

"Those Copelands trust nobody,'' Skinner confided. "Cross Travis, and he turns absolutely feral.''

"Well,'' Jewel said, "I'm certain he already knows about me. Maybe Connellan keeps him posted, just like Amelia.''

"Oh, no.'' Skinner, loyal to his favorite client, ran a finger down his chin. "I've known Keefe Connellan a lot of years. I've seen and heard nothing but integrity. A lot of people say so. Travis, now, is a vile, vile man. If I were you, I'd have nothing to do with him.''

"I don't think I can cope with this,'' Jewel said, vigorously pulling a paper clip apart. "He's supposed to be my *father*.''

"You don't have to respect him,'' Skinner said, concentrating on his own paper clip. "It's Lady Copeland we're interested in. She's a woman who has a lot of power but she doesn't hit you over the head with it every other minute. If Lady Copeland accepts you, my dear, you're in.''

"In *where*, Blair?'' Jewel threw her paper clip away.

"Into riches, my dear. Do you want me to get you the latest *Business Review Weekly?* You can catch up on 'The Rich 200 List.' ''

Jewel leaned across the desk, fixing her gaze directly on his. "Blair, up until recently, I'd been enjoying every minute of my life. I never got bored and I was never confused. I knew who I was and what I was doing. I wish I hadn't even laid eyes on Lady Copeland and that backstabber Keefe Connellan.''

"Well, it's natural to feel like that right now," Skinner replied, "but what you're saying about Keefe just isn't true."

"Even if it isn't, this whole thing is shaping up to be a disaster of monumental proportions." She sighed. "You can't blame Amelia for seeing it that way. Her father will want to run me out of town."

"Or hire someone to push you under a bus," Skinner suggested with a delicate shudder.

"Thanks, Blair." Jewel gave a hollow laugh. "I'll make sure I always have plenty of people around."

Skinner laughed. "You must realize, dear girl, they need time to let the unthinkable sink in. I just knew that Amelia was a bitch. I *knew* it."

"And you still want me to become part of the bunch?" Jewel frowned at him.

"My dear, you'd be like a breath of fresh air," Skinner pronounced. "You could be the salvation of that whole family. Bring them back to reality." He lowered his voice. "Do you want me to help you?"

"How?" Jewel asked, her voice cracking confusedly.

"I'm not without influence in both quarters. Like Connellan, I come from an old Establishment family. My quiet promotion of you should mean something. Everything had gone a bit stale the past year or so, then you whooshed into my life—and now, look! I mean, it's so *rare* to come across a missing claimant to a huge fortune."

"Would you like me to offer you a finder's fee?" she asked sarcastically.

"Not at all, but I *would* like you to be grateful. Remember that when they appoint you to the board of Copeland Connellan."

"Sure. No problem." Jewel groaned. She opened a file. "I might as well get back to work. It never goes away. See you later, Blair."

Skinner went out of the room chortling. "And to think I've taught you so much!"

Twenty minutes later, Jewel picked up the phone to hear a man's voice say, "Ms. Bishop?"

Jewel scowled. The caller's identity was unmistakable. "Mr. Connellan," she snapped. "You must have the hide of a rhinoceros."

"That's right. It's been said before." He laughed, a low-pitched mocking sound. "Are you having a bad day?"

"I'm sure Amelia told you exactly what you wanted to hear. It all went very badly."

"What did?"

"Why, the meeting of course," she said brightly. "You know, the *meeting*."

"Lunch with Davina?" he asked, sounding fully alert.

"Oh, you're so *smooth*," she said disparagingly. "You mean to say you didn't know about it?"

"Bite my tongue if I tell a lie. I don't know any more than you told me."

"Really? I didn't realize you were such a good actor. The first thing you did was pass the information on to your girlfriend."

"All right," he said. "I give up. This is making me insane. Can you unscramble, please?"

"It goes something like this. You're a twister, a very devious person. I'm angry about that. Goodbye, Mr. Connellan. One. Two. Three. I'm hanging up." Jewel slammed down the phone.

It rang a moment later. Jewel waited only long enough for him to say, "I hope I can get a word in edge—" before she slammed it down again.

The man was a rotter. And he could win an Oscar for his performance. She had to forget all about him. The excitement, the humiliation and the anger. A shocking assortment of emotions.

When the phone didn't ring again, she felt almost miserable and couldn't understand it. She would *love* to tell him off! "Face it," she muttered to herself, "George Everett was an angel compared to my so-called family and their best friend." She returned to her preparation of the Hungerford brief.

AROUND SIX, with the summer sun still bouncing off the pavement, she left the building, intending to do some shopping. There was a little party going on at the Heritage. One of the legal secretaries had just become engaged. Jewel thought she might pop in for a while. She felt she needed a little fun. Not to mention support and understanding.

There were lots of people about. In fact, the "River City" was crowded. She stood beneath the green heart of an umbrella tree and slipped on her sunglasses.

The Rolls materialized from nowhere, gliding up alongside her. "Where are we going, Ms. Bishop?" a dark, familiar voice called out.

Jewel considered stalking on, like women did in movies, but at the last moment veered off to the curb,

showing her anger. "Haven't you got anything better
to do?" she asked.

"As it happens, I want nothing more than to have a
conversation with you," he replied suavely. "Our best
yet. Would you like to get in?"

Jewel stared at him, long and hard. "You've got a
nerve."

"Agreed. That's the kind of man I am. Don't let's
hold up the traffic." He got out of the car and handed
her in.

"What is this? Another setup?" she demanded, before her anger drained away. "Same chauffeur, I see.
And once again the window is up."

"We're in need of privacy, aren't we? Actually, I
called you earlier on the off chance you might like to
come out to dinner tonight."

"Good grief!" She moved her back against the
plush, seductive-smelling leather. "That's the last thing
I expected."

"Of course, if you'd rather not..." His eyes slid
over her, giving Jewel a series of violent little shocks
down her spine.

"I wish I knew what's going through your mind."
The disgust in her voice was genuine.

"Nothing that should alarm you. Dinner, then?"

She turned on him, almost calm with despair. "What
do you *want?*"

"To tell the truth, you fascinate me. And you're a
beautiful woman."

"You've met beautiful women before."

"Not one who claims to be Davina Copeland's
granddaughter."

"I don't *claim* anything." Her mouth parted in outrage. "What exactly does this have to do with you? You surely don't want *more* money?"

"What do you mean?" He met those blazing blue eyes, wondering why he was doing this, complicating his life endlessly.

"Your romance with Amelia isn't working out," she said tartly. "It helps to have a backup, doesn't it?"

"Are *you* offering?" He wondered what might happen if he just seized her and kissed her. That luscious mouth! Her silken legs were so close to his, demurely crossed at the ankles.

"No, I'm asking *you* the questions," she said. "You are not a person I want to get involved with."

He nodded. "Sound reasoning on your part. Now, are you going to tell me why you hung up on me?"

"Perhaps I don't like interruptions," she said. "Also, I was furious that you told Amelia about my luncheon date with Lady Copeland. It was very upsetting, especially for Lady Copeland. She told me herself her health isn't good."

He frowned, looking quite daunting. "You're jumping to conclusions."

"Conclusions?" Her voice was rising and she deliberately lowered it. "You've been a step ahead of me all the while. Amelia told us you tipped her off."

"Really? I can't think of anyone who lies more easily than Amelia."

"You deny telling her?"

He gave a near-Gallic shrug. "You're asking me to deny too much these days. I would never do anything to hurt Davina."

"You don't mind hurting me." She spoke sharply.

"Aren't you a woman who can look after herself?" He gave her a brilliant black-eyed look.

"You bet." She nodded in emphatic agreement. "How did Amelia *know,* then?"

He didn't consider for more than a few seconds. "Well...if I had to guess, I think I'd settle on Holly. I imagine she got a big surprise seeing you close up."

"Her mouth stayed open so long, it was a little vulgar. But why would Holly tell Amelia?"

"It comes with the territory. Holly adores her."

"Really? Having met Amelia, I must say I'm surprised. I'd have expected Holly to be more loyal to Lady Copeland."

He glanced out the window as they stopped at the lights. "I think Holly sees herself as a long-term employee."

"What does that mean?" Jewel asked, her heart suddenly thumping with fright. "Lady Copeland isn't ill, is she? I mean, seriously ill?"

"She has a heart condition but medication keeps it under control. She has to look after herself, though."

"Then, I'm even less impressed with Amelia for upsetting her," Jewel said in dismay.

He took her hand. "I like you when you're being kind," he said, stroking her skin. "Don't forget I warned you. Travis and Amelia aren't the sort of people one threatens in any way."

She tried to get her hand back. Couldn't. Tried to control her racing pulse. "Are we talking about accidents? Accidents to me?"

"Don't worry. I'm keeping a close watch on you." His expression turned grim.

"Why, exactly? Your attitude was quite deplorable when we first met."

"And it could be again. I didn't say I absolutely trust you, even now." He linked her fingers with his. "But you're funny. You're sexy. You're beautiful. You're resourceful. You're clever. Do you want me to go on?''

"What I want you to do is give me back my hand.''

"If I can.'' Slowly he released it. ''What time would you like me to pick you up?—although I have to admit I lose all sense of time around you.''

"Would eight o'clock suit?'' She glanced at him. "That gives me a chance to get home, shower and change.''

"What can I say except I can't wait!''

THE RESTAURANT was a luxuriant, softly lit room with perfectly laid tables, silver service, sparkling glasses; small garlands of flowers surrounded the lanterns that held lighted candles. The walls were covered in a deep green shimmering fabric that matched the green leather, brass-studded chairs; the green was also picked up in the striking floral fabric on the banquettes. At various points, gilt-framed mirrors were set into the wall, reflecting the beauty of the room and the female guests, who always wore their most expensive clothing when dining here. On the river side, great windows reached from floor to ceiling, granting a spectacular view of the city by night, all humming lights and glitter, with the City Cats, the ferries, plying up and down, landing their passengers at the base of a broad terrace with leafy trees in large pots. It was the ideal place to be at ease—if one was affluent and well-connected. Keefe Connellan, of course, was perfectly at home.

"So?'' He looked across a riverside table at her with that faint smile she found too darn sexy. ''What did you see in your last male friend? I've heard you were both madly in love.''

"He was nowhere near the catch you are," she retorted, openly taunting him.

"What kind of work did he do?"

"I'm sure you already know that. He was a lawyer, like me. And great in bed. I thought I'd mention it in case you planned to ask."

"Well, that's good." Those attractive little grooves appeared at the side of his mouth. "You certainly can't say it about everybody."

"I'm not tasteless enough to ask about Amelia."

"Very wise. I wouldn't tell you. Anyway, let's not talk about our exes. I can't think why, but a sudden flare of jealousy just hit me."

Of course, he was teasing her. "Why don't you go into movies?" she suggested with a trace of hostility. "You've got the looks—and the talent."

"The problem is, I'm fully occupied in my own world."

"And you're extremely ambitious."

"Famous for it," he admitted. "I also intend to put certain wrongs to right."

Jewel toyed with her champagne glass, but her gaze remained intent on him. "Does this include smacking Amelia's and Travis Copeland's heads together?"

He laughed, looked off across the gently opulent room. "You've got quite a repertoire of little jokes." He paused, then told her grimly, "I hold onto my memories, Jewel."

"I pray I'll forget mine," she responded, then immediately regretted the admission.

"Was it that bad?" His black eyes, heavily lashed, lit with interest and—was it sympathy?

"Yes," she said curtly.

"Yet despite this disadvantaged childhood, you managed to establish yourself in a competitive world."

"And deserved to," she returned with some spirit. "I worked very hard. At one point in my university days, I was even unpacking crates in a warehouse."

"Do you think that hurt you?" His interest appeared flatteringly intense.

"No, not really." She shook her head, which set her hair dancing. "I had plenty of energy."

"And you still have." He smiled, letting his appreciative gaze travel over her. She was wearing a simple one-shouldered dress in a color that reminded him of African violets. The material, soft and supple, lightly skimmed her body yet it seemed to mold every womanly curve. Candlelight enhanced the deep violet of her dress, throwing a shimmering haze around her. It accented up her beautiful coloring and the perfection of her skin. This was a woman who could steal a man's heart…but she wasn't about to steal his. He had too many other pressing concerns. The mess Copeland was making of things. The way he was raising the hackles of important Asian clients with his arrogant manner. This was something relatively new, but when Travis felt threatened, he resorted to these airs of superiority. God knows how Travis Copeland would react to this challenging young woman. She wasn't the type to be easily cowed, unlike Amelia, who, for all her pampered background, was. A few sharp words from her father were enough to send Amelia into an emotional decline. He knew that wouldn't happen with Jewel. She was too much of a fighter.

"What are you thinking about?" Jewel asked, as he continued to regard her in thoughtful silence.

"I was thinking you wouldn't be a woman to cross,"

he answered lightly. "Tell me, what caused the split between you and your last boyfriend?"

"Why don't you phone him and ask? Anyway, 'boyfriend' is a silly term."

"I don't think anyone's come up with anything better," he reasoned mildly. "The guy you were in love with, then."

Jewel quickly looked away. "Maybe my own ambitions overshadowed my romance. He was and is a fine, decent man, but for some reason I couldn't deal with the thought of marrying him. No doubt a result of my dysfunctional early life. Abandoned by my so-called father, losing my true father—all that. Who was the last woman to share *your* bed?" she goaded, unwilling to let him ask all the unsettling questions. "I can see you're having difficulty remembering."

He held up an elegantly shaped, darkly tanned hand. "No, I can tell you exactly. She's an old friend and very charming."

"Married?" She raised her winged brows.

"I don't make a habit of desiring married women," he murmured.

"Do you desire *me?*" It was said in no way seductively but as a straightforward question.

"I'm attempting not to." He couldn't help it; he laughed.

The smile alone would make most women fall into his arms. *But not me,* Jewel vowed. She hadn't the slightest wish to get burned. "Part of you will never forget who you are," she said, slowly tipping her head to one side. "A Connellan, with all the responsibility— and all the privilege—that implies. You won't mess up your meticulously planned life."

"How well you know me," he jeered, eyes unreadable.

"Your life hasn't all been glamour and power, has it?"

"Not at all." His handsome face sobered. "Losing my father was a tremendous blow. I could've searched the whole world over and never found a better role model. My mother and my grandmother went through a long, deep period of mourning. Both of them would tell you they found strength because they had me to raise. They had to put up a fight to retain what we had until I was ready to take over. And then we had Davina on our side. Davina is a woman of honor."

"It's obvious she's very fond of you."

"The caring is mutual," he said. "I'll do anything to protect her, especially now that she's growing older and frailer. It's been very exhausting, even for a woman like Davina, to cope with Travis. For many long years, that house was a battlefield. A complete contrast to the peace and harmony of my own. If Amelia reacted badly when she walked in on you and Davina, you have to remember the Copeland fortune is *everything* to them."

"If that's the case, I should pity her," Jewel said, experiencing anger all over again.

"Maybe you should. Most people think Amelia has it all, but I've seen her go through real misery."

"Because of her father?" Jewel stared at him.

"Travis plays far too important a role in her life," he said. "She's always tried desperately to please him but never really succeeded. Not that anyone could. Travis had a tough time with his own father, so the pattern of oppression and disapproval continues."

"How awful! Why doesn't she simply leave? Why's

she living there? She's a few years older than I am. I'd expect a woman of thirty to have some initiative and a few skills. Why doesn't she learn to support herself?''

"You're not listening, Jewel." There was a hard edge in his tone. "Amelia is the heiress waiting to ascend the throne. She lives for that day. It's the one reason she puts up with so much.''

"Doesn't he love her?" Jewel felt increasingly disgusted with Travis Copeland. "What's wrong with the man? Doesn't he have any sense of remorse, any tender feelings?''

"He *does* love her in his own peculiar way. He wouldn't, for instance, countenance your claim to her throne. Still, he's a bully as opposed to an out-and-out tyrant like Sir Julius. And if you want to know about Travis's tender feelings and his capacity for remorse, you should ask his ex-wife, Amelia's mother. She's a tough lady, but he cut her to pieces.''

"Charming. I don't think I'd like to meet him.''

"You wouldn't, except for one thing. Davina wants her granddaughter," Keefe Connellan told her. "Her other granddaughter. *You.* Much as Travis strains under the yoke, his mother is head of the family. What she says goes.''

"There's still no positive proof." Jewel allowed the bubbling champagne to fill her dry mouth.

"Instinct and a wealth of circumstantial evidence.''

"Why the shift in *your* attitude?" she asked bluntly.

"Initially, I saw you as engineering the whole thing. With Skinner's full support.''

"And now?''

"What I think doesn't matter at all. Davina has taken you to her heart." He gave her that seductive, practiced smile and another faint shrug. "Shall we order? The lobster looks good."

Jewel hadn't realized she was so unashamedly hungry. She even felt reckless, which didn't augur well. No doubt due to the champagne, combined with Keefe Connellan's exhilarating presence. It immersed her in an intoxication the likes of which she'd never known. She had to keep reminding herself that beneath his striking exterior lurked a human calculating machine.

The food was delicious. One incredible dish after the other. A salad of lobster, quickly fried with roasted pine nuts and watercress, dressed sparingly and arranged on slices of warm baby potato. This was followed by steamed Red Emperor served in a banana leaf with papaw chilli and coconut salsa. Afterward, Jewel surrendered to a small ginger soufflé with Calvados cream, while he settled for a slice of almond tart with burnt-honey ice cream.

"That was wonderful!" she said sincerely, finally laying her spoon down. "Just splendid. I've been here a few times before, but it's so very expensive and hard to get in without reserving well in advance."

He smiled without commenting.

"How did you manage it?" she asked.

"It helps to own this block."

"Of course." She rolled her eyes. "I should've known."

"Are we going to have coffee? Or did you plan to invite me to your town house?"

"I don't know." Her brain was reeling at the thought of him inside her home. It wasn't like her to feel so vulnerable. She preferred being contained. "You're a dangerous man." She made the admission. Indeed, his sexual allure was a powerful weapon.

He nodded, his lean face creasing into a smile as though she'd said something totally inoffensive. "Definitely, but not to you. I make it my business never to hurt women."

"As though it were that simple."

"I meant *deliberately*. My mother brought me up to be a gentleman. Having said that, shall we go?"

"Why not?" she agreed briskly. "You know, I'm just the teeniest bit intoxicated. It's…an interesting sensation." And not one she was used to.

"I promise you I won't take advantage of it." He gestured to a hovering waiter, requested the bill, pulled out a card.

"I never said it was affecting me *that* badly," Jewel responded a shade edgily. "I'm absolutely certain you'll have no difficulty whatsoever keeping your hands off me."

His dark eyes swept her briefly. "Let's see if you're right."

WHAT FATE HAD IN STORE for Jewel, she was totally unprepared for: her first view of her father.

Keefe Connellan had maneuvered her effortlessly through the dining room, acknowledging friends and acquaintances along the way. Jewel was very aware that, unlike her, he knew everyone there. Once they'd left the restaurant proper, their exit via the elegant foyer was blocked by a large party of late diners, some four or five couples. The men were all in dinner suits; the women, none of them young, visions of glamour in surprisingly fashionable evening dress. They looked as if they'd come from somewhere else, as indeed they had. A little "do" at Parliament House. Jewel registered their affluent, civilized air but little else. She had never been one to stare, even at people who liked to be stared at. Consequently she was caught off guard when a tall, dark impressive-looking man with the silver temples of a forties movie star strode toward Keefe, holding out his hand.

"Keefe!" he cried indulgently, stopping before them as though he'd sprung a huge surprise. "I *thought* I'd see you tonight."

For a moment, Jewel wondered if she'd simply dissolve. Death by tremendous shock. *Travis Copeland.*

Here was the man she now believed was her father, yet there was no trace of recognition in her. No piercing grief of the abandoned child. Rather, something about him repelled her. She didn't gauge her reaction as extreme, either. Even Keefe Connellan with his habitual air of command seemed about to spin on his heel but must have decided to shake the older man's hand. Whatever Connellan had been thinking a moment before was now masked by a smooth social smile.

"What's happened to Orlando's, Travis?" he said. "I thought it was your favorite dining spot?"

"Some of the ladies figured they'd like a change. Last-minute decision." Travis Copeland's ice-blue eyes, so light against the dark hair and tanned skin, moved on to Jewel, but his gaze was totally devoid of appreciation. "And this, of course, must be your friend, Ms. Bishop." He said it as though it were a joke.

I'm an adult, Jewel thought. *I don't get crushed by some megalomaniac bully.* Yet instinctively she moved closer to Keefe Connellan, who did far more than she'd expected. He put his arm around her in a gesture that was protective without being patronizing.

What grace, what style! There was sadness in knowing they were, in fact, opponents.

Travis Copeland didn't relish Connellan's grace. If eyes could wound, his did.

"My God, she's so much like my mother it's eerie." Obviously warned by Amelia, he yielded to a faint gasp. "Amazing! They do say we all have a double in this world."

"So they do." Keefe's voice was polite. "*This* time, however, the resemblance is of a more personal nature."

Another glimpse of venom. Only in the eyes. The dark, handsome face continued to smile benignly. "You surely don't trust her." He lowered his voice.

"Trust has nothing to do with it, Travis. I have complete confidence in Jewel's story. So does Davina, which is more important."

Travis laughed and glanced at Jewel quickly. "My mother's an old woman. A lonely old woman. At this stage of her life, she'd accept anyone as her granddaughter. Your friend here, Keefe, although she looks like Davina, is probably a real pro."

In other words, a cheap tart. *I should stamp down hard on his foot,* Jewel thought. Aunt Judith would have, and cursed him, as well.

"Some people will do anything to get noticed," Copeland continued in that mock-humorous upper-crust voice. "But eventually we'll get to the truth."

"There are ways of doing that quickly," Keefe suggested in a mild voice.

Copeland shook his big, arrogant head. "I've got no idea what you're talking about, Keefe. No idea at all. Yet I have the feeling you're accusing me of something." He gave the younger man a half droll, half censorious look.

"I'm attempting damage control," Keefe answered,

his expression grave. "For all of us. For the business. I notice that some of your friends are mighty interested in this conversation. I think Natalie Carlyle's about to beckon Jewel over."

"Don't be ridiculous." Travis threw a nervous glance over his shoulder. "Jewel! What an outlandish name," he said. "A made-up name just like your story, Ms. Bishop."

Jewel found she couldn't bear to look into those frozen eyes. She turned her head, pretending to study a nearby flower arrangement.

"I'll get back at you one of these days, Keefe," Copeland murmured in a quick aside, as he prepared to rejoin his party. "Do remind me."

"Hell, Travis. I'm shaking in fear."

They had to run the gauntlet of Copeland's dinner guests, all of them known to Keefe as he was to them. He flashed that charming smile, tossed in a few cordial "good evenings," and then they were out in the star-spangled night, a cooling breeze blowing off the river to cool the turmoil in Jewel's blood.

"That man is *scary*," she said in a heartfelt tone. "It's not often I run into someone who frightens me as much. I thought you were tough, but you're like Sir Galahad compared to him."

"I told you I was raised to be a gentleman. Anyway, he can't hurt you. I promise."

Jewel was having difficulty keeping up the breathless pace. "I'll remember that when I get my first threatening letter. He looked at me like I was a despicable nobody."

"You're infinitely more respectable than that," he said with casual amusement. He recognized another half-dozen patrons, also leaving the restaurant. Smiles and waves. Plenty of curious glances.

"Well, thank you. But didn't you think he might turn up here?"

He pressed his hand to her back as they forged across the busy street. "Actually, Travis and his friends have always preferred the Paxton."

"You mean they don't patronize anywhere else, even occasionally?"

"Don't blame me for this." The uptown traffic stopped at the lights across from where his BMW was parked.

"I *am* blaming you," Jewel said. "That was what my aunt Judith would rather crudely call a 'balls-up.'"

"So it is. So it is." He suddenly burst out laughing. "I'm half in love with Aunt Judith already, but I swear to God, Travis was the last person I expected to see tonight."

"Is nowhere safe?" Jewel's breath was fluttering. "He hates me. More than that, he loathes me. He kept smiling that cold, nasty smile when the steam was nearly coming out of his ears."

"You're a puzzlement to him, that's why." He used his remote to unlock the car. "Why didn't you say anything?" He turned to look down into her face.

Jewel shook her head violently. "I'm never going to say anything to him. Ever. Not a word. He's not the only one who doesn't want him to be my father."

He opened the passenger door for her. "He knows in his heart that you're his child. I've had years and years to measure his reactions. I could tell you shocked the living daylights out of him."

Jewel was incredulous. "You can't be serious."

"Get in," he ordered, using his CEO voice.

"Please," she murmured.

"Get in, *please.* Either that or I'll have to sweep you off your feet."

"I rather think I'd like to be swept off my feet," she told him audaciously, but obeyed, slipping into the passenger seat while he closed the door.

The next moment he was behind the wheel, pulling into the traffic. "So where's it to be? Your place or mine?"

She knew he was joking but her whole body felt saturated in heat. "I can offer you coffee," she said with feigned composure.

"I'll accept it gladly."

"Just coffee. Maybe a little conversation."

"My dear Ms. Bishop, that's understood."

She thought he might have the most attractive laugh she'd ever heard.

It had been a night of very real shock and pure pleasure. Her life was becoming increasingly complicated. Until recently, it had been one long lie. She'd been reared to believe Steven Bishop was her father, and in the ways that counted, she still believed that. Having met Travis Copeland, she felt pity for her mother—young and inexperienced, lonely, confronted by the devil in human form. Travis Copeland was handsome now; Jewel could picture him as a swaggering young man with his intoxicating background of power and riches. She could see her mother made to feel so pretty, so desirable, his hands on her....

"What's the matter?" Keefe Connellan turned his face to her, as she sharply drew in her breath.

"I was thinking how easy it would've been for a man like Travis Copeland to seduce my mother," she said, recognizing both sympathy and anger. "Even easier for him to disappear. I've read everything I could about the day of the funeral. The news reports indicated that he was attacked by an unnamed assailant. A disgruntled employee, they said.'' She swallowed with difficulty. ''Poor Steven Bishop! He didn't rate a name. The rich know how to cover up their mistakes,'' she added bitterly.

''Travis isn't going to be able to cover *you*,'' he pointed out.

''I don't think he's about to let me into the family, either.''

''He was waiting for some response from you.''

''Why do you think I spent so much time staring at the flowers? His broken nose never did heal properly, did it?'' she added with satisfaction. ''One up for Dad. It must have been frightful for him to realize he'd been so betrayed.''

''Add to which he'd learned the truth about the daughter he adored. Still, he should've given himself time—a chance to adjust.''

''That is, if he *did* commit suicide. It might have been an accident.''

''Only, it wasn't. The police were as good as certain.''

''I was so small. I didn't grasp anything that happened back then. I still miss him, you know.''

He glanced at her in the intimate darkness. ''I can understand that.'' After a pause he asked, ''Have you ever been head over heels in love?'' he finally asked, surprising her. ''I mean the passionate, romantic love you read about in books?''

''Have you?''

He shook his head. ''I haven't been married, either.''

"Weren't you almost engaged to Amelia?" She found herself desperate to get to the heart of the matter.

"I've known Amelia all my life," he said, "but in the end, I don't think I know her at all."

"She's that deep?" She affected an astonished voice.

"In a word, no."

"But things were very cozy between you. Still are?"

"And you never really loved your lawyer. Did you live with him?"

"Good Lord, no! I couldn't bear to have a man messing up my house. And I'm not in favor of live-ins without commitment."

"Indeed," he drawled.

"Have your fun."

"On the contrary. I like a woman who demands respect."

ON THE WAY into her stylish little town house, her high heel caught in a crack in the pavement. "Oh!" Damn it, these were her best evening shoes.

"All right?" He caught her to him as she tripped, one arm locking around her waist. "You know, I think you're right. You're borderline tipsy."

"I am not." She denied it indignantly. "It's my shoes. Anyway, even if I were, running into my so-called father would've sobered me instantly."

"Now *that* I believe." He looked about him with interest. "I know the architect who designed this building. A dynamic guy. I'm interested to see how it turned out."

"Well, it's exactly what I wanted," Jewel said, inserting the front door key in the lock. "Fresh, clean, with the illusion of spaciousness and light. Lots of maple, which I like. Come in.''

''After you.''

Jewel reached for the panel of light switches that completely illuminated the downstairs area. She was glad now that she'd spent so much money on several beautiful white Phalaenopsis orchids she'd placed in strategic spots. They floated like exquisite butterflies in the low golden glow, adding their own magic to the furniture, the objects and the various attractive but relatively inexpensive paintings she'd bought over the years.

''I'm impressed with what I see,'' he said. ''Did you do your own decorating?''

''I certainly did,'' she said.

''Then, I admire your taste.'' His dark eyes moved appreciatively around the open-plan area.

''For that, you may get invited again.''

''I'd enjoy that very much.'' He turned to look at her. The lighting gleamed on his thick hair, black as a crow's wing.

''Why? What are you up to, Keefe Connellan?'' She was half smiling, half serious.

''Surely you realize you'll be joining one big happy family.''

''So you've decided to like me?''

''Maybe.'' He smiled, too.

''I think you have quite a capacity for strategic responses.''

''I mean what I say.''

Jewel dropped her evening purse on an armchair. She walked through the living-dining area, defined by free-floating timber panels, on which she'd hung paintings, to the small functional kitchen with its high-gloss steel fixtures and dark green granite countertops, "How about a cheeseburger?" she asked flippantly. "Or I can make you a steak. Or a—"

"I don't think I can fit it in. Just coffee. Unless you want me to stay the night."

Jewel let a few seconds go by, hoping her face didn't betray how she felt. Her dress might had been peeled away, exposing her naked trembling body. This man was taking her places she'd never been, introducing her to sensations she'd never experienced. Nevertheless, she managed to say lightly, "Nice try, but I don't. I trust your ego's not suffering because of it."

"Actually, it's a rule of mine never to sleep with a woman on the first date." He bent to read the signature on one of the paintings. "I like this."

"I'll have it delivered to you in the morning," she joked.

"No, it's very good. Where did you get it?"

"The Young Contemporary Studio." She spooned the freshly ground coffee into the plunger. "That's where I got them all. I love paintings but I can only afford the up-and-coming."

He straightened. "All of these show talent. Is there a terrace?"

She gazed at him thoughtfully. "You're genuinely interested in my house?"

"Of course I am. One doesn't have to pay a fortune to achieve good design. You obviously have a sense of style."

"It couldn't have been inherited from Sir Julius. Nero would have felt at home at the Copeland villa." Jewel paused in her coffee-making to turn on the terrace lights. Paved in slate, it was set with a single recliner and four large Asian pots filled to overflowing with pink flowering hydrangeas and a single contrasting blue agapanthus.

She watched him move out into the starlight, as she struggled with feelings she could only describe as intense. The last thing in the world she wanted was to make a fool of herself with this man. She closed her eyes for a moment, shutting out his deeply exciting presence, deliberately trying to control the heavy beating of her heart.

When she opened them again, he was standing right in front of her.

"You startled me," she gasped.

"Only because you were lost in thought." Watching her, he lifted a hand to grasp a handful of her hair. "You're a very beautiful woman," he said, those brilliant eyes like smoldering lamps.

"And you're a very disturbing man."

"How's that?"

Despite herself, she felt her back arch. "Power has its own high voltage." Wasn't she already scorched?

"You can't be saying I have power over *you?*"

"I wouldn't be fool enough to let you use it." She had the oddest sensation that the whole room was receding, leaving them both enveloped in a heat-induced mirage.

"How would you go about stopping me?"

"By pushing you away." She brought up her hands to place them against the lapels of his suit jacket, acutely aware that they were trembling.

"Desire's a funny thing, isn't it?" he mused, his voice low and absorbed. "Like a moth to a flame. You know you're going to get burned, yet you can't resist it."

With his hand still caressing her cheek, he bent his head until his mouth covered hers.

Peaches. She could taste peaches.

From then on, she had difficulty thinking as the full rush of sexual desire hit her body.

The kiss seemed to go on and on, almost as though she was dreaming, except that the reactions of her body were too real, too convulsive. She was feeling it all too deeply, allowing the entry of his tongue, her own entwined eagerly with his. Her nipples, budded to the point of pain, thrust against the supple fabric of her dress, and the silken place between her thighs began to throb.

God, she had been wanting this for years but had never reached it. And all with a kiss! Her own mouth was nectar, open and molded to his, her body yielding as his hand sought and found the curve of her breast.

How easy it would be to surrender. How easy to let him pick her up and carry her to bed. A fantasy lover taking her from the wildest elation...to possible despair. If you gave someone that power over you, it became almost impossible to protect yourself. She wasn't the first and she wouldn't be the last to experience manic surges of emotion, of passion, that affected the rest of her life. Her mother, for instance. Becoming like her mother had once been her greatest fear.

"You're a siren, aren't you," he accused, as though he, too, was questioning their actions. "The Lorelei, luring a poor sailor onto the rocks."

It was a new view of herself for Jewel. "Isn't it gratifying we've both got good heads on our shoulders." With a supreme effort she drew back, one of the hardest things she'd ever done. "Sexual attraction.

That's all it amounts to. There's no protection against the body's chemicals, hormones, neurotransmitters, whatever.''

"Depend on you to come up with an explanation." His voice was infused with dark laughter. "All the same, I don't think I knew what a kiss was until tonight. You have the most seductive, provocative mouth.''

"Perhaps it's because of you." She was amazed she sounded so normal. "Usually I'm so controlled.''

"So am I. But what a difference tonight." He kissed the arc of her throat.

She almost wished he'd do that forever. "We'll know better the next time. It must be a terrible thing to really be in love." She swept her hair aside so he could nibble her ear. "The power one hands over to another human being is too complete.''

"Agreed, but it's either take a risk or miss out on *this*.''

More gossamer, burning kisses. They were fracturing her determination to end this extraordinary episode. "The coffee's ready." She spoke as decisively as she could.

"Great. I need it." He thrust a hand through his hair, missing a dark lock that fell forward onto his temple. It softened the rather severe look of his face in repose.

They each backed off, staring into one another's faces until Jewel belatedly turned away, lifting the coffeepot.

"My mother stopped living when Dad was killed." She made the confession spontaneously. "He'll always be 'Dad' to me. After his death I had a lot of responsibilities.'' These were the experiences and feelings that defined her, and she wanted him to understand.

"That made you a woman of substance." He found the coffee cups and saucers without being told where they were.

"It's made me very, very cautious," Jewel said. "I suppose I was about ten when I swore I'd never allow myself to be put in the same position as my mother. Grieving terribly for a dead husband. Love meant loss. Pretty much the end of life, even when you were young. Now I know that not only was Mama grieving for Dad, she couldn't rid herself of her guilt and her degrading memories."

He had no wish to defend Travis Copeland. Still, he caught her arm, trying to comfort her. "It may not have been as you think. Only two people know. Your mother and Travis. They could have formed a genuine emotional attachment."

Jewel shook her head. "It was pretty short term. He made sure he stayed away. Davina told me that. Travis Copeland is a cruel person, and I know I could never love him, even if I'd been raised as his daughter."

"Amelia idolizes him despite all her unhappy experience," he said, rather discordantly.

"It must have something to do with her personality. Maybe she's a masochist. Some women are. They love men even when they're brutal and abusive. Not me. I'm not in the market for that kind of humiliation. After tonight, I want nothing to do with Travis Copeland."

CHAPTER EIGHT

HE ARRIVED HOME in a fury, not caring if he disturbed the household. He knocked at Amelia's door first. She'd returned from a private dinner party only ten minutes before, so she was still in her short chiffon slip dress.

"Father, what is it?" she asked in hushed tones, glancing past him down the hallway. He swept past her without a word, so Amelia immediately closed the door behind her.

"I saw that girl tonight. Thea's girl," Travis told her savagely.

"Jewel Bishop?" Amelia's strained half-smile was wiped from her face.

"And you'll never guess who she was with," Travis exploded, pitching Amelia's beautiful expensive evening purse off an armchair so he could sit down.

"Don't tell me. *Keefe*." Amelia's golden-skinned, oval face went pale as she sank into the chair opposite him.

"Yes, Keefe Bloody Connellan," Travis confirmed, looking steadily and harshly at his daughter. "How old are you now, Amelia?"

Inside Amelia withered. "You know perfectly well, Father. I'm twenty-eight."

"And how long have you been trying to get Keefe Connellan to marry you?"

Icy fingers clutched her heart. It seemed now that she'd spent her life on a knife edge, always evading her father's disdain. "It feels like a hundred years," she said with a sigh that might have been a sob.

"Well, that girl had him in tow." Travis Copeland's heavily handsome head shook as though he had palsy. "What does that say for *you?*" He answered himself. "Not much."

"She's very beautiful, Father," Amelia told him. "Any man might fall in love with her."

"Love, love. What's love got to do with anything?" Travis looked back, incredulous at her simplistic thinking. "Keefe's a born manipulator. He's most likely using the girl. Mother's fallen for her story like a ton of bricks. God knows, she's her mirror image. I tell you, I got an appalling shock. I—"

"Who is she, Father?" Amelia interrupted him.

"She's a bloody impostor, that's what she is." Travis, used to deference, shot his daughter a furious look.

"Gran doesn't think so." It took courage for Amelia to say it.

"Your grandmother is in her dotage," he said scornfully. A little more courage trickled into Amelia's veins.

"I've never met anyone less unhinged. Gran gives us all strength. So...you're saying she's *not* your daughter?"

Travis stared at her, his expression malignant. "I have *one* daughter. Everyone knows that."

"You *had* one daughter until Jewel showed up." Amelia heard the nervousness in her voice.

"Don't use that ridiculous name," her father thundered.

"It suits her," Amelia said. She hadn't been able to stop thinking of Jewel. *Those beautiful violet eyes.* "She has Gran's eyes."

"Why don't you accuse me of betraying your mother and be done with it?" Travis snapped. "I couldn't care less."

"I suppose not." When her father wasn't setting out to charm, she realized he didn't really love her. Any affection he showed was for the benefit of an audience. "None of us can keep up with your affairs, Father. Gran said you flew into Mingaree Station often in the old days. Then you stopped."

"So?" Travis Copeland's heavy, muscled body went rigid and intense. "I did many things for my father. I was his right hand."

Even Amelia knew that wasn't true. "The question is, what are we going to do about her? Pay her off?"

"Frighten her off is more like it." Travis Copeland swore beneath his breath, his face twisted with emotion. "She never said one word, but you should've seen her eyes. How dare she look at me as though I were beneath her contempt! Who does she think she is, the little nobody? Who's she plotting with? Keefe? He'd do anything to ruin me."

Amelia pressed her hands together so tightly they looked bloodless. "That's not true, Father. I hate to hear you talking about Keefe like that. He's a good man."

"He's a top-notch wheeler-dealer, you mean. Mark my words, he's got some plan going. You obviously don't interest him, for all the time and money that's been spent on you. My God, you've got the looks but you're just like your mother. Frigid. Not a trace of sex appeal, let alone fascination. That girl has it. Even I

could see that. I tell you, Amelia, I couldn't be more
disappointed in you. I had great hopes for our two families to be united. Keefe would owe me his loyalty then.
But you couldn't get him to propose. Great God, it
doesn't have to be a love match! Surely you understand
that. Families like ours have to think in bigger terms.
We have to think of the Fortune. You enjoy being rich,
don't you?''

"Of course I do, Father," Amelia said. "But being
rich is *all* I am," she whispered with unusual honesty.
"You've never encouraged me to use my brain. But I
know we have real trouble this time."

"You know that, do you?" He mocked her cruelly.
"Why do you think I'm here? I don't usually start up
a conversation this time of night."

"Gran is going to recognize her," Amelia told him
carefully.

"Over my dead body." His anger was so intense he
kicked Amelia's evening purse out of the way. "Or
hers."

Amelia felt ill. Her father was such a violent person
he sometimes terrified her. "Gran is still a powerful,
mentally strong woman. She's head of the family. Not
only that, she has an ally in Keefe. Keefe and his family. They won't be swept aside, Father. Keefe is going
to get back every last penny the Connellan family
lost."

The icy eyes, cold and hard, flashed. "Whose side
are you on, my dear?"

"*Yours,* Father. I'm always on your side." And that
had been her whole life up to date.

"As I expect you to be," he told her. Indeed, Amelia's blind loyalty was important to him. "I can't have

this girl destroying our world. Making a spectacle of me.''

''Even if she *is* your daughter?'' Amelia's heart was hammering so hard she was short of breath.

''I will *never* recognize her.'' Travis looked squarely into her eyes.

''So she *is* your daughter,'' Amelia blurted, feeling her own identity had been wrenched from her. ''I wanted to have her thrown out of the house today, but I knew in my bones she had a right to be here. The look on Gran's face wounded me terribly. The love that was in it. For *her*.'' She shook her head. ''There's no trace of Gran in me. You've had such a hold over me, Father. I used to hate Mother for saying I spent my entire life trying to please you and no one else. But it's true. And…and Jewel is my half sister.''

''Whose mother is feebleminded,'' Travis shouted back, startling her. ''An emotional wreck. So even *you* have betrayed me behind my back? Now, at this time of my life.''

''I told you tonight that Jewel was here at Gran's invitation,'' Amelia reminded him desperately. ''But you were on your way out, and there wasn't time to talk about it further.''

Travis Copeland came to his feet, glaring. ''I'll get rid of this girl,'' he cried. ''Have no doubt about that. *You* are my heir. The child of my marriage. Your inheritance is safe. You had a chance to please me by marrying Connellan. In one swoop, a marriage would've put everything to rights. United families can't fight each other. Keefe would've seen sense. An alliance was crucial, still is, but on *my* terms, which means you. After tonight I've come away with the feeling that you're not up to it.''

The disappointment in his voice was so bitter, Amelia felt like collapsing at his feet, begging forgiveness. "There might be a chance, Father. I know Keefe cares for me."

"Then, why doesn't he marry you?" Her father let out a growl of frustration, then started walking to the door. "Dear God, that it should come to this...."

"You're not going to disturb Gran, are you, Father?" Amelia was plunged into the depths of anxiety. Anything was possible with her father in this mood.

"Oh, go to bed." He spoke as though he disliked her intensely. "The meeting with my mother can wait until morning."

"OKAY, TRAVIS, what is it?" Davina, who was standing in front of an exquisite French *secretaire* looked critically at her son. She had known perfectly well that Amelia would inform her father of Jewel's visit. Consequently, she was prepared for this confrontation. Travis had inherited all Julius's worst qualities, including the rages, but few of his strengths. It was an arrow in her heart, for she continued to love him despite the conflicts that had filled their lives.

"I wanted to speak to you about the girl, Mother." Travis Copeland instinctively began carefully. His awe of his mother had been well-hidden for many years, yet he felt compelled to swallow his anger and bitterness. It was now nine o'clock and his mother had kept him waiting for an hour while she dressed.

"Your *daughter,* Travis?" Davina, being Davina, stripped away all pretense. "She is your daughter, isn't she, Travis? Thea Bishop's child."

Travis licked his dry lips, his expression changing

to one of self-loathing. "She isn't the only woman who's tricked me."

Davina laughed grimly. "You mean there might be more grandchildren tucked away somewhere?"

Travis snapped his fingers. "Of course not, Mother. She was just a silly little girl. I was kind to her, and how did she respond? She was all over me every time I turned up."

"You mean she was ready and waiting for an affair?"

"Aren't they all!" Not sweet little Thea, no. Both of them had surrendered to a powerful impulse. Travis shook his head to clear the memory that survived.

Davina sighed heavily, hardly guessing her son's thoughts. "You have a callous hand with women, Travis. Even your father didn't have that. Riches can spoil. They spoiled you. Had this Thea been the sort of young woman to have easy affairs, she wouldn't have let you get away with fathering her child. She'd have slapped a paternity suit on you and fast. She wouldn't have spent the past twenty years bitterly regretting an act or acts that tore her family apart. I should've known to go further when I saw that tragic young man, Steven Bishop, strike you at your father's funeral. I guessed you'd taken advantage of his wife, of course. Sonia thought the same thing. Neither of us knew about the child. But *you* did."

"I didn't know there was a child." Not at the beginning, anyway. That part was true. He swallowed on a hard knot in his throat. Didn't anyone realize he had his own capacity for pain? "I didn't believe for one moment she was mine."

"That won't hold up as an excuse, Travis." Davina was shaking her head, every pearl-white hair in place.

"Jewel is the living image of me when I was young. You don't often see resemblances like that. You don't see natural blondes with black lashes and brows."

"I never saw any resemblance," Travis said, moving his eyes away. This was becoming unbearable.

"You're lying. You're not a fool, Travis, whatever else you are. You abandoned her and her mother."

"What else was I supposed to do?" he cried, not concealing his feelings of impotence. "Tell me, Mother. Go to Father? Tell you? Tell that cold bitch of a Sonia who offered me her body exactly like a sacrifice? All three of you would've torn me to shreds. The scandal would have been shattering. God Almighty, Father thought he was Caesar." He shrugged helplessly. "Do you really think I'm the only man who's had to turn his back on his child?"

"No, I don't. I'm a woman of the world. But you were bound to help them financially, Travis. Your father's been dead twenty years. You and Sonia are divorced. And why would you ever think *I'd* turn my back on my own granddaughter? I'd be damned forever if I did."

Travis gazed at his mother with wondering eyes. "So you're going to ruin all our lives?" he challenged, his strong jaw thrust out. "Yours, mine, Amelia's? You've never really loved her, have you."

Davina's hand went to the dull ache in her breast. "You've twisted Amelia's character, Travis. You deliberately took her away from her mother and me. You wouldn't let our relationship flower. You're wrong when you say I don't love her. I love her very much. That's why I don't want to see everything that's good in her disappear."

"Why is it, Mother, that you blame me?" Travis

asked in a hoarse voice, going far back into his childhood and adolescence, remembering his virtually arranged marriage to a woman who'd turned out to be
frigid in bed. She *hated* it. Nothing like the desire that
had flowed between him and…and…the sort of woman
he'd really wanted—sweet, soft, sensitive to his needs.
A woman who actually used to hang on his every
word…. Unlike his father and mother, who were too
brilliant, too motivated and too self-disciplined, too tremendously sure of themselves and their place in the
scheme of things. Both of them had turned him into
the man he was, full of frustration and fury. Sometimes
he thought he couldn't bear what he had become.

Now he tried to explain his strong dependence on
his daughter, Amelia, who sprang to his defense, no
matter what. "Anyone would tell you I've been the
most indulgent father on earth to Amelia, Mother," he
said, truly believing it. "She's wanted for nothing."

"Except your *unconditional* love, Travis," Davina
pointed out. "There are always strings attached. If she
doesn't please you, you're sarcastic to her, even hostile.
You've given her hell over Keefe. Don't you know you
can't make people fall in love on demand?"

"Why would you be telling *me* that?" Travis
showed his profound resentment. "Father as good as
forced me into marrying Sonia."

"She really loved you, Travis." Sonia had never
been Davina's choice, but she tried to be fair.

"She *screamed* the first time I tried to make love to
her on our honeymoon. How do you think that sits with
a man, Mother? I've had plenty of affairs since then,
not a one of any consequence, but at least no one's let
out a scream."

This was news indeed to Davina. She sat down as

though she'd suddenly lost the power of her legs. "I'm very sorry, Travis. You never told me that before. I know you had a difficult marriage, but you must remember you ignored my advice. I told you not to get mixed up with the Watson Smythes. They're such an odd family."

"My God, and ours isn't?" Travis said. "By the time I was married, Father had me convinced I was an idiot. 'Boofhead'—isn't that what he called me? Sonia carried on in the same vein. No wonder I fell in love with Thea. She was a different human being altogether. Gentle and loving. Full of mercy."

"Oh, my dear boy." Whatever Davina had been expecting, it wasn't this. She'd even faced the worst possible scenario—rape. "Why didn't you come to me?" She stared into her son's wretched eyes.

"I couldn't." Travis recalled how he had tried. "Father would've heard about it eventually. He'd have cut me off without a moment's hesitation. That's the way he was."

Davina drew a short, shallow breath. "He wouldn't have done it, Travis. I wouldn't have let him. He used his power over you like a whip. I think he thought it would make you stronger. Extraordinary, isn't it? You've always been insecure and your way of confronting it has been to put terrible pressure on others. Amelia's particular terror is that you'll cease loving her altogether. You've made her feel she *has* to get Keefe to marry her as part of that deal. But Keefe and Amelia don't suit each other at all."

"Really?" Travis was livid. On his own and Amelia's account. "So what's *your* dream, Mother? Bring this girl into our lives and let her marry Keefe?"

"This girl, Travis, is your daughter," Davina said

once again. "As much your daughter as Amelia. I want you to meet her."

Travis laughed in his mother's face, his own expression ghastly with pain.

"For once, Mother, I've beaten you to it. I met her last night. Well, not exactly *met*. We weren't properly introduced. She was out dining with your beloved Keefe."

"Was she?" For a moment Davina felt faint. "Now the whole thing's out in the open. You were at the same restaurant?"

"Yes." Travis nodded uncontrollably like a puppet. "We were arriving. They were leaving."

"I suppose all of your party saw her?" The scene flashed before Davina's eyes.

"They saw her, all right, but no one passed any remark. Not to me. They left that for later. She's the very image of you, Mother. She has nothing of me or Thea."

"You sound disappointed." Davina's tone was ironic. She had tried so hard to win her son's love, but he'd never really responded. Too much like his father, believing men ruled the world.

Now he confirmed it, if only to his mother. "I've never liked women who feel they're equal to men," he confided, in the genuine belief that male superiority had been carried unanimously. "You should've seen the way she looked at me."

"You've had your share of approving nods, Travis," Davina said. "Don't be so mean-spirited. Perhaps you should consider Jewel's point of view. She hasn't had an easy life. Far from it. Thea apparently still suffers from severe depression. We'll have to make things easier there, Travis, if they'll let us."

"So you're determined to bring her into the family?" Travis stared at his mother as if she'd gone mad.

"For God's sake, Travis, can't we put things right?" she begged, her eyes bright with unshed tears.

"You're not seeing the implications, Mother," Travis said. "This is the child of one of my mistresses. It was over long ago. Now you want to subject us all to long-term punishment. Where's your pride, your sense of family?"

"It's my sense of family that's speaking, Travis." Davina had recovered her composure. "Blood ties. This family has done bad things. I want to make amends. Compensation, if you like. I want this with all my heart. But let's look at this in a way that might suit you better. Many people will admire you for recognizing your child. Even after all these years. No one needs to know you haven't provided for them."

"What do you mean by that?" he asked sharply.

"I mean we should offer Thea Bishop compensation for raising your child. The burden fell totally on her and her sister. Given her state of mind, she couldn't have done it by herself. These women need some sort of settlement. It's only justice, and we must persuade them of that."

Travis was seized by a mad desire to laugh. "Why don't I just visit Thea in her jungle home?" he said. "Maybe we could even get together again. I could marry her in one of her lucid moments. That would solve the problem, wouldn't it, Mother? Why didn't I think of it before? Thea and I could marry and legitimize our daughter."

"Travis, please stop," Davina implored, holding her head. "It doesn't help to talk crazily."

"What's so crazy about it?" He'd had his arms

crossed over his chest, and now he threw them wide.
He was a big, powerful, angry man. "It's no crazier
than introducing my bastard to society."

"Nobody talks about bastards anymore, Travis,"
Davina pointed out coldly. "If a child feels unloved
and unwanted, the damage can never be repaired."

"Then, you'll have to accept some blame there,
Mother," Travis said. "I barely saw you and Father
when I was a child. My God, most of the time I was
left with Rosie Lennox, a servant in the house."

"Rosie was a tower of strength." Davina looked
down at her hands, beautiful once, now knotted with
arthritis. "A lovely, kind, woman. I didn't leave you
with just anyone. I had to accompany your father ev-
erywhere, Travis, whether I liked it or not. It may not
have been right or for the best, but your father became
my universe."

"You wouldn't attempt this if he were still alive,"
Travis challenged her.

"I suggest you didn't know your father as well as
you think. Julius went ahead with whatever he believed
in and to hell with everyone else. He acted according
to his own judgment and he acted swiftly. I'm certain
he would have made the decision to bring Jewel, his
granddaughter, into the family. I think that, unlike me,
he would've gotten to the bottom of what went on at
Mingaree Station all those years ago, and you wouldn't
have escaped. You must have found your father's death
a great relief."

Travis's face lost color. "I never expected you to be
vindictive, Mother. I idolized Father, as you very well
know. I revere his memory. I'm only saying this new
development might destroy us. Certainly our high
standing in society."

Davina rose and walked to the open doors that led to her private balcony. "Travis, we'd lose our supposedly high standing in society tomorrow if Copeland Connellan crashed. We're powerful because we're rich. The Connellans are powerful because they're universally admired and respected. That's why you've been trying to get Amelia and Keefe married off."

Travis recoiled. "I know my duty. I wish to see my daughter married well."

"Far better she be happy," Davina said wearily. "I married well. So did you. Where did it get us?"

"Are you saying you didn't love Father?" Travis looked his shock.

"Travis, dear, your father was magnificent but he wasn't lovable. In my next life, I'm going to choose someone quite different."

"There is no next life, Mother." Travis shook his head. "This is all we've got. Meeting that girl gave me an enormous shake-up. I'm not the ruthless, heartless bastard you seem to think. I want to love, but I don't seem able to. It's like you say—I see myself with Amelia, giving her the same awful time Father gave me. It's almost as though I was programmed in childhood." He fell silent for a moment, then started up again in quite a different tone. "Keefe put his arm around that girl last night. I know a protective gesture when I see it. He put his arm right around her when I reached them. Just like a shield."

"Keefe is a born gentleman." Davina sighed and returned to her armchair.

"Oh, and I'm not?" Travis lifted his head.

"Maybe as your father's son, it's been beyond you. Without your father there, both of us would've been completely different people."

There was great truth in that.

"But everyone loves you, Mother," Travis assured her, suddenly struck by her frailness. "They all look up to you."

"I don't deserve it," Davina answered quickly. "And I certainly won't deserve it if I turn my back on my own granddaughter. I haven't got all that much longer, Travis. I feel a strong need to put our house in order. I want you to phone your daughter Jewel and persuade her to come to us this weekend. It's a long weekend, so that gives us three days to get to know each other. You and Amelia will remain at home all that time, so you can both cancel your engagements. I want you to invite Keefe, as well, and that nice young man who works for us, Greg McCall. I know for a fact that Amelia enjoys his company, and he's a very pleasant young man to have around the house. Better yet, he's loyal and discreet. The young people can swim and play tennis. There's plenty to do."

Shock and horror clouded Travis's eyes. "You can't be serious, Mother. Even if I wanted to, which I don't— My God, she'd never speak to me."

"Then, you'll have to use your charm, Travis." Davina refused to back away. "You *do* have it when required. Aside from everything else, I want us to sort out our strategies before the press get hold of this thing. From what you tell me, you and Jewel were seen in conversation last night."

"She never said a word to me." Travis knew he sounded fierce and full of indignation.

"That's beside the point. Jewel's resemblance to me, even if I am an old woman, is striking. People aren't fools. Some of them remember me from my prime. Most of them love scandals. You can guarantee the phones have been ringing off the hook. What I'm suggesting to you now is that we beat them all to it with an announcement. That we act as *one* family," she urged.

"Dear God!" Travis buried his head in his hands. "You're ruthless, Mother, once you get started."

Davina shook her head. "Travis, don't you think I feel for you? I know you hide behind that mask. I know all your insecurities. But I love you. Nothing will change that. You are my son. We can't let our wounds fester—we have to bring them into the light of day. The world is a changed place, far more tolerant. Less hypocritical. I promise you, this will be no more than a nine-day wonder. Jewel isn't someone to be ashamed of. On the contrary—she's a daughter to be proud of. It is my dearest wish that you'll come to see that. Do this for me, Travis. It may be the making of us all."

JEWEL WAS STILL IN HER NIGHTGOWN, drinking her morning coffee and reading the newspapers, when Travis Copeland's call came through.

"Hello?"

His voice was so clear, so immediately identifiable, Jewel almost dropped the phone. "It's Travis Copeland here," he said. "And there's a good chance I might be your father."

She didn't know whether to be shocked or infuriated by his offhand announcement. "Thank you for ringing, Mr. Copeland, but I simply don't care." Jewel put down the receiver as if it burned, her whole body trembling. What right did he have to call her? In her own home, yet. She picked up her coffee cup and drained it, going to the kitchen to get more. What did he expect? That she'd forgive him for his paternal shortcomings? For the hard life she and her mother had led?

The phone rang again ten minutes later. Jewel swept up the receiver and spoke in a rush. "I'd appreciate it if you didn't ring my home."

"With no hint of the caller?" Another voice. A different kind of jolt. This one she liked. "How are you, Jewel?" Keefe asked. "Since it's Saturday, there's no chance of getting you at the office."

"I'm fine. Really," she said automatically, trying to disguise a certain breathlessness. "I've just had a phone call from someone you'd never guess if you lived to be a million."

"Travis Copeland, right?"

"I'm impressed. Yes, it was Travis Copeland."

"Actually, it's not a guess. He called me."

Jewel propped herself up against the wall. "Not about me?"

"I was too astounded to make it all out" was the response. "Apparently, he and Davina want you to come and stay with them for the long weekend. Travis was about to issue the invitation, when you hung up on him."

"I admit it. I did. Has he gone mad? Last night he looked like he wanted to hit me over the head with a blunt instrument."

"He's a different man this morning." The low attractive laugh was hard to resist. "I'd say he's had a session with Davina."

"So his mama snaps her fingers and he jumps? I haven't the slightest intention of going back to that house."

"Not even to see your grandmother?" he asked.

Jewel considered. "I'm sorry about that, but no. The

whole idea of it dismays me. For one thing, Amelia couldn't have been any part of that decision."

"Amelia hardly knows what it is to make a decision. If you decide you *can* do it when Travis rings again, give me a call. I've been invited, as well."

Jewel straightened her arm to reach a chair. "If you're trying to confuse me you're doing a darn good job," she said, sinking down.

"Think about it, a foursome. You. Me. Amelia. And a very nice guy named Greg McCall."

"And how's he involved in all this?"

"It's a house party," he explained. "Greg and I get on well together. I have the impression he's keen on Amelia. She certainly likes him. He's in our legal department, so you two should get along, too. He's well-bred, well-educated and he knows where all the bodies are kept."

"Quite. Such is life in big business," she said crisply. "I'm not going, so you can cease your blandishments, Keefe Connellan."

"It really isn't my kind of event, either, but if you're there... Are you sure you don't want the opportunity to beat me in a game of tennis? They have a grass court. Amelia is very, very good. And Travis might be past his prime but he still plays a mean game."

"Absolutely not. I've won my share of games but I haven't played for ages."

"We can still have fun," he cajoled. "We could have lunch together. Lose ourselves, if we wished. It's an enormous place."

"Why do you want me to go?" she asked point-blank.

"I'm not entirely sure." Suddenly he sounded serious. "I'm not close to Travis, but he's a complex char-

acter. I never really knew Sir Julius. I do know there
were a lot of people pleased to say farewell to him.
Though he'd never admit it even before a firing squad,
I'd say Travis was one of them. I'm very fond of Davina, as you know. I've known Amelia all her life. She
could be my cousin.''

She sat there, rejecting that. ''It didn't seem that way
to me. Lovers might be more accurate. I can't decide
whether or not you're on the level. I know I've kissed
you, but I don't know you very well.''

The laugh sounded in his voice. ''That's why I'm
eager for us to spend the weekend together. So we can
remedy that.''

''I really don't believe you.'' Jewel sighed.

''Shall I come over? Try to convince you?''

She shook her head although he couldn't see her.
''I'm still trying to get over what happened last night.
You're not the man I want to get involved with,
Keefe.''

''I'm afraid you already are involved,'' he said. ''I'll
get off the line. Travis is going to ring back. When he
does, for all our sakes, give him a chance.''

CHAPTER NINE

KEEFE FOUND HIS MOTHER in the lush tranquillity of the garden, discussing new design ideas with Arnold, their head gardener. Arnold, "a happily transported Pom," as he described himself, had once worked as a landscape designer for rich clients around the world. He'd been with the Connellans for ten years or so, and under his direction the extensive grounds surrounding the family home had turned into one of the country's great gardens. Year after year, his mother and Arnold opened the garden to the public during the full glory of spring; now they were planning for the year ahead. Serious business. Neither of them seemed to run out of creative ideas, which they discussed endlessly and enjoyed passionately. They were standing in the scented shade, looking toward the river. The brilliant morning sunlight was shining on the deep broad stretch of water, lending the dark green surface a remarkable quality, with bright flashes of color like the heart of a fire opal.

"Hi, there," he called, his shoes sinking a little into the plush emerald-green carpet of lawn.

"Darling!" His mother turned, throwing out her arms in welcome. "Where did you spring from?" Keefe maintained his own inner-city penthouse apartment but called in on his mother and grandmother almost every other day.

"Hi, Keefe, how's it going?" Arnold asked, preparing to move off so mother and son could talk.

"Fine, Arnold." Keefe smiled, putting his arm around his mother's waist, while she stood on tiptoe so she could kiss his cheek. "More plans in the making?"

Arnold, a big, well-set man in his early sixties, nodded. "We have rather a splendid statue coming in. Came out of a Sussex garden. A lady Sphinx. Your mother and I are trying to hit on the best site. It will be enormously heavy, so when it goes down, it stays down."

Keefe, who felt privileged to have this man working for them, said, "Why not place her exactly at the center of the break in those trees across the river? It could be an impressive backdrop."

His mother's dark eyes smiled into his. "We'd more or less decided on that, darling," she said happily.

"Great. I like to get it right. I can't tell you how pleased we are, Arnold, with what you've helped us achieve."

Arnold couldn't control a pleased blush. "There's nothing I've enjoyed more. I mean that. This is a fine place to work and your mother's the best boss in the world."

"Not boss, *colleague*," Rebecca Connellan corrected affectionately.

"Well, I'll be off." Arnold smiled and doffed the cap he always wore. "I have a couple of helpers coming in this morning. We're going to dig a narrow canal running the full length of the west wing, with a fountain at the end. The sight and sound of playing water is wonderful in a hot climate."

"I'll look forward to seeing it," Keefe called. He knew to the cent the considerable amount of money it had taken to establish such a garden and maintain it, but the pleasure provided by these lawns, these trees and formal arrangements and flower beds was worth the expense.

"So, where are you going this weekend?" his mother asked. "Sailing?" She knew Keefe loved his boat, which he kept at a bayside marina.

"That was the intention, but something else came up. Come and sit down for a moment." He took his mother's arm, guiding her to a stone bench set beneath a huge jacaranda. "Travis rang me earlier on, inviting me over to the house for the weekend."

"How absolutely extraordinary!" Rebecca stared at her son, fascinated. "Why did he do that?"

"Davina." He shrugged. "She's put pressure on Travis to meet his long-denied daughter."

"Oh!" Rebecca reeled slightly. "That's going to cause problems."

"It is."

"How did dinner go?" Rebecca patted her son's hand. She and his grandmother, Lady Connellan, had been kept informed of the whole business from day one. "I'd love to hear."

Keefe told her. He left out only that one unplanned, heart-stopping kiss. He might be able to talk about it in a day or two. Not now. Not even to the mother he adored.

"Good grief! It'll be all over town, I suppose." Rebecca sounded somewhat aghast. "Natalie Carlyle is never happier than when she's spreading gossip. This is going to create quite a scandal, Keefe. Are you sure this girl had no real idea of who she is?"

Keefe looked at his mother and half smiled. "Jewel's story is that her mother kept her secret well locked away."

"Do you believe her?"

"Yes and no. A man could believe anything looking

into those dazzling blue eyes. She's very beautiful.
Very sexy. And a whole lot more. Make no mistake.''

"A multilayered woman," Rebecca murmured,
pleased in one way but a little fearful, too.

"A clever, stylish, ambitious woman," Keefe said.
"Who knows what secrets lie behind that beautiful
face?"

Rebecca stared at her son thoughtfully, seeing the
intrigue in his eyes. "It sounds very much as though
she's going to overshadow Amelia."

"Could be," he agreed wryly. "She won't do it on
purpose, though. She's very likable." He caught her
eye and gave her his beguiling smile.

"Then, I have to meet her," Rebecca responded.
"She seems to have made quite an impression on
you."

"And here I was trying to conceal it. Don't get any
ideas, Mother. Neither of us is taking the other seriously."

"That's a relief. The implications could be quite
staggering. Amelia's been madly in love with you for
years."

"Oh God, when I was hoping it had all worn off.
We grew up together. Copeland Connellan—it's almost
incestuous. My relationship with Amelia was finished
a good two years ago, in spite of her father's pressure.
She should turn her attention to someone else. There
are plenty out there."

"Amelia doesn't want to be loved for her money,"
Rebecca said with sympathy.

"Then, she should develop her talents in more fruit-
ful directions," Keefe suggested with a shrug.

"The first step would be to get away from her father.
Travis is a throwback to the Dark Ages. Amelia's
bored, unhappy, unfulfilled. She's finding it extremely

difficult to get over you.'' Rebecca, who cared for Amelia, was worried about her.

"And I'm sorry for her. But I don't love her. I tried. Mostly I pity her. Travis has built this whole thing up, encouraging Amelia to think the two of us would be gloriously happy. Pure fantasy.''

"That's sad. I feel sad,'' Rebecca said. "And somewhat concerned. Amelia would be devastated if you ever found yourself in love with her half sister. Travis wouldn't like it much better. He loves Amelia, as much as it's possible for him to love anyone.''

Keefe compressed his mouth. "I think I'll wait a while, Mother, before I fall in love with anyone.''

"Not too long, darling,'' Rebecca said. "Nan and I are so looking forward to a wonderful romantic wedding. Followed by two or three christenings.''

"Let's get the wedding over first,'' he suggested dryly. "Sure you both haven't picked out baby names?''

"All we want is for you to be happy.'' Rebecca rested her head onto her son's shoulder. Keefe was the source of her greatest happiness in life. He'd been so special since he was a little boy. "When you meet the right woman, I'll be able to tell just by looking at her,'' she said with genuine conviction. "The past has left a mark on all of us. The future is all that matters now.''

Gracefully Keefe picked up his mother's hand and kissed it. "As long as you and Nan need me,'' he said.

TEN O'CLOCK SHARP, he picked up Eugenie Bishop, aka Jewel of the golden hair and glorious blue eyes. With very little effort this woman could bewitch him, he thought, but he wasn't going to allow it to happen. Threats surrounded them. His mother knew it. Nan knew it. So did he. Davina was so desperate to find the grandchild of her heart that she was turning a blind eye to the world she lived in.

Jewel was waiting for him outside her town house. He was acutely aware of her—physical beauty, plus all those other assets that, in the end, a man needed for a lifetime if he was going to find any happiness.

"You're right on time," he said, slamming the door of the BMW and moving to the pavement to collect her single medium-size suitcase. Quite a departure from Amelia, who needed half a dozen pieces just for a weekend.

"I'm always on time," she said. "The business world does not embrace people who are late."

"You look gorgeous."

"If so, I'm not the only one." She cast an approving eye over him.

"How are you feeling?" he asked, stowing her luggage in the trunk.

"Confused." Her whole existence had been turned upside down. And not the least of her confusion was due to this man. There was something so compelling about him, so complex and potentially dangerous, she instinctively found herself trying to repress her natural feeling. Which was to gravitate to him as if he were a magnet.

"Don't worry. So is everyone else." He smiled at her, sending a ripple of excitement, like a warning, the length of her spine.

A moment more, and they were both inside his car, silent as he circled the cul-de-sac and purred off in the direction of Coronation Drive, which ran parallel to the magnificent river on which the city was built.

"It appears Lady Copeland is shaping all our lives," Jewel remarked eventually, looking out at the picturesque paddle steamer plying weekenders and tourists up and down the river.

"She's certainly trying to," he agreed wryly, giving the impression that he shared her concern about where these various relationships were going.

"I hope she's aware that the best laid plans go awry," Jewel said. "Disaster might be staring us all in the face."

He shrugged, as though to minimize her worries.

"Just so long as we don't start killing each other," she said.

"God forbid!" He didn't even smile.

"Tell me, is this Greg McCall my real or fake partner for the weekend?"

He glanced at her briefly. "Greg is more susceptible to beautiful women than I could ever be."

"Being in your position, the heir to a considerable fortune, would keep you from doing anything too extreme," she reminded him.

"I kissed you, didn't I?"

"Ah, yes, but you're well able to deal with that." Her warm, clear voice was almost sardonic.

"Well, I'm giving myself a couple of days for the effect to wear off."

THEY DREW INTO the Copeland driveway some twenty minutes later.

"Nice place!" he said.

"Do I detect an element of friendly contempt?"

"I'm sure most people would consider this a palatial home."

"Would anyone have the money to buy it even if it was offered?" she asked, and brushed back the fall of her hair.

"Not unless it was a Hollywood movie star, but perhaps they wouldn't be interested in the address." He stopped speaking to lower his side window and press the brass button on the stand. "Jewel Bishop and Keefe Connellan," he said.

Immediately the towering gates swung open, and Jewel's jaw clenched.

"*What* am I doing here?" she asked.

"It'll be fine, don't worry," he assured her.

"Fine for *you*. You're Keefe Connellan. Most people think you're Amelia's boyfriend. You're also a business partner of theirs, someone they need. While I'm sort of...a threat."

He turned his head. "Jewel, you can be sure Davina has made it very clear that she intends to bring you into the family, regardless of their views on the matter. And Davina's the one who counts."

"What about me?" Her eyes flashed. "With all due respect to my grandmother, regardless of her power over the rest of the family, she has no power over me. If I'm nothing else, I've learned how to be my own woman."

He let out a soft laugh. "Now, that's something I find very attractive. Relax, Jewel. All the evidence points to your true identity. You're a Copeland, whether you like it or not. You've accepted your father's invitation—"

"Only because you came along," she cut in.

"All right. I've agreed to be your white knight, but unless you plan on moving overseas, this issue has to be confronted. The *family* has to be confronted."

"Don't I know it." She gave a heavy sigh. "But I don't have to be a Copeland to have a life. The life I want."

He stopped the car at the base of the low, broad flight of steps, switched off the ignition and turned to her, one arm lying along the back of the seat. "You want to know who you are, don't you?" He stared into her eyes.

"Yes!" God, if she wasn't careful she'd fall crazily for this man. And where would that get her. "I want to discover the truth," she said, trying humor to cover her nerves. "If I can't get it from Travis Copeland, I'll have to drag it out of my mother."

THE DOUBLE-DEALING HOLLY was at the door to greet them. She addressed Keefe with a face full of admiration, telling him the family was gathered in the atrium. It turned out to be yet another grand space, this one enhanced by a stained-glass domed ceiling, four very large Palladian glass doors that led out onto the terrace and the most spectacular Venetian chandelier Jewel ever expected to see. Davina, beautifully dressed and coiffed, sat regally in a sumptuous armchair that more than encompassed her fragile frame. She was flanked by her son Travis and Amelia—for all the world like two griffins holding up a shield. What made it so extraordinary for Jewel was the fact that they all smiled.

"Jewel, Keefe, how lovely you've arrived." Davina remained seated, while Travis rose slowly and Amelia made a graceful swoop across the marble floor to embrace Keefe Connellan warmly. The main thing accomplished, she then turned to Jewel, holding out her hand.

"Hello there, Jewel. We're all so glad you could come. Father?" She inclined her head as her father approached, a near identical smile to his daughter's painted on his lips.

"Jewel, my dear. Welcome to our home." To her shock he kissed her, bending to brush her cheek. "For-

give me for the last time we met. Shall we start over?''
He looked very persuasively into her eyes.

"I'd appreciate that, Mr. Copeland,'' Jewel said.

He grimaced. "Why don't you call me, Travis?''

"As you wish.''

Travis turned next to Keefe, extending his hand for
the ritual shaking. "Many thanks for coming, Keefe.
Greg won't be here until lunchtime, since we have
things to discuss on our own.''

Jewel moved on to where Lady Copeland was sitting
so expectantly, her eyes full of a blue radiance. "How
are you, Lady Copeland?'' Jewel asked gently.

"I feel wonderful now that you're here,'' Davina
said. "You can't keep calling me Lady Copeland, my
dearest girl. For the time being, you may prefer to call
me Davina. Amelia alternates between Davina and
Gran. Now, won't you both sit down. We were waiting
until you arrived before I rang for morning coffee.''

It entered a few minutes later, on a large trolley
wheeled in by the multipurpose Holly. The trolley was
covered by a starched white damask tablecloth overlaid
by another of very pretty palest pink lace. A small posy
of pink roses rested on top, as well as a silver service,
tea, coffee, delicate bone china cups and saucers and
little wafer-thin sandwiches. Nothing so homely as
scones, but a range of delicious, bite-size sweet con-
fections to indulge in.

"Would you like to be mother?'' Amelia exclaimed.
Her heavyhanded attempt to be witty suggested that she
was desperate to be friends. Jewel and Keefe had been
supplied with little side tables, while the family faced
a banquet-size coffee table. "Gran's hands are a little
shaky these days.''

"Sometimes they're shaky,'' Davina said. "But yes,
Jewel, if you would?''

"My pleasure," Jewel answered easily, not given to pretensions or excessively formal rules of social etiquette. Besides, she was well aware of the challenge behind Amelia's sisterly smiles.

All the photographs she'd seen of her half sister didn't do her justice, Jewel decided. Amelia was very good-looking with her clear golden skin, her large dark eyes and long flowing ribbon of dark hair. She was also naturally very stylish, as tall as Jewel but thinner, pared down to the bone. She was wearing a jade-green silk shirt tucked into boldly printed silk trousers that picked up the color of her shirt. Her flowing hair was slicked back behind her shell-like ears. *Daddy's girl,* even if Daddy was an ogre from time to time. It was perfectly obvious, too, that Amelia was still hell-bent on pursuing Keefe Connellan. Amelia openly adored him with her eyes, she seemed almost to be paying homage, and Jewel found she didn't like it at all.

For several minutes she was kept busy playing "mother," showing her own brand of confidence. Surely one didn't have to study pouring tea? She had learned all about it watching her aunt Judith, who actually did most things right. The little lemon-cream cheese tartlets were so delicious, had she been at home Jewel would've licked her fingers. As it was, she was hungry enough to eat a second when Davina pressed it on her, but Amelia extravagantly shook her head to all offers. She drank her coffee strong and black. Unsugared. But then, she was a young woman conscious of her figure to the point of obsession. The pressures on the heiresses of this world to stay very thin had to be huge, Jewel thought.

"This is so extraordinary for me," Amelia said, reaching out to touch Keefe's arm. "I've never had a sister."

"I wasn't aware I had one, either," Jewel remarked mildly. "We all seem to be agreeing that I'm part of this family, but there's been no proof."

"You surely don't expect me to present you with some?" Travis Copeland gave a wolfish laugh. "You are the image of Mother. I knew you were my daughter the moment I laid eyes on you. I can't believe your mother's never spoken of the past, but then, I understand she suffered a nervous breakdown."

That set Jewel's teeth on edge. "I wouldn't express it exactly that way. My mother has suffered her private hell."

"I'm deeply sorry," Travis managed to say thickly, avoiding her eyes.

"A normal reaction," Jewel said, continuing to look straight at him. "You never thought my mother might have borne you a child?"

"Of course he didn't!" Amelia's dark eyes flashed outrage.

Jewel ignored her. "Then, why do I keep thinking of myself as abandoned?"

"My dear, it would have created so much misery," Travis explained. "My father would have ensured that. But the fact is, I had only Steve's suspicion to go on."

"Which should have been more than enough. You never thought of checking? Confirming his suspicion? Providing a bit of money for my education?" Jewel was aware of Keefe's eyes on her.

"My dear, I really couldn't do that." Travis threw up his hands, as though self-interest was entirely reasonable.

"Forgive me, but I can't help thinking of that as wicked," Jewel said. "You had a responsibility to find out, and if—"

"Aren't you being overemotional?" Amelia broke in, suddenly fanning her hair out wildly.

"Not at all." Jewel shrugged. "It's a professional judgment. I think a jury would conclude the same."

"A jury?" Travis Copeland's handsome face turned cucumber-green. "What on earth are you talking about, girl?"

"Jewel is talking hypothetically." Keefe intervened, giving Jewel a keen glance. "You must appreciate, Travis, that she spends her life as a lawyer. A very good one."

"It sounds like blackmail to me." Amelia flew to the defense of her father, her eyes betraying jealousy at Keefe's intervention on Jewel's behalf.

"We'll ignore that," Davina said, sitting very straight.

"No, it *could* sound like blackmail," Jewel responded, looking at her grandmother, "but that's not what I'm here for. Please, all of you be assured of that. My integrity is very important to me. And, needless to say, I'm not such a fool that I'd go around threatening blackmail. What I want is simple. I know hardly anything about you and I want to know more. I want to be able to come to terms with the injustices of the past. My mother's been the real victim in all of this. She stopped living twenty years ago. That short affair and her husband's tragic death all but destroyed her. Now, twenty years on, I think my biological father should be made to admit to a lot of the blame." Jewel turned her eyes to Travis. "When did you first realize I might have been your daughter?" she asked quietly.

"Until you turned up in this house, we didn't know about you at all," Amelia said furiously and got to her feet, only to be told to sit down by her grandmother.

Jewel smiled and shook her head. "That might be

true for you, but not your father.'' She turned to Travis, gazing directly into his eyes. ''I think you must have wondered from the very beginning.''

Travis jerked his head away. ''I couldn't afford to know. It would have ruined me, my dear.''

Sadness touched Jewel's expression. ''If you'd searched all your life, you'd never have found a more vulnerable woman than my mother. She would never have made trouble for you. She wants no part of you now.''

''I'll make it up to her,'' Travis promised in a surprisingly remorseful tone.

''How?'' Jewel's voice remained quiet.

''I'll acknowledge you. Is that what you want? I'll pay compensation.''

''You'll never get my mother to take money from you.'' Jewel shook her head again. ''I don't think she'd accept your heartfelt regrets, either. After all, she denies to this day that she even had an affair.''

''She loved me,'' Travis suddenly said, something about his expression intimating that floodgates inside him had opened up.

Amelia stared at him in horror. ''What are you saying, Father?'' she demanded, flashing an aghast look at her grandmother, who seemed unmoved.

''I loved her,'' Travis repeated. ''I still carry an image of her in my heart. She was the sweetest, gentlest little thing. I could have found happiness with Thea. God knows, I found it nowhere else.''

Amelia wasn't the only one who was shocked. Jewel suddenly reached over and seized one of her father's hands. ''You loved her and you deserted her? How could you do that?''

Travis gave Jewel's hand a stiff little shake. ''My dear, we were both married at the time. My first concern, I admit, was to keep it all from my father. To keep it out of the papers. Things are a lot easier today than they were twenty-odd years ago. A whiff of scandal would have ruined us.'' He sighed heavily. ''You have no idea what my wife was like. The Antarctic should've been her home. She didn't want me, but God help anyone else who did. I admit to numerous affairs over the years, but not a one of them she didn't unearth. At least my women friends knew the score. All of them women of the world,'' he added wryly. ''Except Thea.''

''So, are there any more sisters I should know about?'' Amelia asked bitterly.

''No—and I don't think you were listening, Amelia. Thea Bishop was the only woman to ever touch my heart. I'm not a brutal man. I didn't rape her. It was love. Love on both sides. It wasn't premeditated, either.''

''You're just saying that,'' Amelia accused him, her dark eyes full of tears.

''It's true.'' Travis's voice was low and urgent. ''I want you to believe that, Eugenie.'' He turned to Jewel. ''I know that's what your mother called you. You were conceived in love. Illicit love but love all the same. Thea may have agonized, thinking I was glad to be rid of her, but that was far from the truth. If I'd been even half a man, I would've taken steps to protect her. Instead, to my everlasting self-contempt, I cut you both out of my life—Thea and the child I suspected was mine…. I told myself you'd be all right. That our affair didn't happen. After a while, I really believed it. I had my rightful heir. My only child. And that's not the worst of it. I heard along the way, maybe eight years ago, that Thea was virtually a recluse in her family home.''

"Any more confessions?" Amelia's tone was glacial. For once she was staring at her father with open criticism.

"Maybe you and I should talk in private, Eugenie," Travis suggested, looking so woebegone that Jewel started to feel sorry for him.

"Well then, you won't need me!" Amelia jumped up from her chair, ready to bolt.

"Don't run away, Amelia," Davina begged. "Please, dear..."

"I'll go after her," Keefe offered. "It'll work out but there might be a bit of drama first."

"Tell me about it!" Travis said wearily. "I'm already having nightmares."

After Keefe had gone looking for Amelia, Davina turned to her son. "You want to talk? Then *talk*."

"It's all too bloody late." Travis swallowed. "Eugenie probably despises me."

Which just happened to be true until moments ago.

"I did." Jewel shot him a pitying glance. "But I hadn't known you'd once loved my mother. Is it true? Don't lie to me, please. I won't forgive this lie." She gazed at him fixedly but he didn't back away.

"You could put me in front of a firing squad but now that I've proclaimed my true feelings for Thea, I'd never recant. I was very much in love with her. She made me feel good about myself. If she'd been unmarried, a young woman of my own circle, I would've married her in an instant. And you know why? Thea would have shown me how to be a man. How to be a husband and father. Instead, I did something that destroyed us all. But consider how it was all those years ago. I was a married man with a child already. Amelia. A girl, incidentally, I've helped ruin. I know that—I admit it. I should've divorced Sonia years ago and been honest about my relationship with Thea. None of it would've been easy and I was a coward. I took the easy way out."

"That's true, but at some point you could've put things right. Or made them better at least. Maybe it's better if I don't stay," Jewel said abruptly, seeking her grandmother's eyes. "Amelia is very upset."

"We *all* are, dearest girl." Davina nodded. "But we have to move on. Your father and I have agreed that we want the world to know you as a Copeland. You are my son's daughter. My grandchild. Regardless of the distress and confusion, I'm excited about it. We need to be a family. *Right away.* We need to make up for all the wasted years."

"It can't be done overnight, Grandma." Jewel spoke spontaneously, almost demolishing Davina. Tears jumped to the older woman's eyes.

"We need to *celebrate,*" Davina cried, wiping her eyes with a linen napkin. "You should try to approach Thea, my boy," she said eagerly to her son. "Beg her forgiveness. Tell her that what existed between you was good. You should talk to her."

Travis studied his mother, as if she'd imparted the greatest truth.

"She's *exactly* the one I want to talk to," he said, almost rapturously. "If anyone will forgive me, it's Thea."

CHAPTER TEN

JEWEL WAS UNPACKING in the vastness of the guest suite allotted to her, adorned and patterned in every shade of blue, when a knock came at her door. She went to it, straightening her already-straight shoulders. This could be her half sister, Amelia, in a fighting mood.

Keefe stood on the threshold, a wry expression on his face. A face she found so attractive it made her head spin.

"I hate you, Keefe Connellan," she said.

He sauntered past her into the room, tall, lean, superbly athletic. "Did I say I labored for your love?"

She gave an amused little laugh and returned to her unpacking. "We've already agreed the last thing you intend to do is abandon yourself to love. Did I ask you to come in, by the way?"

"Now, now, you weren't going to keep me outside." He walked through the open Palladian doors onto the balcony, which looked out over the garden. "Did you ever start something!" he said in a low, mocking voice.

"There is nothing but nothing like the feeling of power," she said, equally mocking. "But what did you expect me to do? Sit there like a good little schoolgirl?"

"I didn't expect you to suggest putting a noose

around poor old Travis's neck. When you mentioned juries, I thought he was going to be ill.''

"Poor old Travis!" Jewel scoffed in an unsympathetic voice, feeling she could disappear completely in the room's towering armoire. "It might've taken a while to reach this point, but—wait for it—he's planning on taking a trip to see my mother. He'd better go armed," she muttered. "Aunt Judith might shoot him just for being on the premises."

"Is this something Aunt Judith does regularly?" And then, in a more serious tone, he asked, "Do you mean that about Travis?"

Jewel clutched a pair of tennis shoes to her heart. "Every word of it. Did you manage to comfort Amelia?"

"I'm famous for my comforting powers," he said smoothly, sinking into an antique armchair.

"Really? Then, you're going to wind up as her husband one day."

"Would that matter to you?"

"How do *I* come into it?" she retorted, snapping the lock on a suitcase.

"It can't have slipped your mind that we shared a brief passionate interlude," he said. "Kiss after kiss. And never for a moment did you pull away."

"I'll make sure it doesn't happen again," she said, lowering her eyes but unable to restrain a slight laugh.

"So, are you jealous of Amelia?"

"I avoid jealousy at all costs. But I will admit to a slight flutter when I saw you both in the garden."

"I was merely being kind," he informed her, watching her every movement. "Were you by any chance spying on us?"

"You learn a lot that way." She paused to shrug.

"But, no, I was just taking in my surroundings. Both of you were too absorbed to notice."

"Amelia is in a state of shock," he told her. "Emotions all over the place. She doesn't know her exact position in the world anymore."

"You mean she's horrified by the thought of a scandal," Jewel corrected.

"That, too." He stretched out his legs, crossing them at the ankles. "I found it very touching that Travis has been holding onto tender memories of your mother all these years."

"I could've passed out when he said it. Actually, now it's all about my mother. Nothing to do with me. Mama, apparently had a talent for getting the best out of him. To be honest, I would never have guessed. I don't think he fancies me as a daughter at all. I'm probably too much like Grandma."

One black eyebrow shot up. "*Grandma,* is it now?"

"Yes, it is." Jewel turned to look at him. "She's so frail. I want to care for her. I want to save her more pain. It'll be easy to love Davina. My hopes aren't so high for my dear father. Or your girlfriend, for that matter."

"Tut, tut." He stood up and came to her. "I think I should kiss you again. You need sweetening up."

He brought his hand up beneath the thick golden fall of hair.

"Are you intending to transfer your affections to the prodigal daughter?" she challenged him, her mind filled with images of him and Amelia in the garden, only ten minutes earlier.

He swooped and kissed her. A hard kiss. So weighted with emotion it sent shock waves to every pressure point in her body.

"It won't help if you're suspicious of my every move," he said with an edge.

"How are you asking me to interpret the things you do?"

"I would never want a woman who didn't trust me."

"Where does that leave me? Or can't you distinguish between kissing and sparring? I looked over the balcony in all innocence a few minutes ago and I saw you sharing a very tender moment with Amelia. That's okay. I understand there's a lot of feeling between you. You've told me you don't love her, but I'm finding it a little difficult to believe."

"And why exactly is that?"

"You have the most frightfully arrogant expression on your face," she said, without answering him.

"And your eyes are as blue as a blowtorch," he returned caustically. "Please don't misinterpret my motives. I do care about Amelia, but I was never destined to fall in love with her. Does that clear up your confusion?"

"Just so long as you don't tell me you're prepared to take a chance on the second daughter?"

"The nerve of you!" he murmured very quietly. "The fact is, Jewel, you're turning into a Copeland right before my eyes."

That hurt her, as was intended. "All right, I'm sorry." She sank her teeth into her lower lip. "Confusion seems to be the order of the day."

"Hell, yes," he agreed. "If we want to fight, maybe we should take to the tennis court. I saw you with a pair of tennis shoes. Do you want a game?"

"Like I told you, I haven't played in ages," she answered casually.

"I have a feeling you're bluffing."

"You're not a poor loser, are you?"

"I don't ever see myself as a loser, Ms. Copeland."

"That's good. Neither do I. And it's Bishop."

"All right, Ms. Bishop. Tennis court in about twenty minutes." He walked to the door, paused. "See you later," he said with a breezy wave.

JEWEL WAS ALMOST READY to go downstairs, when she had another visitor. This time it was Amelia, whose brown eyes widened when she saw her. Jewel was dressed in snappy white shorts that showed off her small shapely bottom, matched to a snug navy-blue T-shirt with a white designer logo emblazoned across an equally pert bosom. Jewel's golden blond hair was caught back in a businesslike ponytail. She wore white socks and white navy-trimmed tennis shoes.

It took Amelia a few moments to speak. She seemed quite thrown off, whatever it was she'd come to say. Finally she looked up from her examination. *"Tennis?"* she burst out, as though it were a blizzard outside and not a piercingly bright day.

"Yes, would you care for a game? I am told you're very good."

"I excel at most games," Amelia replied with no attempt at modesty. "Who are you playing *with?*" She appeared flustered.

"Actually Keefe has challenged me to a game."

"Keefe! Good Lord," Amelia said sharply. "Keefe could go five sets with Pat Rafter."

"That's okay." Jewel turned back to collect her tennis racket, resisting the urge to rap Amelia on the head with it. "I'm hoping not to make a complete fool of myself. Can I help you with anything, Amelia?"

Amelia moved to stand directly in front of her.

"Don't take Keefe from me, will you, Jewel?" she pleaded in an unexpectedly girlish voice. "Don't, okay. I couldn't bear it."

Jewel could understand that. "I've only known him a very short time," she said gently, feeling a wave of pity combined with frustration.

"It only takes one glance." Amelia nodded sorrowfully several times. "Keefe is *mine*. He's always belonged with me. I just wanted to ask you not to take him from me. You're very beautiful and sexy. I don't have that, the sexy bit. I think you have to be born with sex appeal. Just look at you in that gear," she complained. "I can't look like that."

"Why would you want to?" Jewel said. "You're very attractive, very stylish."

"I don't have your flair." Amelia shook her head. "I have people to help me put my wardrobe together. I bet you don't bother."

"I couldn't afford it, Amelia. Besides, I think I know by now what suits me. It just takes a little time and experimentation getting things together."

Amelia was obviously finished with the small talk. "This is a momentous time for our family," she said darkly. "You know the news is all over town. It spread like wildfire."

"What news?" Jewel demanded. "Tell me *exactly*."

"That you're the result of one of Father's affairs." Amelia seemed happy to oblige. "Well, the only one to surface so far. Father has betrayed me—" Her voice cracked.

"Try not to see it like that, Amelia. Things happen in life. People do lots of things they regret."

Amelia scarcely heard her. "I'm going to find it very hard explaining this to my friends."

"Then, don't explain," Jewel suggested. "It's none of their business, anyway."

"And Father telling us he was in love with your mother! Did you ever hear anything to equal *that?*" She said it as though her father should be delivered to the nearest asylum.

"Strange to say, I think it must have been true. You can't see into your father's heart, Amelia."

"He told me once that I was the only person he loved."

"Amelia, you can believe that he loves you, but— forgive me—you're too fixated on him. You need a life of your own. A family of your own. There must be a dozen eligible guys wanting to rush you to the altar."

"I—only—want—Keefe." Amelia spaced the words very carefully. "That's why I'm begging you not to take him away from me."

Jewel held up a hand. "If he loves you, Amelia, I couldn't. *Wouldn't.*"

Suddenly Amelia relaxed, rushing to hug Jewel. "Oh, thank you," she said. "I really am sorry for the way I spoke to you that first day. I thought you probably were after money. Most people are."

"I'm not most people, Amelia. I'm your half sister."

"I know!" Amelia gave her a brilliant smile. "I just need a little time to get used to the idea. It's been such a *shock.*"

"For me, too," Jewel reminded her. "But it makes our grandmother happy. You're pleased about that, aren't you, Amelia?"

"Yes, yes, of course I am," Amelia cried, but it wasn't reflected in her eyes. "If you wait a few minutes, I'll go and get changed into my tennis outfit. I could give you a few tips to polish your game."

"That would be great," Jewel answered promptly, playing humble. "But I'll go ahead, if you don't mind. Keefe doesn't strike me as a man to be kept waiting."

"How *does* he strike you?" Amelia returned swiftly.

"Very masterful," Jewel said honestly. "Charming, clever, high-voltage, very polished, given to arrogant moments. But one can't help being impressed."

To Amelia, all of that must have added up to infatuation because she frowned. "He's practically a genius. Father says he's going to end up running the whole company. I might as well tell you, Keefe's extremely wary of you." This was said with a very solemn expression.

"Wary? In what way?" Jewel asked, thinking her half sister had all the attributes of a troublemaker.

"I don't know, actually." Amelia looked a little bewildered at Jewel's challenging expression. "I think he had you investigated. Gran would agree to that if you were to come into the family."

"How very commendable," Jewel said, tilting her chin. "I suppose you were all afraid I might sell the story of how I grew up to the *Women's Weekly*," she muttered furiously, receiving a troubled look from Amelia. "Then there's the question of my inheritance. What do you think? A lump sum? A generous yearly allowance? Something in line with yours. I'm fairly reasonable."

With a horrified expression, Amelia retreated, moving backward. She fell over the same antique armchair Keefe had sat in, flushed with embarrassment, then sprang up again. "I must ask you to speak to Gran about these matters, Jewel," she said in a rush. "I can't help you with anything. It has nothing whatever to do with me."

"Of course it has," Jewel answered decisively. "We're half sisters, aren't we? We share the same blood. But to put your mind to rest, I promise you, Amelia, I'm only fooling." She laughed. "If the family went to such lengths as employing snoops, I'll have my bit of fun, too. See you on the court. I just might have a few tips of my own."

KEEFE WAS WAITING FOR HER by the time she arrived at the beautiful grass court. Palm trees, golden canes and tree ferns flourished in this section of the garden, with two sides of the wired enclosure completely covered by a climbing vine with beautiful white flowers.

"Hi!" Keefe greeted her casually, but his eyes sparkled with appreciation. "It took you a while, but the result was worth it."

"I should hope so!" Jewel unzipped her racket a little more forcibly than necessary. "I can't *believe* these people are my relatives," she said.

He came to sit on the bench, relaxed and vibrant in a red T-shirt he wore loose over white tennis shorts. "This is only a guess, but I think old Julius had something to do with it. What's the problem?"

She shook her head as though to clear it. "I don't think either of us was predicting a great weekend, but Amelia deserves good marks for a spot of troublemaking. I've just been listening to her tell me how I've been investigated."

"Darling, wouldn't you investigate me if I were in your position?" he asked, drawing her down onto the bench beside him.

"Who said you could call me 'darling'?" she chided.

"There's just something about you, I guess. Darling comes easy. Why worry about it?"

"I don't think *you'd* be very happy about being investigated." She studied him severely.

"I think I'd recognize that there's a fortune involved."

"I've told you—I don't want their money," Jewel protested. "Or if I got some, I'd start giving huge donations to my favorite charities."

"Which are?"

"Oh, the Children's Hospital, Leukemia Foundation, breast cancer research, the Salvation Army, RSPCA. I could go on."

"My dear girl, the company is quite involved when it comes to philanthropy," he pointed out, contemplating her long satiny legs. "Surely you know the tremendous charity work Davina has done over the years?"

"What about the others?" she retorted.

"The others are a lot tighter with their money," he admitted. "However, my own family has done a lot of work in that area."

"Well, good for you." She couldn't resist slapping his tanned knee. "I must apologize for my lapse in manners."

"That's okay," he said.

"However, that doesn't give you permission to go on spying on me."

"Not anymore." He threw back his head and gazed heavenward. "I have all the proof I need."

"Good thing *you're* not a fortune hunter," she said, her eyes on the clean cut of his jaw. "You'd be way too good at it."

"Oh, nothing like that. Are you going to give me a

game?'' He stood up and grasped her hand, pulling her to her feet.

"Sure I am. But we'll have to be sharp. Amelia's changing into her tennis gear as we speak."

"What?" He didn't sound pleased.

"She's also going to help me polish my game."

"How exhilarating! Let's go!"

They were enjoying a prolonged warm-up, each evaluating the other's game, when not one but three people arrived at the court, all smartly outfitted in immaculate tennis whites. Amelia, flanked by her father and an attractive young man who flashed them an engaging smile. Greg McCall.

"How's it going?" Travis called, looking so good for his age Jewel couldn't help but be impressed.

"Fine," Keefe answered for both of them. They left the court so he could introduce Greg to Jewel. Greg had brown hair and hazel eyes, with pleasantly rugged features. He proved charming but in no way ingratiating to his bosses and the super rich, and Jewel would have liked him for that alone. His steady handshake warmed her, she also liked the way he was able to keep any trace of curiosity out of his eyes as he spoke to her.

"What about you girls having a quick game?" Travis suggested, giving Amelia's shoulders an encouraging squeeze. "You can learn from her, Jewel. Amelia is an excellent all-around athlete. No need to feel badly if you're outmatched."

"What about a little bet?" asked Keefe somewhat dryly, caught between warning Amelia and letting Jewel's racket talk for her.

"Keep your money in your pocket, dear boy,"

Travis murmured. "Ask anyone how good my daughter is."

"I know," Keefe agreed lazily, "but you have *two* daughters."

"Don't worry about me, Keefe," Jewel said. "I'll try my best."

"Let's get down to business." Amelia spoke in a brisk tone. "I'm a very good coach, Jewel. For all you know, I might be able to uncover some ability in you."

Ah, the optimism of ignorance, Keefe thought, watching the women walk out onto the court. They looked beautiful, both of them, in different ways. Both thoroughbreds, natural athletes, although Travis and Amelia had a nasty habit of seeing the tennis court as a battlefield. He was sorry he hadn't been able to get a bet on with Travis. He'd been prepared to wager Amelia would crack first. Once deprived of her overriding confidence, Amelia had a tendency to collapse.

But Amelia was on her mettle. Her father's highly critical eyes were watching her. So were Keefe's and although she wasn't worried about him—Greg's. Having won the toss, Amelia elected to begin the game without benefit of a warm-up. She knew what she could do. She knew the number of good players who'd lost to her, so she wasn't prepared to waste time. This was destined to be one very short, very educational game for the half sister she would've been happy never to meet. Whose very existence was threatening.

Jewel wasn't quite ready, but that didn't stop Amelia. She sent down a center line ace Venus Williams would have died for. A shot even she had never produced before. "Fifteen love," she called, trying not to smile. After all the recent trauma she and her father had suffered, Amelia was looking forward to this. This

was something she could do. This was something that
made her father proud. Being a winner was everything
to him. Her next serve she belted so hard it slammed
into the net. The follow-up she put at Jewel's feet,
scarcely able to credit the way Jewel picked it up, con-
verting it into a sharply angled crosscourt winner.

"Fifteen all," Jewel called, giving Amelia a warm
smile.

"That was lucky."

Jewel didn't reply.

In a way, it was the worst possible scenario, Keefe
thought, his back pressed against the bench. Neither
Travis nor Amelia had learned not to jump to conclusions. Since Jewel had lived her childhood and adolescence without material advantages, they automatically
assumed she'd missed out on all the extras provided
by top schools. In point of fact, Jewel had won a full
scholarship to just such a school, which took into account both her academic and sporting prowess. Amelia
wasn't the only natural athlete in the family. Jewel was
a very good tennis player; had she made it her career,
she might have reached the international circuit.

It was a three-set match none of them was destined
to forget. Jewel took the first set 6–3, with Amelia so
accustomed to winning, it rattled her badly. Instead of
receiving encouragement from her father, she was
forced to endure a barrage of criticism that was like a
whip on raw wounds. Travis had grown into a professional bully, Keefe thought as he glimpsed Jewel's expression. It suggested clearly that Travis had better not
try harassing her.

The young women returned to the court. It was obvious to everyone that Amelia had to improve her
game. Which, thanks to her fighting spirit or fear of

her father, she did. She hung in there to take the second set at 7–5. The third set, the decider, saw Amelia over-extended, just as Keefe had predicted. Jewel brought her brains to the game. Also, she had so much energy, so much commitment, so much natural focus, that she stuck to her game plan and polished off the set at 6-2.

"That's one darn good player!" Greg jumped to his feet, clapping vigorously. "They're both great," he added hastily, catching Travis's ferocious frown, "but Jewel has incredible speed around the court."

"Amelia simply threw in the towel," Travis fumed. "I can't for the life of me think why Jewel was holding out on us." He looked affronted. "She's obviously an experienced player."

"She'd have told you if you'd asked her," Keefe said, hoping poor Amelia wasn't in for another tirade. She really didn't deserve such a father. And he'd prefer not to watch Travis humiliate his daughter.

"Amelia has a lot of work to do." Travis was still muttering. "She's getting downright sloppy. Of course, she's not used to Jewel's serve-and-volley game."

"Jewel would beat me," Greg admitted freely, looking at Keefe with loaded eyes.

"We can believe *that!*" Travis threw him a glance full of contempt. "I believe Amelia's beaten you every time you've played, dear boy."

"And you, too, sir," Greg said with a grin.

Those were the occasions when Amelia, carried away by the killer instinct she'd inherited, forgot herself to the point that she didn't allow her father to win.

Jewel put a friendly arm around Amelia's shoulders as they left the court. "That was wonderful!" She smiled. "I really enjoyed our match, Amelia."

Amelia eased away. "I'd call it an out-and-out attack," she said almost accusingly.

"Oh, come on!" Jewel realized she didn't fully understand the pressures put on Amelia by her father. "I wanted to win. Didn't you?"

Amelia stopped, gazing into Jewel's eyes. They were of a height. "Why don't you be straight with me, Jewel? You were showing off."

Jewel stared back at her in astonishment. "That's insane! I was having a good time. You're taking this too seriously, Amelia. There's no need to get so upset. I thought what we had was a healthy competition. Next time around, you'll probably beat me."

"I expect I will," said Amelia, who looked as if she might fall over any minute. "You took me off guard. I'm not used to your type of game."

"Oh, you can study it easily enough," Jewel said, all pleasure in the game draining away.

When they joined the men, Travis gave Jewel a smile that was almost savage. "Well, well, well," he jeered, breathing rather hard, "you are a dark horse, Eugenie."

"Ignorance is bliss," Keefe remarked suavely, standing up to offer the women a drink. "That was a great match. We enjoyed it."

Travis stared at Keefe as though he'd betrayed the family. "*You* may have enjoyed it, Keefe. I certainly didn't. Amelia didn't play intelligently at all."

"Why don't you give her a break," Jewel said, patting a cushion so Amelia could sit down. "That wasn't the Wimbledon Final, you know."

"Allow me to advise my own daughter. Amelia was raised to be a winner." Travis glared at Jewel with outraged eyes.

"But surely there has to be more to life?" Jewel picked up a hand towel and pressed it to her heated face. "Like discovering one's identity."

Keefe gave her a quick glance that said, *Don't press too hard*, but Jewel had had enough of this domineering man.

Travis's throat worked convulsively. It was clear that he took offense at Jewel's remark. "You have a great deal to say for someone so young." He gave Jewel an icy glance that was meant to be intimidating.

"Surely you recall I'm twenty-six, Travis," she said. "Not so young."

Do be careful, Jewel, Keefe thought. Travis Copeland could be dangerous. "Why don't you and I have a game, Travis?" he suggested before all goodwill disappeared.

Travis responded with his wolfish smile. "I'm not ready for you, Keefe," he was forced to concede. The last time he had attempted to play Keefe, he'd suffered a distressing bout of tachycardia. "What about you, Greg?" He turned to the younger man with confidence. Greg McCall was an employee. He wouldn't be fool enough to beat Travis. Even if he could.

"It'll be a real pleasure, sir." Greg had long been recognized as a diplomat.

After the two had taken the court, Amelia quietly burst into tears.

Jewel, who'd been enjoying her cold drink, scrambled up. "Amelia, what is it?" She put a comforting hand on Amelia's bare arm, but Amelia shook it off.

"Can't you learn some respect when you talk to my father?" she said, gulping down sobs.

"Not when he's so cold and cheerless, Amelia," Jewel replied. "So cruel to you."

Amelia wasn't going to accept that. "My father *adores* me! He's only trying to be supportive."

"God, is that how you describe it?" Jewel turned away, disgusted.

"You *do* have to take charge of yourself, Amelia," Keefe remarked gently, stroking Amelia's cheek. "I've never understood why you allow your father to bully you."

"It's discipline." Amelia raised drowned eyes to his. "I stop thinking about myself and concentrate on what I should be doing. If anyone was cruel today, it was Jewel. She tried to make a fool of me in front of everyone." Amelia's voice was raw with emotion.

Jewel's own temper came up like a gale. She watched Amelia pitch forward into Keefe's arms, burying her shiny dark head against his chest, begging for the comfort apparently only he could provide.

"Is she for real?" Jewel demanded angrily, looking over Amelia's shaking figure into his eyes. She pulled the clasp from her ponytail, shaking her head so hard her hair flew about like a golden cloud. "Why doesn't she just tell Travis to get stuffed?"

Keefe tried but failed to bite back a laugh. "I think she'd be a little fearful of using that word."

"Well, I don't need her picking on me." Jewel grabbed her racket decisively. "I thought *I* had a rough childhood, but Amelia's must have been hell."

She was outside the court walking at a swift pace to the house, when Keefe caught up with her.

"Jewel." His voice was deep and cajoling. "This sort of thing goes on all the time. Amelia's been the victim of emotional domination since she was a child. By her father and to an extent by Davina. Don't pull away." He closed his fingers around her wrist. "Davina's a very forceful, dynamic woman.'' He tried to explain. ''Amelia had to live in her grandmother's shadow. Which isn't to say Davina hasn't always loved her and tried to influence her in the right decisions. It's her money. Never forget that. Their whole lives are defined by it. The Money. Amelia and the money can't be parted. I honestly think she'll put up with anything so long as she's not cut off from the source. Her clothes alone must cost a fortune. I've never seen her in the same outfit twice.''

''Am I supposed to *envy* her? I don't. Go back to her,'' she said, her whole being alive with nerves. ''She obviously arouses protective emotions in you.''

''Oh, don't be stupid.'' He gave her arm a shake, a muscle twitching along his jaw.

''I'm *not* stupid!'' Waves of anger and frustration emanated from her. ''Why did I let you talk me into coming here? These people are crazy. You're talking *stupid?* Amelia acts like a silly schoolgirl. It's pitiful. I'm ashamed of her. I'm ashamed of myself for coming here.''

''It's a dilemma, all right.'' He moved her along, his tone somber. ''The only trouble is, you can't back out. You're one of them.''

''It's too bloody dreary. I don't *want* to be one of them. It'll never work. There's no dignity—they're all unbalanced.''

''Darling, you're preaching to the converted.'' His voice was as ash. ''So what are you going to do?''

''I'm not going to sneak away, if that's what you think,'' she said quickly. ''I'm all for doing the right thing. I'll speak to my grandmother. Tell her I've seen enough of the Copeland brand of family love. Travis

Copeland is cruel and Amelia's like a greedy helpless child.''

''That's the way he raised her.''

''Well, it didn't work out too well, did it? I'll have to warn my mother. I think she'd lose her mind completely if he ever turned up at the farm.''

He let out a laugh. ''Don't worry. Aunt Judith will fend him off.''

''Aunt Judith works most of the time—I have to get away,'' she said abruptly. She felt too flushed and hot, dazed and defenseless against his sexual aura. ''I have to clear my head.''

''Why don't I take you out on the bay?'' His vibrant voice turned seductive, effortlessly charming her.

''And *you* really disturb me, as well.'' She brushed her hair from her face. ''What is it you want from me?''

They stood in the brilliant sunlight, staring at each other, Jewel with bitter pleasure. Half in love with him, half resentful of his power.

''God, you're a fire-eater, aren't you.'' He gave a soft grunt of amusement.

''And what about you? What's all this about? Why do you look at me like that? I'm a working girl. There's an heiress back there waiting for you. Why are you wasting your time on me?''

''We're in this business together,'' he said, resorting to mild humor. ''You could almost say our... partnership was inevitable.''

He had a talent for sending her into a frenzy. ''*What* business?''

''You may be a working girl today, Jewel, and a very successful one, but you're entitled to a good slice of the Copeland fortune for *who* you are and what you've suffered. Your mother and aunt are entitled to compensation, as well. You may talk disdainfully now about how you don't want their money, but it's *your* money as well. Make no mistake. Sir Julius was all kinds of a bastard who did unimaginable things—but he would never have turned his back on you. How could he? Not only are you his granddaughter, you're the living image of the only woman he ever loved. For his pains, he died knowing she never loved *him*."

"How horrible!" Jewel had difficulty taking all of this in. "I can't believe she married without love."

"One could almost pity him," Keefe remarked rather bleakly. "Maybe Davina was waiting for it to hit her, and it never did. Their marriage was virtually arranged. She was already in love with someone else."

"This is unbearable." Jewel threw back her head. "I don't know a damn thing about these people."

"What you need to know I can tell you," he offered quietly.

"There are times you make me feel I'm talking to a real Cesarea Borgia," she said with narrowed eyes.

"Never!" He shook his head, and his beautifully cut black hair settled instantly back in place. "All his plans failed and he died in battle. You, however, are beautiful enough to have been the legendary Lucrezia who managed to turn pious. And could even have been pious all along."

"Cesarea, on the other hand, lived and died evil," she pointed out, her bones melting when he suddenly took her hand and carried it to his mouth.

"I'm not evil, Jewel," he said. "I'm a man determined to right the things that are wrong."

AMELIA, stalking them through the garden, was blasted with shock when she saw them on the path ahead of

her. She squeezed her hands together in dismay, her
dark eyes glittering like glass. They were standing absolutely still beneath the shade of the overhanging
golden canes. Not talking, just staring at each other.
Caught up in each other's eyes. The atmosphere between them was so highly charged it singed the air.
That any other woman had the erotic power to do that
to Keefe! It was more than she could bear. Here was
the destruction of all her plans.

In that moment she hated Jewel. Hated her with all
the pent-up rage and bitter resentments that were in her.
Tears ran down her cheeks to her chin. She had tried
so hard, as hard as anyone could imagine, to get Keefe
to love her. She knew she always looked wonderful,
poised and charming. They were bonded in so many
ways. Friends from childhood. Heirs to the very rich.
Now she found she couldn't escape her lack of self-
esteem. Most people thought of her as the girl who had
everything, but she lived with terrible feelings of de-
pendency on her family, as though without them she
was nothing. To please her father she had sacrificed
her personal freedom. She'd failed to continue her education, just frittering away her life, without the qual-
ifications to carve out some sort of career that might
have made Keefe respect her.

Instead of accepting any blame, she now turned it
on Jewel, the usurper. The viper in the nest. In almost
one stroke, Jewel had taken her grandmother from her,
and even her father had relented his entrenched position. Jewel would soon lay claim to a share of the family fortune at least equal to Amelia's own. But far beyond those grievous considerations, she was turning
her large beautiful dazzling blue eyes on Keefe. She

had a way with men. Greg had difficulty keeping his
eyes off her, in those skimpy shorts and the figure-
hugging T-shirt. She was so ostentatious! *Jewel*. Pre-
posterous, like her name. If she could've had Jewel
annihilated at that moment she would have done so.
This was someone who didn't belong.

Amelia shrank back, giving full rein to the demons
that had grown up with her. She couldn't get over it.
Keefe didn't love her. He had never loved her. Her
tragedy, her great ocean of pain, was that she'd never
cease loving him. Even now, she knew she absolutely
had to have him. Only one woman could win, and it
was going to be her. She had to talk to her father.
Really talk this time. If they gave Jewel enough money,
she might go away. Perhaps forever. The one thing she
could never be allowed to have was Keefe.

Amelia wiped away her tears with the back of her
hand. She had to act on her heart's desire, and to hell
with the consequences.

CHAPTER ELEVEN

JEWEL FOUND HER GRANDMOTHER in the plant-filled solarium, quietly reading a book. She glanced at the title. Margaret Atwood's *The Blind Assassin*.

"Enjoying it?"

"Loving it." Davina looked up, her face radiating welcome. She marked the page, then closed the book, setting it down on the small table near her. "I've read everything she's written."

"That makes two of us." Jewel smiled, regarding her grandmother with equal pleasure.

"We share the same taste," Davina remarked. "Amelia has no time for reading, alas!"

"That's sad." Jewel sank into a chair. "I think people who miss out on reading must be somehow deprived."

Davina sighed. "Of course, Amelia's very sports-minded. She excels at tennis and golf, and she's very handy on the yacht. Which reminds me, why aren't you with the others? I thought they'd all gone off to the tennis court."

"Most of them are still there. Keefe and I sort of left them to it." Jewel exhaled, finding it hard to free her mind of all the rebuffs. "I'm afraid I committed a cardinal offense. I beat Amelia. She didn't take it too well. Neither did her father."

"Oh!" Davina pursed her lips, obviously getting the

full picture. "Can't you think of Travis as *your* father?" she asked quietly.

"No more than he can think of me as his daughter." Jewel shook her head. "I accept you completely as my grandmother. I think I connected with you almost immediately, but I don't think Travis and I are ever going to be close. I have too much to say for myself and he's not a man who approves of freedom of speech in women."

Davina laughed aloud. "My dear, he's famous for it. Even his father didn't portray such grandiosity, if there's such a word. Pomposity. It's Amelia I'm concerned about. Travis gives her hell when she loses."

Bullies do indeed know how to choose their victims, Jewel thought. "Why does Amelia let him?" she asked, frowning. "She's a woman, not a child who has to stand there and take it."

"It's all too much for me, my dear," Davina lamented. "As I've told you, Travis has always ruled Amelia's life. I tried for years and years to do something about it, but now I've learned not to interfere. There's sorrow in it, but Amelia has to break her own bonds."

"I certainly hope she succeeds," Jewel said with feeling. "If she doesn't, he'll never see her as an adult. He absolutely trashed her every time we came off the court, yet she took it as the most constructive form of criticism."

"I know. I know." Davina closed her eyes. "I also know how odd it is, but that's Amelia's usual reaction. Sonia opted out of the marriage. She opted out of trying to steer Amelia in the direction of escape. Whatever either of us said, Amelia only resented it. She worships her father."

"How awful!" Jewel burst out honestly, but her grandmother didn't seem to mind. "The thing is, Grandma, I don't think I can stay here the whole weekend. Travis doesn't want me. Neither does Amelia. I feel I'm here under false pretenses, since Travis will never see me as his daughter. I'll always be someone foisted on him. I don't think Amelia will ever care about me, either. We'll never be on equal ground. I can understand what an embarrassment both of them find me."

"But Keefe? What about Keefe?" Davina studied her granddaughter closely.

"Keefe is an enigma." Jewel glanced away so Davina couldn't see into her eyes. "Being involved with him would have far-reaching consequences. I've been in control of my life up to date, and that's how I plan to continue. Nevertheless he wants to take me out on the bay."

Davina inspected her with love and sympathy. "Then, why are you sitting here? Go!"

"You don't object?" Jewel met her grandmother's blue eyes. "We're not asking the others, which could seem very rude except that they've been uncivil to me. Greg McCall excluded. He's very pleasant."

"Yes, he is." Davina inclined her head with approval. "You go, my dear. But please come back for dinner. Will you do that?"

"For you, yes." Jewel rose to kiss her grandmother's cheek. "I have to tell you, Grandma, I'm very attracted to Keefe. And if I'm any judge, he's attracted to me. I'm proceeding as cautiously as if I were in the middle of a minefield. For one thing, I know Amelia might take any relationship between us as a derailment of her plans. Her plans and her father's ambitions."

Davina grasped Jewel's hand. "It's pretty much about winning, Jewel. Marrying Keefe has always been Amelia's goal. It's not about being happy. It's getting Keefe to marry her. End of story. So unrealistic. Travis has convinced her she has to do it so things can continue the way they have. Keefe is working toward taking over as executive chairman of Copeland Connellan. He's got most of the board in the palm of his hand, especially since he was the one who pressed to buy Borodin Gold Mine. It's proved very profitable for us, relatively low-grade but a huge field. Keefe's full of ideas, but there's Travis as Julius's only son and heir."

"Who do you want as chairman?" Jewel was nothing if not direct. "Your opinion must count for a great deal."

"That's true. There's no question in my mind about Keefe's capabilities. He's young, that's all. I don't want to burden him too soon. And there are other matters.... Matters from the past that have never been resolved. Keefe as a Connellan is determined to take back everything his family lost through my husband's maneuvers. This was after Stafford died. I did everything I could to make restitution but I couldn't force my son's hand."

"So it's a power struggle," Jewel said. "If Amelia were to marry Keefe, that would put Travis in bed with them, as well."

Davina laughed outright. "That's one way to describe it. Travis believes that cozy arrangement will ensure him the top spot. He'll keep the position until he allows Keefe to take over."

"Mightn't Keefe do better marrying me?" Jewel's eyes became watchful and shadowed.

"Is this a hypothetical question, my dear?"

"Yes, it is. I've just suggested to Keefe he's a modern day Cesarea Borgia."

"Dearest, he's nothing like that." Davina shook the hand she was holding.

"All right, Machiavelli. After all, Machiavelli modeled *The Prince* on Borgia."

"You think Keefe, too, is making plans?" Davina held Jewel's eyes steadily.

"You just told me he was."

"He'd never marry a woman he didn't love. You can believe that, my dear. I know Keefe very well indeed. I've gotten to love him as if he were my own grandson. He's very much like another man I knew, his grandfather Stafford."

"You must talk to me about him someday," Jewel said. "Can't the two of us be family without involving anyone else?"

"Impossible!" Davina shook her head. "Once people see you, everyone will know. I couldn't call any of this off, Jewel, even if I wanted to, which I don't. I realize some things are going to hurt—there are complications already—but I must act according to my conscience. You are my granddaughter, just as Amelia is. As a family we must take responsibility for you and what has been done to you and your mother. I've been reflecting long and hard about your financial situation."

Jewel sat down again suddenly. "Grandma, don't think I'm ungrateful but I'm not here for money," she protested. "I'm here to open my heart to my family. Unfortunately my family, apart from you, seems hell-bent on driving me away. Amelia has already begged me not to take Keefe from her."

"Really?" Davina looked dismayed. "Do you see

Amelia wearing Keefe's engagement ring? No. For all that Travis and Amelia want it—as though everything they want has to happen—Keefe has never succumbed. He doesn't love Amelia. I've told her that as gently as I can, but she insists he hasn't turned to anyone else. Which is true, and it's giving Amelia false hope. Keefe could have anyone he liked. I think one could safely regard him as one of the most eligible men in the country.''

"Amelia wouldn't love me for taking him from her,'' Jewel said soberly.

"Jewel, she never had him.''

"Try telling *her* that.'' Jewel's voice was wry. "She'll never believe it. The idea's too deeply entrenched. Perhaps she's even a little emotionally unbalanced as far as Keefe is concerned. Not that anyone could blame her. He's that kind of man.''

NO WONDER THEY CARVED WOMEN into the prows of ships, he thought. While he sat in the flybridge nosing *Odysseus* into a sheltered inlet, she stood up front, a strumming breeze making a crackling pennant of her golden hair. A few moments before, drenched in brilliant sunlight, she had unselfconsciously stripped off her T-shirt, exposing the brief bra top of a bikini patterned in a swirl of turquoise, navy and white. She still wore her white shorts, but he hoped he was going to see the rest of her. She was a beautiful creature, yet *beautiful* wasn't enough to describe her. She had so much warmth, intelligence, life. She carried herself with the confidence and inherent poise that came with such a physical gift. Davina had it, too. So did his mother.

He knew Jewel was upset, although she was hiding

it extremely well. He was upset, too. Mostly on her account. He was disgusted with Travis and Amelia. There—he had to say it. He'd spent years on Amelia, urging her to develop her own identity. She wasn't even trying or she *couldn't,* so powerful was her father's hold on her. Keefe had to recognize that part of the problem was Amelia's addiction to being an heiress. That was all she knew, but it didn't entirely explain her emotional attachment to her father, which his own family considered crippling and extreme.

Amelia, not generally given to bouts of anger, would be furious at being left behind. A natural enough reaction—had she and Travis not gone out of their way to make Jewel feel unwanted. An outsider. For his own part, he had to accept that it was pretty risky bringing Jewel out with him today. They were entirely alone in a world that was suffused in glorious blue—the dense cloudless blue of the sky and the sparkling sapphire of the fifty-mile spread of deep water, as precious to the inhabitants of the river city of Brisbane as their beloved Harbour was to Sydneysiders.

The bay was dazzling, famous for its mud crabs. Nothing to match them, except maybe the delicious delicate Moreton Bay "bugs"—like a cross between crayfish and crab. The waters of the bay were teeming with fish. He should know. He'd made plenty of hauls. Red Emperor, pearl perch, snappers, black bream, whiting and the humble mullet; prawns of all kinds, huge jumbos, banana and tiger, king prawns and tiny school prawns just waiting to be caught. The oysters, too, were superb. The locals found them even more delectable than the famous Sydney rock oysters. Children learned crabbing and prawning at an early age. In their teens they went on to yachting. Almost everyone owned a

boat of some kind, working through all the weekly
chores so they could get out on the bay during the
weekends and revel in all that it had to offer.

Even the trees and the vegetation on the small island
Odysseus was approaching were overgrown with larkspur. On a summer weekend like this, with the weather
perfect, the boaters were out in force. Every type of
vessel was on the water: fishing dinghies powered with
outboards, the more up-market family cruisers, most
impressive power boats, one magnificent super-yacht
belonging to a super-rich Southerner he knew, luxury
motor launches like his own *Odysseus*. One day he'd
take Jewel out on his fast little sailing yacht, *Sea
Change*. It had been designed to run. And run it did.
He took it out in all weather, thrilling in its performance. Off to their left, near one of the three large
islands that almost enclosed the bay and kept it so safe,
was a flotilla of graceful sailing ships from the local
yacht squadron, rearing and plunging like racehorses.
About the only thing missing was a submarine.

They dropped anchor less than ten minutes later,
grateful for a lovely, secluded spot. He knew the bay
like the back of his hand.

"Can I dive in to cool off?" Jewel called, looking
into the crystal depths. "Or should I be worried about
the sharks?"

He laughed. "Only the odd Great White."

"No jokes!"

"You're quite safe here. I go in all the time. So does
everyone else."

"Great!" Like before, she unzipped her shorts and
stepped out of them as unselfconsciously as if she'd
been alone, folding them neatly before turning her attention to her windswept hair, which she pinned into a

high knot. "Coming in?" She turned her head, a mesmerizing figure silhouetted against the lush tropical
background of the island.

"When I'm finished admiring you," he told her
dryly, although the expression in his eyes was without
reservation.

"Don't be long." Her pleasure in her surroundings
was radiant. Her large beautiful eyes were extraordinarily luminous, close to the color of a gas flame. Today he could happily have drowned in the color blue.
This was what he loved, what he had always been
deeply involved in, like his father and grandfather before him. *The sea.* Jewel loved it, too.

In this horseshoe-shaped inlet, the water was dead
calm, the dazzling blueness of the bay giving way to a
deep bewitching green. He watched her go over the
side in one graceful dive that didn't even create a
splash. As an athlete it appeared she was very, very
good. Something she and Amelia appeared to have inherited from their father, though Jewel mightn't like to
hear about it.

After a moment or two he joined her, the two of
them moving through the water as sleekly as seals.

"Heaven!" She turned on her back, treading water.

Yes, heaven. He could see *Odysseus* reflected sideways in the water. He could hear the faint creaking
from the hull. They stayed in about fifteen minutes before returning to the boat. He'd called a restaurant near
his city marina, asking them to make up a fairly simple
picnic lunch, which they'd delivered right on time.
Fresh caviar, chicken sandwiches, fruit and cheese,
some little sweet things—he'd let them choose—a
chilled bottle of Riesling. Very much his choice. Davina wanted them back for dinner, so best make it light.

Amelia and Greg might be enjoying—well, hardly *enjoying* under the circumstances, which he realized he didn't give a damn about—a more elaborate lunch back at the house. He knew where he preferred to be.

Jewel went below to dry off and dress. She was back within minutes, wearing a different bra top. This one was fuchsia pink with the same white shorts. Her wet hair she'd scraped back from her face into a ponytail, revealing the perfection of her bone structure and small, close-set ears. He remembered the sweetness of those ears, their satiny texture. He remembered the curve of her breasts, though he'd never seen them so provocatively revealed. Not that it was intentional. He had the feeling Jewel shied away from being deliberately seductive. Which was just as well. Even spending a few hours together was complicating their lives. Endlessly...endlessly... The very thought tightened his nerves to an exquisite pitch. At that moment, he wanted her so badly the sheer pleasure of it was agony.

She, however, was deeply absorbed in setting out their picnic lunch, commenting as she did that *Odysseus* was easily the most luxurious high-performance motor yacht she'd ever been aboard. Brought up in tropical North Queensland alongside the eighth wonder of the world, the Great Barrier Reef with its immense Grand Canal, she'd spent a lot of time on all sorts of boats and found it great fun.

"You'll love *Sea Change,*" he said, knowing she would.

"I expect you've taken Amelia out on it?" She bestowed a swift glance on him.

"Not on *Sea Change,* no."

"Good."

He went below, sliding a quick comb through his

hair before changing. There was no other boat in their general vicinity. They had this whole place to themselves.

By the time Keefe returned to the saloon, Jewel had lunch all arranged. She'd even opened the wine, finding an ice bucket inside a cupboard in the streamlined galley.

"Okay, then, sit down." She kept her voice and expression calm. She was determined not to give much away. She'd always been in control of herself, of her male friends. Until now.

This was such a beautiful place. So lonely—no, not *lonely,* it was too bright, too sunlit for that, but alone. It might have been a lost world. She was in love with this man and she'd never felt less secure. Maybe that was what made things difficult about loving, she thought. The loss of self. The almost reluctant passing over of one's heart. Once given, she knew she'd never get hers back.

"What are you so serious about all of a sudden?" he asked, his brilliant eyes perceptive, almost reading her mind.

"I'm fighting something," she confessed.

"Could it be fear of me?"

"Something like that." She delicately licked at wine on her lips. "You're a remarkably unsettling person."

"I thought we were having a wonderful time."

"We are. Perhaps that's the trouble. These sandwiches are really good." She bit into one. "Here—" She passed him the plate.

"Thank you." He let his eyes roam over her. Her hair was so glittery it was casting a gilded veil over her skin. He felt if he touched her now, he wouldn't be able to stop himself from making love to her.

They ate slowly and quietly, in apparent harmony, both of them beset by a sun- and sea-drugged excitement. Both of them continually on edge.

Afterward they took the few dishes to the galley, where Jewel insisted on washing them up and putting them away. The galley, indeed the whole fifty-footer, seemed too small for both of them. Finally, she polished a couple of glossy red apples and took them to where he was sitting, looking out at the ever-changing colors of the water. From cobalt to the shallow lulls of emerald with a little amethyst mixed in.

"Want one?" She passed him an apple playfully, having taken a single crisp bite.

"Don't tempt me, Eve." His vibrant voice suddenly altered.

"It was an innocent gesture." Only half true.

"Was it? I can hear your heart pounding."

There was no way either of them could deny the tremendous sexual charge between them. Sensations curling over and over, like waves.

"If we make love, Keefe, our lives will change," she said, basking in his strong male beauty.

"They've already changed in a thousand ways," he pointed out.

"For the good? Can you say that? I never started this quest for a family. I thought I had my family. My mother, my aunt, my father who'd died at an early age. Now I have Travis and Amelia staring at me like I've smashed their world to pieces simply by appearing. Then, there's *you*." Momentarily she closed her eyes. "Whatever's happened between us, it's happened too fast."

A breeze ruffled his hair, pushed that lock onto his forehead.

"You want to fight it. Is that what you want?"

"I *want* to." It should have sounded final. It didn't.

"Is that a yes?" A crooked smile.

It shook her so much she thought she'd lost the ability to breathe. Her whole body felt weak, and she pressed back against the cream-colored leather upholstery. "Don't do this to me, Keefe," she begged.

"Me?" He paused for a moment, then moved to support her. "I just need to kiss you." He turned her face to him. "I could abandon myself to you, to your whole body."

He opened her mouth with his own. "Let's go and make love and the rest be damned," he urged, aware of the faint shaking in his arms, his hammering pulse. He had never felt such an overwhelming need for sex. Not just blind sex. He wanted to merge himself with this woman with the thick golden hair and skin that tasted of honeyed nectar and sea salt.

She exposed him, his masculinity, to the point that he felt adrift and unprotected in an ocean of elemental power.

"You want this, Jewel?" he whispered, staring down at her, her every feature so revealing of the turbulence within her.

A hushed "yes," a whisper of breath against his cheek.

They rose together, he keeping his arms around her, bodies connected, both of them lost to the tyranny of passion.

EVERYTHING CHANGED for Thea Bishop in the days that followed.

Alone in the old colonial the next week, with Judith at her craft shop in town, and the kettle bubbling in the kitchen, Thea went hesitantly to the front door to answer the chimes. Afterward, when she'd had time to absorb all that had happened, she wondered why she hadn't fainted dead away.

Fully expecting to see their neighbor or perhaps their handyman, Tom, she found herself looking into a face she'd never expected to see again. A face that even after all these years, she knew as well as her own.

"Thea, little Thea," the man said in deep cultured tones. "Don't be frightened. Don't run away. I know you haven't been well, or happy. It's all my fault. I can never forgive myself but I'm here to beg forgiveness of you."

Her voice when it came was dry and cracking, like an old woman's. "Travis."

"Such a job to track you down." The handsome face was working with emotion. "Eugenie wouldn't tell me."

"This is a dream, isn't it?" Thea asked. "I'm asleep."

"Not a dream. I wanted to come to you and I have. Will you let me in?"

"For what reason, Travis?" she asked faintly. He hardly looked twenty years older, if anything, he was more handsome, more substantial, his shoulders beneath his light jacket broad and well-set. The only real giveaway was the silver wings in his hair, and even they seemed distinguished rather than a sign of age.

"Don't look at me like that, my dear," he begged. "I'm not an apparition. I want to say I'm sorry. So sorry. Why did you never tell me about your daughter?"

She felt so dizzy she had to clutch at the door. "But Travis, you didn't want to know. You had to return to your wife, your child, your marriage. Your father was a very important man.''

''My God, I've regretted it all the days of my life,'' he groaned. ''Please, Thea, can't I come in? I've had such a trek. Why, oh why, have you buried yourself in this godforsaken wilderness? It must be alive with snakes.''

''There are snakes, Travis. We see them from time to time but they don't bother us. This is my home. My refuge for the past twenty years. Come in.'' She moved away from the door, staggered a little, and just as he used to, he gathered her up in his arms, carrying her into the house.

''Oh, Travis!'' She directed her gaze upward to his handsome face. After the years of agony, nothing had changed at all.

''Shh! Be still, my little love,'' he cajoled. He didn't understand why she should forgive him, given the magnitude of his sin, but he knew in his heart that she already had. It made him doubly aware of the great wrong he had done her.

He set her down in a deep chintz-covered sofa that had seen far better days, coming to sit beside her, taking her soft hands. She was every bit as pretty as she used to be. That lovely innocence, the sweet vulnerability. Thea, his Sleeping Princess. Her body, though still tantalizing through the funny old-fashioned dress she wore, was almost childlike in its slenderness. Eugenie had nothing of her mother in her. Eugenie was the dominant female, like his own mother. He liked women who played the passive role, like Thea.

''Now tell me, dearest girl,'' he whispered, gazing down into her small face framed by the same glossy mane of curly dark hair, ''how I can possibly make amends. I'm ready to do anything, *anything*,'' he repeated, genuinely believing it, ''to return you to a full life. I know what's best for you. Listen to me. Trust me.'' He took her into his arms as she began to cry.

WHEN JUDITH RETURNED HOME that evening to find the man who'd been the cause of so much pain and unhappiness sitting like a lord in their living room, with Thea literally at his feet on a velvet stool, she did something she hadn't done in a long while. She erupted like a small volcano.

''I don't believe this!'' she screamed, staring incredulously from her middle-aged-going-on-teenage sister to the wickedly impressive roué who was staring back at her as though at any moment she'd sail around the room on a broomstick. ''We've had twenty years of hell! Sheer hell, with *you,* Thea, not giving a tinker's damn about your daughter, always holding your head in despair. And now you're sitting like a handmaiden at this man's feet. It defies *belief.* How could you possibly have the gall to come here, Copeland? And without permission. This is as much my home as Thea's. Good God, man, you've given me legitimate reason for murder!''

At that, Thea and Travis shot up, Copeland taking Thea's hand as though they were about to exchange marriage vows before execution. Though it killed him to apologize to this truly dreadful woman who reminded him of Sonia, he endeavored to do so.

''Please, Judith—may I call you Judith?'' he appealed to her, using all the charm that had helped him out of many a bad situation in the past. ''No one could be more ashamed of my actions years ago than I am. Ashamed because I took advantage of Thea's vulnerability. But I never regretted our short time together. I say this before God. Thea is the only woman I have ever loved.''

"Oh, yeah?" Judith gave him a cold scathing glance. "It's a wonder the good Lord doesn't strike you dead. I've had it on excellent authority that your life's been one affair after another.''

"None of which touched my heart,'' Travis continued, while Thea looked on in faint bewilderment, as though she'd never heard any of this before. "Only Thea managed to do that,'' Travis said in the grip of repentance. "This is the first time we've been together in twenty years and it's been a marvelously healing experience. I understand your shock at my coming here, Judith. It may seem incomprehensible, but I had to act. My mother is determined to bring Eugenie into the family.''

Instantly Judith's green eyes narrowed. "Ah, I figured there was an angle. You mean there's a conflict of interests. Right? You don't want Jewel?''

"Of course I want her,'' Travis stated with a heartfelt expression. "What must you think of me?''

"Why worry about my opinion?'' Judith said sternly. "It was Thea who was the victim. Thea and poor tragic Steven Bishop, whom you've failed to even mention. You're a weak, vain man, Travis Copeland, with no self-discipline whatsoever.''

Thea couldn't stand that; she stirred restlessly, tugging at her ankle-length muslin skirt. "Oh please, Judith, have some mercy,'' she pleaded, not wanting to see the man she'd once been so desperately in love with stripped of his pride. "Travis is not the same man who walked off and left me.''

"*Walked* off?'' Judith's voice soared. "I thought he

took a fast ride home in his private plane. You're a fool, Thea! It worries me that you don't seem to have learned a thing.''

This was going badly. Thea and Travis turned to stare at each other, as though one or both were waiting for a signal.

"Please, Judith, won't you sit down?'' Travis suddenly said soothingly. He'd always been known how to charm women. Well…perhaps not Sonia. "Thea and I have some news for you.''

"Yes, Jude,'' Thea chimed in promptly, looking so small and soft that most people would have hesitated to touch her in case they left a bruise. She smiled at her sister encouragingly.

"I don't think I could take your news right now,'' Judith said. "How long have you been acting crazy, Thea?'' she asked, deeply troubled.

The extraordinarily youthful-looking Thea stared back, wide-eyed. "I've never been crazy, Jude. I really haven't. I was depressed.''

Judith collapsed into a sagging armchair. If she stood a moment longer, she felt she'd lose the power of her limbs. "Has Jewel heard your news?'' she demanded. "I really can't imagine what it might be, unless you plan to run away together.''

"But that's it!'' Thea cried joyfully. She let go of Travis's hand to dash over to her sister. "It's what we both want.''

"God Almighty!'' Judith warded off her sister, pressing her hands together.

"It will solve such a lot!'' Travis came to add his pleas. "I know Thea can make me happy.''

Judith's chin shot up. "I'll settle for you making *Thea* happy, thanks very much.''

"I will, I will," he promised, as though that settled everything. "I'll take Thea to a friend of mine. She'll outfit her from head to toe and spare no expense. Thea is still a remarkably pretty woman. When she's dressed properly, with her hair cut and styled, it would be hard to find a prettier little thing."

"God!" Judith moaned, hanging her head. "Is this what you want, Thea. To be cleaned up and made presentable, just like Eliza Doolittle?"

"Why do you always put things so crudely, Jude?" Thea asked with resigned good humor. "Travis tells me he's always loved me, and I've never forgotten him."

"Aw, hell!" Judith was the picture of disgust. "I don't know what line he sold you, Thea, but he's really just thinking of himself. As usual. When Lady Copeland launches Jewel as a family member, her granddaughter, there'll be quite a scandal. I know people. They love to talk. If you and your one-time lover here decide to marry, that'll take the steam out of things. His PR people will dress it up as one of the great love stories of the century. So long as they remember to leave out Steve," she added bitterly.

"Steven loved me. I loved him. He would have wanted me to be happy." Thea lifted her small chin proudly.

"Okay! Fine. You deserve one another," Judith said, shaking her head. "Don't waste your time inviting me to the wedding. But you'd both better watch out if I discover that Jewel's suffered in any way," she muttered fiercely. "Jewel's the only one of us who matters."

Judith went to her room to put through an urgent phone call to her niece—one of many to come.

She reflected ironically that Travis Copeland might very well end up paying for his sins in taking on Thea. After all, Thea had worked hard most of her life making *them* miserable.

CHAPTER TWELVE

"IT'S QUITE POSSIBLE your mother's gone mad," Judith concluded after she'd put Jewel in the picture.

"Obviously, she knows something we don't," Jewel said, her mind reeling at Judith's news. "You really think they were in love?" She asked the question with faint optimism. It would make everything so much better.

"Let's say they had the hots for one another at the time," Judith answered, then relented swiftly on Jewel's account. "They both say so, darl. We're dealing with something outside my comprehension. I've begged your mother to give it careful thought, but that didn't do much good. She and I suppose her fiancé have gone over to dinner with—wait for it—Sheila Hungerford."

"Wh-at?" Jewel was staggered.

"I expect Thea's going to ask her to be bridesmaid," Judith said with black humor. "Sheila's an old friend, at any rate. And she doesn't gossip. I suppose she'd be a good person to have on side. While I think of it, how are you doing with Sheila's affairs?"

"The brief will be ready in about three weeks. The case will be heard in the Supreme Court, but I don't anticipate it'll come before the court in under a year. Sheila knows all this. I keep in touch with her and the boys."

"Well, it all worked out there. Good old George has disappeared."

"They'll find him when they're ready," Jewel said. "So will I. I proceeded with the assault charge."

"So you should. He asked for it. Just one thing, love. People stupid enough to commit crimes, to risk going to jail, are dangerous people."

"He's been warned off, Judith. Don't worry. It's Mama we should worry about."

"I'm done with that, sweetheart," her aunt said. "I'll never allow myself to be caught up in Thea's affairs again. Including her wedding."

"But you *have* to come," Jewel protested. How would her mother even get to the altar unaided? She'd had to be supported in everything for twenty years. "Anyway, if you don't go, I don't go. I mightn't go even if you are there. Travis Copeland hasn't made a good impression on me. I'm not anxious to have him for a father, let alone see him as Mama's husband," she said disgustedly.

"He's only got one thing going for him," Judith added in a near-cheerful tone. "He has lots and lots of money."

"Money doesn't do much good if you're desperately unhappy," Jewel said. She loved her mother even if Thea was totally unreliable.

"Maybe he's been just that," Judith suggested, as though she was thinking it over. "At the risk of sounding like a lunatic myself, I couldn't help noticing that he appears to be genuinely fond of our little Thea. He's been holding on to her, and her to him, like they're both frightened the other will disappear. Like I say, when it comes to love, I haven't got a clue. By the way, your mother rang you, but she couldn't get hold of you.''

''She could have left a message on the answering machine,'' Jewel said a little sharply. ''I never in my wildest nightmares figured that Travis Copeland would want to marry my mother, take care of her.''

''It might help shut the tabloids up,'' Judith offered cynically. ''Their little affair will be dignified by marriage. I just know I'm going to read that they were childhood sweethearts. The way he agreed so readily to go over and meet Sheila makes me think they discussed it. Sheila and the Hungerford name is part of his plan—I'm sure of it. Then there's the fact that Sheila's father was a highly valued employee of Copeland Connellan and a rich man in his own right. I swear they're thinking along those lines.''

''Maybe Mama *should* be locked up,'' Jewel said, rolling her eye expressively.

SHE HAD TO SPEAK to Keefe. Underneath, he was intensely passionate, as she'd found to her pounding excitement, while on the surface he maintained an elegantly cool, analytical and decisive mind. He just might be her means of staying sane. This was a serious quandary. Hadn't her mother been damaged enough? Perhaps that was the problem. It was her role in life to protect her mother. Like her aunt Judith, she'd come to regard it as a long-term responsibility, a personal obligation. And now her mother was planning to marry the man she'd been desperate to keep out of their lives.

It made no sense at all. Her mother, the victim, had turned to the source of her pain. For all Jewel knew, she could be going through some form of dementia. She agonized until she could get hold of Keefe. It was well after nine o'clock, but he'd already told her he'd be working late on a deal with a Southeast Asian mining syndicate. A tough deal, he'd added. In the days since they'd made such passionate, shattering love—the memory of which still gave her a rush—their relationship had deepened so dramatically, it was as though half a lifetime had passed. Indeed, the thought of him was interfering with her work. She actually wondered if Blair Skinner knew about this powerful shift in her emotions because he'd been surprisingly kind to her, not burdening her, as usual, with additional workload.

"I was just about to ring," Keefe said when he answered the phone. "Negotiations aren't proceeding as cordially as we'd hoped. I'd appreciate your input on this. Women often make better negotiators than men. More finesse, more diplomacy when dealing with difficult situations. Why don't I pick you up? We could have a late supper. Or we could arm ourselves with food and go back to my place. I badly need to see you. Touch you. Have you beside me. That's all."

"I need to talk to you, too," she said, fully aware of her own yearning. It must have sounded in her voice.

He laughed, his tone deepening. "Is it trouble?"

"*Trouble* is too soft a word."

Seconds ticked by. "I'll be there soon."

Thirty minutes later, the BMW was outside. When Jewel was seated in the car, inhaling a lungful of expensive leather and of sexy, dangerous *him,* he turned to stare at her.

"You're all right, aren't you?"

"Did you think I was pregnant?" She looked at him searchingly, and color flooded her cheeks.

"Well, if you were, I think my heart would melt."

She swallowed hard, startled by the tenderness in his voice. "Do you mean that?"

"Jewel, you're going to have the most beautiful baby in the world," he assured her. "I'd be genuinely delighted to father it."

"Then, you'll have to be very patient," she warned him. "I'm not as wild and irresponsible as all that. My mother's the wild one. Turn off the engine so you can hear this," she urged, and waited for him to do it.

"Right, fire away." He traced her lovely features with a glance, feeling no longer an observer but her lover. This was the woman who had assuaged his every hunger, his every want, his every need. He was burning to make love to her again. She seemed to be trembling, so he reached out to stroke her hair. "It can't be that bad. Obviously you're upset."

"You will be, too," she said. "Aunt Judith called tonight. Mama and Travis Copeland intend to marry."

Complete lack of interest. "Are they eloping?" The way he said it, she could tell he took it for a joke.

"How do I know?"

"Are you serious?" he demanded.

"Yes." She nodded. "Travis is up in North Queensland as we speak. Mama carried him off to Sheila Hungerford's house for dinner. Sheila is a woman of taste and discernment. Most of all, she's highly regarded in the district, even when she was living with the notorious George. Her father was—"

"Darling. I know who her father was." He began to gently massage the nape of her neck, still staring at her with his brilliant black eyes. "I don't believe this."

"That makes two of us. Three, including Aunt Judith." Jewel shuddered. "I'd rather not know what Amelia will make of it. Now my mother's in on the scam—that's how she'll see it. Not only will Amelia have to take a big cut in her eventual inheritance, possibly even her trust fund, but Mama, as Mrs. Travis Copeland, will be entitled to something, as well. Like two hundred million.''

"How come you're so accurate?'' he asked dryly. "Anyway, Travis is doing it for a reason. He's always got a reason. He wants to put a respectable spin on the whole affair.''

"I remind you that I'm the result of 'the whole affair,''' she said emotionally.

Empathy flashed through him. Empathy and an overwhelming desire. "Come back to my place,'' he urged, turning on the ignition. "We can stop at a deli down the street. They stay open until ten. I'm hungry. I haven't eaten all day. And I'm starved for *you*. God!'' It was halfway between a groan and a sigh. "When I think of the way you've changed my life...''

And I've let myself fall in love, Jewel thought.

TRAVIS COPELAND and Thea Bishop were married very quietly by a minister at the old colonial farmhouse where Thea had been born. Only family and close friends attended. Twenty people in all. Trusted people. Secrecy was understood under pain of being struck off the Copeland social list. The bride looked ravishing in a cream lace and chiffon gown reminiscent of the twenties. She wore it with panache. It suited to perfection her almost boyish figure. Her abundant dark curly hair had been expertly cut and styled, caught back at one side by a starburst of diamonds. Diamonds were at her ears, and around her throat she wore a necklace of very large, very lustrous South Sea island pearls. Her small ivory embroidered shoes were handmade. With twenty pairs of wondering eyes on her, she looked and acted as though this was the happiest day of her life. Even Travis stayed absolutely charming, every so often cuddling, kissing and touching his new bride, who smiled with newfound contentment as he tucked her into his tall, splendidly fit-for-his-age body. The happy couple were to honeymoon on a small exclusive Barrier Reef island, where the guests' privacy was so valued the staff eventually went cross-eyed from trying not to make eye contact. Or so Jewel had heard.

Jewel, as bridesmaid, wore a dress of palest pink chiffon over ivory silk, cut like a slip, the delicate fabric embroidered all over with bead-encrusted rose-pink flowers. There was no adornment in her golden mane, but an outsize pink silk rose trailing sequined ribbons was pinned to one shoulder. Judith, dramatic in her favorite emerald, had declined the position of bridesmaid, but Sheila Hungerford, who'd dropped the "Everett," stood in as matron of honor, looking very attractive in a silk dress and matching jacket the color of a good chardonnay.

Travis insisted the wedding guests be driven to the splendid Sheraton Mirage at Port Douglas for dinner and an overnight stay, to celebrate his wedding. But after joining their guests in a glass or two of champagne, husband and wife were anxious to fly out to their fabulous island so they could start their twenty-year-deferred honeymoon.

"Give me your blessing, darling," Thea whispered into Jewel's ear when it was time to leave.

"Do you really need it, Mama?" Jewel kissed her mother's sweet-smelling cheek.

"Of course I do, darling," Thea said. "I've lived for so long in so much pain."

"We *all* hurt, Mama." Jewel couldn't help pointing that out. "But all Aunt Judith and I want is for you to be happy."

"Thank you, darling." Thea's green eyes were a dazzle of tears. "I'm not so sure about Jude. I think she's cloaking a lot of anger behind the bright smile and brittle manner."

"You couldn't have managed without her." Jewel, loyal to Aunt Judith, kept on smiling. "Judith's straight as an arrow."

"Travis thinks she's one tough lady."

"What woman *isn't,* who can answer back?" Jewel quipped, trying to keep it festive. "I just can't believe he's stolen you away."

"I love him," Thea said, blinking the teardrops from her long lashes. "I always did, deep in my heart."

So much for twenty years of hell, Jewel thought. She wondered how her mother had the gall to say it. This wasn't the day to remind her mother of Steve Bishop, either.

"What will you do now, Judith?" Sheila Hungerford asked later when the happy couple had flown away.

Judith slapped a palm down on the dining room table, laughing shortly. "I may catch up with my own life," she said.

THE NEWS HAD SCARCELY BROKEN that Travis Copeland had secretly married a woman from his youth he'd never forgotten and who had borne him a child, when Davina decided to launch Jewel upon society as Travis's daughter and her grandchild. The great occasion—so what if Davina and Thea were the only ones to see it that way?—was to be in the form of a masquerade, the guests' costumes to depict legendary characters from literature. Chaucer to Capote and all stops in between. Three hundred invitations had been sent out. Not a single soul declined, including Travis Copeland's first wife, Sonia, who was currently expecting a marriage proposal from a distinguished career diplomat touted for an important overseas posting.

"Ever want to go back to where you were?" Blair Skinner, who was on the invitation list, asked Jewel one morning when she turned over the Hungerford brief and several others before they were sent to counsel.

"Just about every day," Jewel confessed. She was feeling depressed, plagued by myriad doubts and on the receiving end of Amelia's seething hostility.

"Sorry, dear, you're stuck with it. I suppose it's only a matter of time before you change your name to Copeland—or is that Connellan?" Skinner asked slyly.

"Forget it, Blair. I'm not telling." She waved him away.

"I'll bet your half sister, Amelia, is livid about your liaison with her ex-boyfriend."

"She sure isn't happy about it," Jewel said, "although he never cared for her in *that* way."

"I suppose I have to believe it, dear, if you tell me so," Skinner responded archly.

"All right, they went to the movies together. All I know is that nothing is ever as it seems. Anyway, I've got something that's really going to shock you."

"Really? What?" At the door, he turned back, an avid look on his face.

"My mother and f-father—" she could hear herself stammer "—are blissfully happy."

A bemused expression crossed his face. "How very strange."

"I knew you'd be interested."

"My goodness, yes. I never cease to be amazed at how little we humans know ourselves. Especially when we're talking about matters of the heart. I say," he said wistfully, "wouldn't it be nice if Travis turned into a nice guy under your mother's influence?"

"Do you actually think we could be so lucky?" Jewel was absolutely convinced it was never going to happen. Not to her, anyway. Her mother, who had acted irrationally for years, was the only one Travis Copeland wanted to care for.

His wife, not his daughters...

IF THERE WERE BIGGER PARTIES around the country, none got more media attention than the masquerade to be given by Lady Copeland at the family's riverside mansion. The city's social elite were expected to vie for the spotlight in an extravaganza of costumes. The women naturally would want to look their most beautiful. There was a lot of speculation about Natashas, Laras, Scarletts, Becky Sharpes, plus heroines from Jane Austin, Edith Wharton, perhaps Du Maurier's Rebecca, and the expected contingent of Shakespearean heroines and various Greek and Roman goddesses. A few women had apparently misunderstood; their costumes, already delivered, depicted historical figures like Cleopatra, Elizabeth I and Marie Antoinette.

Jewel had solved her problem with relatively little bother or expense. A couturier friend had run up a simple white toga that actually looked very good when she tried it on. The fabric was particularly soft and supple. With her hair swept off her face, her features rather than her golden mane demanded attention. She skillfully used makeup to accentuate her eyes, full mouth, skin and bone structure. A gleaming rhinestone-encrusted gold band encircled her head in classical Greek style—she'd had to let her hairdresser do it that morning—allowing her to call herself Helen of Troy.

Thirty minutes before the revellers were due to arrive, she was staring at herself in the mirror of her guest room, turning this way and that, when her grandmother called through the door.

"Open up, darling. It's only me."

Outside, Davina stood in her four-thousand-dollar gown of midnight-blue silk taffeta and lace, a dazzling diamond choker around her throat, diamond pendants at her ears, rows of pearls cascading down her front, her hair dressed in a high roll and supplemented with a double chignon at the nape—Oscar Wilde's Lady Bracken.

"You look fantastic," Jewel said, falling back to admire.

"I love playacting." Davina laughed. "'Is this the face that launched a thousand ships and burnt the topless towers of Ilium?'" she asked, studying Jewel with great pleasure.

"Either that, or I've just come from the bath. You don't think it's too simple? I didn't have the time for the Lady of the Camellias."

"You look wonderful!" Davina said. "So beautiful you're not quite human."

"My God, I am human!" Jewel protested, turning back to the mirror.

"Of course you are. That's what they used to say about me." Davina smiled. "Beauty can be a load to carry. It can be deeply resented, intimidating to some. But you have a lot of warmth in your face. You aren't the ice queen I used to be."

"Your life hasn't been happy, has it, Grandma?" Jewel said, looking into her grandmother's blue eyes.

"Not really, darling, but things have changed since you came into it." Davina made a visible effort to brighten. "Your father's the Great Gatsby, by the way. Needless to say, your mother's Daisy. She looks extremely appealing in her costume, and Travis has decked her out in very expensive jewelry."

"Oh, well, one of us had to get some," Jewel quipped, not really caring.

"Jewelry wouldn't suit the classical perfection of that gown," Davina said. "Otherwise, I'd go get you a few pieces. It's a superb cut."

"Of course it is. Daniel's very good." Jewel smoothed the toga over her hips. "And what's Amelia wearing? She wouldn't tell me."

Davina's expression was both sad and puzzled. "I'm not actually sure, dear. I only know she's got on a great deal of makeup and a magnificent ruby-red period costume with a big crinoline skirt and very little bodice. She doesn't look like herself at all."

"I wish she was happier about things," Jewel lamented. "The marriage has put a lot of pressure on her. She was her father's great favorite, the 'woman' in his life. Now Mama's completely taken over that role. Amelia must be feeling it."

"Well, she is." Davina could scarcely deny it. "But Travis is entitled to a life. I think your mother's going to demonstrate, not only now but in the future, that she can keep him happy."

"Such is the power of love," Jewel said, shrugging ironically. "My mother tortured herself for years. Travis stopped all that just by turning up at her door.

It's going to take time for Aunt Judith and me to come to terms with that.''

"But Judith's feeling better isn't she, dear?"

Davina and Judith had met at the wedding, taking an instant liking to each other. In fact, over the past week, with Judith in Brisbane for the masquerade, they'd become real friends. It had even been suggested that Judith sell the farmhouse—Thea had gone on record as saying she wouldn't take her share, something Judith didn't feel at all guilty about. Judith could then come and live in Brisbane to be near her sister and niece. Davina had promised Judith she'd find just the place.

Now Jewel agreed. "Yes, she is feeling better, and she deserves to. I would've had no life without Aunt Judith. Both of us are still worried about Mama. I know she seems radiant but I don't think she could face any more mental stress. It's crucial that Travis treat her well.''

"Do you know, my dear, I think he will," Davina said not only to comfort her granddaughter but because she believed it. "In his own way, Travis has had a frustrating life. Anyway, I'm not concerned with Travis and Thea at the moment. It's you. This is *your* night. Travis and Thea have made their lives. You have a future, and I won't die happy unless I set things right. I've already told Travis and Amelia that I intend to change my will. It'll be taken care of this coming week. You will become one of the major beneficiaries, as you should be.''

Jewel drew a deep, steadying breath. "Grandma, all I've wanted is to have you really care for me. Life is meaningless without family and love.''

"Well, my darling—" Davina took Jewel into her

arms and gently kissed her cheek "—I love you. I love you so much it makes me dizzy. Sometimes I think you're my own little girl come back to me, but of course you're a completely separate person. Your own person. My granddaughter." She sighed. "Very few of us can go through life without traumas. Some of them terrible. Money can't stop people from dying."

"Why are we talking about dying?" Jewel asked her grandmother in alarm.

"I'm not dying, darling." Davina shook her head. "I'm just speaking about the way life is. Whatever is ahead for you—and I wish you all the good things in life—you won't want for money. That's all I wanted to say. Your share will be equal to Amelia's. I have some jewelry, too, that I want you to have. You're entitled to a little extra. I'd also like to reward Judith, although I know she wouldn't hear of it. I'm good at getting around people, however. Both of you had a long struggle. It's not going to continue. Now, my darling, I must be off. Our guests will be arriving soon, and we all have to stand in the receiving line. What's Keefe coming as?" she asked as she moved in regal fashion to the door.

"There's another one who wouldn't tell me." Jewel smiled. "He'd be devastating as Rhett Butler."

"But of course! *That's* who Amelia is," Davina exclaimed. "Scarlett O'Hara. One usually sees the green-and-white costume that opened the film. It's the sensual red one she wears when Rhett makes her confront Melanie. I should've guessed."

"I hope things go well, Grandma," Jewel said. "People can be awful."

"Not in my house," Davina said, fine features tightening. "Not to me or mine. I'm honored to have you for a granddaughter, Jewel. I'm even happy about your mother. She's taken over the burden of Travis. Anyway, this is going to be a marvelous night. A night to remember.''

Amen.

AMELIA WAS GLIDING DOWN to the hallway in her blood-red gown, when Jewel stepped out of her room. It was impossible for either of the women to ignore the other, but Jewel was convinced Amelia was about to try.

"Hello there, Amelia. You look magnificent,'' she called. "I hope you've got your Southern accent down pat?'' Jewel moved toward her half sister smilingly, hoping that tonight of all nights Amelia would relent her harsh stand.

"And what are *we?*'' Amelia retorted, her dark eyes whipping over Jewel's white-clad figure and classic gold sandals. "A vestal virgin?''

"Just the opposite,'' Jewel said, determined to be pleasant. "I'm supposed to be Helen of Troy.''

"Ah yes, the most beautiful woman in the world. How vain!'' Amelia said darkly.

"Don't you ever let up?'' Jewel sighed. "I'm not in the least vain. I just didn't have the time or money to go in for a more elaborate costume.''

"Money.'' Amelia's brows furrowed slightly. "But that won't be a problem for long. I understand that by this time next week, you'll be an heiress.''

"Being an heiress hasn't helped you.'' Jewel didn't delight in saying it.

"I'd advise you, Ms. Integrity, not to cross me,'' Amelia responded, her expression the spitting image of one of her father's.

"I'm not trying to cross you, Amelia. I wish you could understand that. The last thing I want to do is make you unhappy."

"Unhappy! Dear God!" Amelia muttered. "There's no way I'm ever going to accept you or your silly little mother. God, she's not even fully grown, just an itsy-bitsy flower child. I don't know how Father could be remotely attracted to her."

"Actually he *was,* years ago. And just about everyone else likes having her around. I understand your feelings, Amelia. So does Mama. But you'll get married, too. You'll have your own life."

"You enjoy mocking me," Amelia cried. "You've done everything in your power to take Keefe from me. Stabbing me in the back. But then, Helen of Troy was a deceitful woman driven by passion into betraying her family."

"Actually, most writers regard her as the innocent victim of her own beauty," Jewel said. "And I haven't taken Keefe from you, Amelia. But I can't deny that our relationship has deepened."

"You're sleeping with him," Amelia accused her. "I *begged* you to leave him alone. Your behavior's been monstrous!"

"Amelia, you're shouting," Jewel warned her, fearing Amelia would be overheard. "Grandma is so looking forward to tonight. Please don't upset her. You'd only enrage your father. He doesn't want any trouble in the house."

"Father will never love you," Amelia pointed out vengefully, glaring at her half sister.

"I can live with that." Jewel shrugged. "Anyway, I had a father. A great father. His name was Steven

Bishop. But I might get to love *your* father a little if he makes my mother happy.''

''*Your* mother!'' Amelia almost spat the words. ''*My* mother is a lady. I despise yours.''

''I wouldn't make that obvious to your father,'' Jewel said. ''He just might take a different view of you. We have to go downstairs, Amelia. Please compose yourself. People will be arriving.''

''You go ahead,'' Amelia ordered, quaking in her outrage. ''I want no part of you.''

''Then, that's your loss.'' Jewel moved away, trying to leave bitterness behind. ''We could've been friends.''

But never with Keefe between them.

BY TEN O'CLOCK, the gala was in full swing. Round white-clothed tables had been arranged throughout the solarium and the rear terraces, the floodlit gardens and the aquamarine swimming pool. Glorious floral arrangements were placed strategically, and hundreds of potted cymbidium orchids had been brought in to grace the house. The huge billiard room had been cleared of its furnishings, transformed into a ballroom where dancers whirled in the brilliant glow of antique bronze-and-glass chandeliers.

Everyone appeared to be having a wonderful time, having taken in their stride Travis Copeland's new bride, so youthful and fetching in her exquisite pale-green chiffon gown—and did you see those emeralds? The near-unanimous verdict was that she was entirely socially acceptable, indeed, several society matrons planned on inviting her to their homes in the immediate future. And the daughter! After all the gossip and its implications, Jewel was considered a huge success, not

to mention the very image of dear Davina. No wonder
Amelia seemed to have her nose well and truly out of
joint. She'd get over it, though. God knows, there was
enough money to go around. The motto of the evening
soon became *Enjoy every minute.* Especially the sumptuous supper that was to come. Most of the guests had
taken a peek at the delectable dishes being brought in.
Davina Copeland had always been famous for the high
quality of her food and drink. Despite the excellence
of domestic champagne-style wines, the guests were
more than happy to drink Moët all night.

Keefe, who'd had a lot of work on his agenda, had
decided to come as James Bond. He wore an excellent
dinner suit, already in his closet, and easily acquired
from his mother's garden the red carnation dictated by
the early Sean Connery movies. He already had the
height, the dark hair, the dark eyes and the tan. It was
the easy way out, but he'd never been one for fancy
dress. The only concession he made was to slick back
his hair, Connery fashion.

It was to prove a decision that caused many a
woman's heart to flutter. They found themselves continually watching him in the crowd. He had such enormous style. Not a man there to compare with him, and
many were powerful and handsome.

Fully realizing how unpredictable Amelia might be
in her present mood, Jewel decided the smart thing to
do was adopt an easy attitude with Keefe, dancing with
almost every man who beat a path to partner her. Keefe
noticed. He could scarcely help it, but he divined without too much trouble that Amelia's attitude was the
cause of Jewel's casual manner. Amelia, in fact, was
bothering him to distraction, following him from room
to room, leaning on his arm at every opportunity, play-

ing to an audience of three hundred. *She* was the one
Keefe Connellan was in love with, or so she meant to
proclaim. Not the dazzling blonde with her grandmother's extraordinary aura. Amelia was the woman in
his life. Or would be if only he'd come to his senses.

Finally Keefe had had enough. He took Amelia's
elbow quietly and drew her out onto the terrace, walking some distance along so their voices wouldn't carry.

"Amelia, what's up?" he asked, not wanting to hurt
her but not wanting her to follow him around, either.
It was becoming impossible to capture a moment with
Jewel, the object, the sum total of his passion. The
moment he'd laid eyes on her in her white gown, her
beautiful hair bound Grecian-style, he'd felt such an
assault of sexual pleasure he thought it must've been
apparent to everyone massed in the entrance hall. Judg-
ing by the knowing smile on his mother's face, his
feelings were transparent.

Now Amelia raised her dark eyes to his look of
feigned bewilderment. "I don't understand, Keefe.
What do you mean?"

"Oh, cut the act. You do understand." He tried unsuccessfully to keep the hard impatience out of his
voice. He'd known Amelia all her life; he did care for
her. But not in the way she wanted. Now he had to
explain. "You've been twining yourself around me all
night. You should be off enjoying yourself. You're giving out entirely the wrong message. Surely you realize
that?"

Here she grasped his hand, her voice impassioned.
"Keefe, I love you."

His anger died. "And I love you, Amelia. But as a
friend."

"You slept with me," she burst out.

His face turned intimidating. "Keep your voice down," he told her sternly. "When did I make love to you? Years ago. God knows, it was all a mistake."

"A *mistake*. How cruelly put."

"Amelia, I don't want to be cruel, but there's danger in your obsession. You can't cause a scene."

"You're in love with Jewel," she accused him flatly.

"Jewel has opened my eyes to so much." He could scarcely tell her Jewel was the image of his heart's desire.

"She'll bring you no happiness," Amelia warned, her dark eyes glittering.

"You know you're acting like a bad loser. That's what it amounts to. I've tried many times to let you down lightly, but it didn't work."

"If you don't love me, I'll *die*," she said through clenched teeth.

"Oh, rubbish." Keefe was disgusted. "Honest to God, Amelia, sometimes you sound insane."

"I'll destroy her," she threatened. "I'll destroy every chance the two of you have at happiness."

Keefe stiffened, reached out and held her arms. "Cause Jewel any harm and you'll answer to me. Understood?"

But Amelia, hysterical in her efforts to connect with him, threw herself forward and kissed his mouth. That beautiful cruel mouth. There was no one for her but Keefe. No one. No future. To lose him would be intolerable. To lose him to her half sister, a defeat she couldn't live with. There had been too many defeats already.

JEWEL WAS WEIGHTED DOWN by her own need to be with Keefe, despite her half sister's unreasonable demands, and she finally went in search of him. Her passage through the main reception rooms was marked by frequent stops as guests went out of their way to show their approval and acceptance. Her rise from nowhere to the top of the social tree was what fairy tales were made of, after all.

Keefe was nowhere to be seen. That left only the length of the rear terrace. Guests in all manner of costumes—including, for some reason, a plethora of the ghastly Hannibal Lector—were gathered outside the great ceiling-high doors, but just as she was about to go back inside she caught sight of Amelia's darkly glowing red gown.

As her eyes adjusted to the dimmer light, she realized Keefe was with her. They appeared to be caught up in a wild clamor of conversation. She couldn't hear a word but intuitively knew it was profoundly confrontational. Their public kiss came next. The classic ploy. Planned in advance. It could have come straight out of a romance novel. No expression of affection, but a greedy, gloating, defiant statement. On Amelia's part. Jewel wasn't such a fool she didn't know that. She'd read the books, seen the movies. The only hitch was that Keefe wasn't fighting it the way he should. *Was* he? It was a long kiss. Three thundering heartbeats. No hint of censure or revulsion there. Cooperation aplenty. Most men regarded kissing women as an extremely pleasant pastime. Few felt a sense of guilt; they believed it their right. However, Jewel spared that fact little thought. She focused on finding out exactly what was going on. Her own half sister! Shameless hussy!

Another idea struck her. Was it possible that Keefe, as a Connellan, wanted *both* Copeland sisters to belong to him? It might just be bizarre enough for him to find it exciting. Even as she thought it, she had to reject the idea.

In her cloud-white gown, Jewel sailed down the terrace toward them, prepared to confront them directly. She had no intention of creating a scene; she simply wanted to set the situation straight. Her mother had been the victim of an unscrupulous man—even if he'd married her twenty hellish years later. Jewel's life was going to be different. Let the rapture depart if it had to. Her progress, noticed by everyone on the terrace, provoked a near-ecstasy of anticipation. Most of the guests had seen that impassioned kiss. Most of them secretly thought Amelia Copeland a cold bitch. For all her polished good looks, she was perceived to be strangely lacking in sexuality. Now *this!*

Jewel's eyes when she directed them at Keefe were ablaze with blue light. She looked stunning, imperious....

"May I speak to you, Keefe?" Her voice was subdued, but it came out a little too much like a command. He could just walk away.

"Why don't you leave us alone," Amelia cried, flooded with jealousy. "Get out." The words spilled hoarsely from her throat. "I'm the only one who can make Keefe happy. The only one. All *you* can offer—"

"Be quiet, Amelia." Keefe's voice was filled with muted fury. "Why don't I take you upstairs?" he suggested, handsome face taut. "You're not feeling well. Jewel, take her other arm."

"I don't want to touch her." Jewel had had just about enough of Amelia.

Though Amelia gasped, enraged, she didn't fight being led away. Her big moment had been exciting and frightening at the same time.

"You can let me go now." Once upstairs she struggled to be free, wondering if it wouldn't have been wiser to keep her mouth shut.

"All your life you've known how to behave. And now *this*," Keefe said, his voice so disgusted it hurt her.

"You're the whole world to me." Amelia turned to him and started to sob. "I know you better than she ever will. You've abused me, Keefe. Abused my trust. You told me you loved me." She leaned forward again to kiss him, but this time he fended her off.

"Cut it out."

"Is this true?" Jewel rounded to face him. Perhaps it was. Amelia when she was behaving herself was an extremely attractive package. Perhaps they'd shared a deep commitment.

"Of course it's true!" Amelia put a heavy hand on Jewel's shoulder. "I begged you not to come between us. Why did you do it?"

From nowhere, Aunt Judith appeared, a mesmerizing figure as Miss Havisham, her wealth of dark curly hair realistically frosted with silver and what appeared to be cobwebs, her green eyes heavily mascaraed, aglitter. "What's up, sweetie?" She looked quickly at her niece. "Everything okay up here?" Judith's antennae, honed to perfection over the Thea years, swiftly summed up the situation. A frozen tableau—the impossibly snobbish Amelia in a magnificent sexy gown that didn't suit her, Keefe Connellan who made even her poor old battered heart beat a little faster, and her beloved Jewel, whose lovely face had paled to the snow-white of her toga.

"Who asked you here?" Amelia responded with a rudeness Judith didn't regard well.

"Your grandmother, actually," Judith shot back, a power to be reckoned with. She gave Amelia a head-to-toe inspection. "You might tell me why, with a grandmother like that, you've got so few manners."

Amelia stared at her, momentarily speechless. Something about Judith instantly stripped all defiance away. She was no longer the self-assured heiress. She was a young woman tottering on her feet. "What is it you want?" she asked more agreeably.

"I've spent a lifetime looking after my niece's interests," Judith informed her grandly. "As for you, young lady, it seems one of the guests has had a little chat with your father. Apparently you've been drinking quite a bit."

"Like a fish," said Keefe, who found Judith's presence bracing. "I've just suggested to Amelia she lie down for a while."

"Rather lie down than fall down," Judith commented, not unsympathetically. "Why don't you and Jewel return to the party, Keefe?" she said. "I'm sure Travis will be up here in a moment. I'll keep an eye on Amelia. That way I can get between her and her father."

"Has someone *really* spoken to him?" Amelia nervously bit her lip. "Or is every word you say a lie?"

"Well, you'd know about lying." Keefe turned away, looking utterly fed up.

"I rarely lie, my girl," Judith said, looking decidedly formidable. "Maybe your father will forgive you. Anyone can overindulge."

"I haven't had *that* much." Amelia shook her head, feeling suddenly exceedingly foolish and hugging her body fearfully.

"Why don't we pop along to your room," Judith

murmured, sounding genuinely kind. She took Amelia's arm. "Don't worry—I'll stay close. I've never yet met the man to intimidate me."

"Isn't that the truth!" Jewel gave her aunt a grateful smile.

A moment more, then they heard footsteps along the corridor. From the heavy tread, a man's footsteps.

"Wonderful. That'll be Travis," Keefe said, hastily throwing open a door and drawing Jewel inside. "Such dreadful people, the Copelands," he groaned.

"Are you including me?" Jewel spoke into the darkness, intoxicated by his very touch. *Possessed.* She didn't want to be. Not yet. There were nagging doubts in her mind.

"Of course not." He leaned close to her, licked her earlobe with the tip of his tongue, igniting her flesh.

"What room are we in?" she asked, so close to him it was no more than a breath.

"I've no idea." He pulled her back against him, slowing caressing her breasts. "But I'm not going to risk turning on the light. God, I've missed you, missed you." This through clenched teeth. "You've been keeping yourself from me all night."

"Amelia is suffering." She said it as though it was his fault. And hers.

"Let her suffer," Keefe answered almost ferociously. He was still disgusted with Amelia's Academy Award–winning performance. "She needs to get her life sorted out." His hand fell to Jewel's hips, gripping them with the urgency of his hunger.

"Did you ever love her?" Jewel pivoted in his arms, putting her hands against his chest to fend him off.

His frustration was unrestrained. "For the last time—we had a brief, ill-advised affair. I don't want to sound like an utter cad, but it left me with the feeling that I'd been trapped.''

"So you dumped her?''

"You wanted me to go ahead and marry her?'' he challenged, lowering his head to barely kiss her. A warning.

"Might you at some stage want to dump me?'' she asked with a heavy heart.

"Only if you pushed me into it by constantly talking about Amelia,'' he answered crisply. "Amelia is my friend. Maybe she's not even that anymore. I told her many times it was over, but she refused to listen. It's all so Goddamn boring. Amelia's trying to sell you quite a story. I'm surprised she hasn't offered to show you an intimate video.'' Now his voice was caustic.

"The affair must have been fairly intense to cause so much misery,'' Jewel persisted, not knowing where this was leading. Maybe a first-class argument.

"Actually, Amelia moved through it like a somnam-bulist,'' he said. "You don't know what you're dealing with here. There's a kind of paradox to Amelia. She's passionate with words, but she might as well have been Joan of Arc in a full suit of armor in bed.''

Her breath was unsteady in her throat, her nipples drawn to painful peaks by his ministrations.

"Not like you. Never like you.'' Now he kissed her. "What do you want me to do, go down on my knees?'' He did so pressing his face against her body, his arms encircling her hips, drawing her to him.

"Keefe!'' Flames crackled and burned.

"You're beautiful. So beautiful!'' Slowly he stood up, still holding her, bringing his lips to the base of her throat. "You feel like silk.'' He moved his mouth over hers, causing a great surge of emotion. "I want you so badly. Feel me. I'm hard with it.'' There was a sharp catch in his breath.

She couldn't stop her hand from sliding down, her whole body trembling as she curved her hand over him.

"I want to fill you with my need." He withdrew his mouth from hers to look into her eyes. "I want to make love to you for a thousand years. You have to come home with me tonight, my Jewel."

Everything in her was rising to him like sap to a tree, when suddenly, without warning, the door opened and the light in the room flashed on, exposing paneled walls, a bar, deep armchairs and enough electronic equipment to blow half the fuses in the city. Travis Copeland was staring at them with such disapproval that he might have caught them rolling madly around a bed, stark naked, disgorging frenzied cries.

"When it pleases you," he said icily, as though he had a bishop's miter on his head, "you might come downstairs. I have to tell you, Keefe, you've upset Amelia terribly."

"You're one to talk," Keefe drawled, in no way impressed.

"I see you've transferred your affections to my other daughter." Travis looked at the wordless Jewel.

"I don't know how it's any of your business, Travis. Your attitude toward Jewel could hardly be called fatherly."

"She is nevertheless my daughter," Travis said. "What I'm not sure of is *your* strategy." With that he stalked off, pointedly leaving the door open.

"I have a feeling that, given the opportunity, both Travis and Amelia would have made terrific actors," Keefe said. "They seem to be able to take on any role at will. Glenn Close wasn't half as menacing as Amelia. Now Travis is *your father*. The man destined to give you away. What a thought!''

"No one is giving me away," Jewel snapped, one moment overwhelmed by passion, the next perversely hostile. "As far as I can see, it's difficult to believe a single thing any man says."

HE'D BEEN FOLLOWING HER for weeks, watching, waiting. He knew where she lived. He knew where she worked. He knew her daily schedule—what time she got up, what time she left for work, what time she left her office building in the evening. He knew about her affair with Keefe Connellan. He knew they slept together. Most of all, he knew that her grandmother, the high and mighty Lady Davina Copeland, had received her into the family. He knew all about the gala masquerade at the Copeland mansion, thrown in her honor. He'd seen the photograph of her with her grandmother in that morning's paper.

Today he'd tracked her to the Copeland mansion where he supposed she might stay for the night or, he fervently hoped, go home. Connellan would probably drive here in his bloody expensive BMW. Chances were, Connellan would stay. Then again, he might not. They tended to be a bit erratic. Connellan was a high-flier who probably had plenty of early-morning calls.

At the moment he was sitting very uncomfortably in his car outside the Copeland place, lost in the shadows, hoping she and Connellan would drive out. It was past two in the morning—he'd been parked down the road since seven. He'd been watching a lot of guests finally depart. They must have had a wonderful evening, damn the lot of them. There was much laughing, many happy calls of good-night. If he had to, he'd wait until those massive wrought-iron gates finally closed. He had plenty of time on his hands now that she'd ruined his life.

Bitch! She wasn't getting away with it. He didn't care about anything anymore except getting even. He'd waited so long he was growing impatient. Ten minutes later, off guard for a moment while he lit another cigarette, he lifted his head to catch sight, first of her gleaming hair, then of her in the passenger seat of a big Mercedes. He didn't know the driver. Who the hell would? He had a damn deerstalker on his head, the fool. He couldn't see the face but it certainly wasn't Connellan. No one could miss *him,* arrogant bastard. They were a pair, those two. He gave them a few moments, then turned on the ignition and drew away from the curb.

At least she was going home.

AT ALMOST THE MOMENT Blair Skinner, with Jewel in tow, drove through the gates of the Copeland mansion, Keefe was asking Judith, who was having a very good time with a Mad Hatter aka Queen's Counsel, what had happened to Jewel. They couldn't finish the evening like this, more or less estranged and all because of bloody Amelia. He'd seen his mother off a good hour before, and Davina had long since retired.

"But she's gone, darling." Judith paused, champagne glass halfway to her mouth. "She left with that fellow she works for."

"Skinner," the Mad Hatter said. "You think there's something between them?"

"Isn't my niece gorgeous?" Judith smiled.

"I know someone else who's gorgeous." The Mad

Hatter gathered Judith up for a dance. Judith was loving it.

Keefe, however, felt on edge, under a lot of strain. He hurried to his car, fully intending to pay Jewel a visit. He *had* to straighten out the situation. Amelia got her kicks stirring things up. But Amelia had problems—and so would he if he couldn't convince Jewel she was very important to him in every way. He'd waited a long time to fall in love. It was the most wonderful feeling in the world. At the same time, it was an agony. In his corporate life he'd been trained to conceal most of his feelings. A negotiator knew better than to show his hand, but he'd made no attempt to hide his desire from Jewel.

Maybe that was it. She knew, couldn't fail to know, how much he wanted her. He had to make it abundantly clear that he loved her, too. He loved her, although at the beginning he'd struggled *not* to love her. He had expressed in every possible way his physical hunger for her; now he had to communicate his love. He was a great communicator on the job, but he'd be a failure if he couldn't convince Jewel she was the best thing ever to happen to him. He wanted to marry her. His mother had suggested he do so quickly.

"She's a wonderful girl. Someone special. Don't let her get away," Rebecca had said.

Up ahead, he saw Blair Skinner's Mercedes stopped at a red light. A small beat-up car was behind it. For some reason he noted the number plate, filing it away in his mind. The car was heading in the same direction as Skinner. Nothing unusual about that. So was he. At this time—he glanced at the clock on the dashboard—nearly two-thirty, there was very little traffic. In many ways it had been a wonderful night. A triumph for

Jewel. It wasn't just that she looked beautiful, though no one could fail to be moved by her beauty, but she was so warm, friendly and intelligent with a sense of humor that people found contagious.

What was that guy *doing?* Twenty minutes later, the question resounded in him. Skinner had stopped in front of Jewel's town house, and she got out, waving to him as he drove away. Skinner could at least have pulled around to the right side, Keefe thought. Now Jewel had to cross the road, even if it was quiet and hushed.

Keefe knew the moment before she stepped onto the pavement what was going to happen. "God Almighty!"

The guy was trying to kill her. Keefe sensed it immediately. The small car accelerated, quickly picking up speed. Startled, Jewel looked toward it, half dazzled by the high beam, an easy target caught in the spotlight. Without the slightest thought for himself, Keefe trod on the accelerator, and the BMW responded with a real burst of power, smashing into the back of the small car ahead, sending it careering off the road and plunging into a tree. Within seconds, Keefe was out of his car, running toward Jewel who was standing there in shock.

"Are you all right?" He put his face right up to hers, as if she were deaf. "Jewel? Are you all right?"

"Fine." But she shook her head. "God, this is a nightmare."

The horn of the small car was blaring. The driver's body must be pressed against it.

"Get back," Keefe ordered. "I have to move him out of there. The car could catch fire."

"Oh, Keefe, oh no!" She clutched at him with desperate urgency, but he broke away, going straight to the crashed car. Already he could hear the sound of a police siren. Natural human curiosity was drawing people in night attire onto the street.

The man was alive but his breathing was labored. His head and torso had struck the wheel. At first, because the assailant was so disheveled, Keefe didn't realize who it was. Then it struck him.

George Everett.

A long second passed as Keefe considered leaving him there. The man was an attempted murderer. But leave him to God. Leave him to the police. Keefe pulled Everett clear, although it didn't seem likely that the car would catch fire. The police siren was closer now. Everett was coming round, groaning tortured obscenities.

Keefe glanced up as a police officer approached, shining a torch. "You'd better get an ambulance," Keefe said.

"On the way. Here, let me get a look at him. Mr. Connellan, isn't it?" The policeman was staring.

Keefe nodded. "And this is George Everett. I've had dealings with him before. Tonight he attempted to run down Ms. Jewel Copeland as she went to cross the street to her town house. She's standing in front of it now. I'm ready to make a statement. You might have to wait a little while for Ms. Copeland's. She's had a tremendous shock."

"We'll take care of it, sir," the officer responded, and Keefe walked back to the woman he loved.

It was almost daylight before the street had settled. Everett's car was a write-off. Keefe's car had come off much better, but it was in no condition to drive. He'd already decided to sell it after repairs and buy another.

Not that he intended to go anywhere. He felt he could never again leave Jewel's side. At least, not until George Everett had been safely locked away. Both of them had made statements to the police. It would be all over the newspapers; no way to avoid it. No way to avoid the necessary phone calls, either. They decided Davina and his mother should be allowed to sleep. Travis took the call at the house, sounding absolutely shocked. He then asked to speak to Jewel, confounding her with a truly fatherly response.

"This is one weird night," Jewel said after she put down the phone. "Weirder and weirder. Travis sounded so...different. Like he really cared. He's going to call later to make quite sure I'm all right. He wants us both to come over to the house when we're ready."

"Just as I figured," Keefe said dryly. "You're starting to get to him."

"Did it really have to take almost getting run down? Anyway, I wouldn't be here except for you," Jewel said. "He was really going after me! Trying to kill me. Isn't that dreadful?"

"It is and he was," Keefe agreed grimly. "He'd been tailing you from the house. Probably watching you for weeks. Losing the good life has obviously turned his mind."

"It's a horrible feeling knowing someone hates you so much they want to kill you," Jewel said, deeply disturbed.

"Try to remember he's an ugly character, my darling." Keefe came to sit beside her on the sofa, drawing her into his arms. She'd taken off her white gown and freed her golden hair. Now she was wearing a pink satin robe. "We'll have to tell Sheila before she gets it from elsewhere," he murmured.

"Why didn't she see the menacing quality in him?" Jewel asked, settling her head on his shoulder with a deep sigh.

"I can guarantee he was on his best behavior until they were married." Keefe turned his mouth to kiss her hair. "Anyway, I don't want to talk. I want to hold you. I want to love you. I want to keep you safe forever. Life can be very fragile."

"It can indeed." A faint shudder ran through Jewel's body. "I love you, Keefe," she said, lifting her head to press a kiss on his jaw. "I love you with all my heart."

"Then, you'll marry me?" His dark eyes looked long and full into hers.

"No one in the world could stop me. You're my destiny. You're the one person my guardian angel handpicked for me at birth."

"And I've had you locked away inside me," Keefe responded. "I've had an image of you all my life."

"A blue-eyed blonde?" she teased, shifting in his arms so she could stare up into his face.

"Believe it or not, yes." He bent to kiss her. The kiss lingered and lingered. Finally he swept her up into his arms, carrying her through to the bedroom.

They made love for a long time. Until the terrors of the night subsided into the past. The future was what mattered. They were going to live it together.

EPILOGUE

Six months later

Mingaree Station, Southwest Queensland

SEEING THE DESERT IN FLOWER was a transcendent experience. Like a day trip to heaven. Jewel reveled in witnessing the rebirth of countless millions of wildflowers that spread for miles across the fiery red sand dunes and the dark golden spinifex plains. The vast area of the Channel country, the riverine desert, had been flooded for weeks courtesy of tropical cyclone Norman. The floodwaters from the far north of the state had poured their bounty into the great central Three River System, the Georgina, the Diamantina and Cooper's Creek, carrying liquid gold to the wild heart. It was this that ensured the survival of the magnificent desert flora.

Once the floodwaters had subsided, they'd decided to make their trip. This was the place where Jewel had been born. Where she'd lived until age six. This was a kind of rebirth for her. Rebirth and an end to all the closely guarded family secrets. She had wanted her mother to come, if only to pay homage at Steven Bishop's grave—for Thea *had* loved him, until Travis Copeland entered her life—but Thea had chosen not to resurrect the old painful memories. The past was the past. Just that. Besides, Travis—although happy for Jewel and Keefe to make the trip—had been opposed to his wife's going. He had shunned Mingaree for many years now. An excellent manager was in place. Thea these days was a happily married woman—beautifully dressed, pampered and cosseted. She adored being Mrs. Travis Copeland. Thea had assumed the role like a great actress might assume the role of some fictional heroine. Thea had always been pretty. And she was still youthful looking; Judith said it was because her sister had left all the strains of living to *them* for the past twenty years. But they both loved Thea as they might love a fey child. They had lived to protect her, and now it was Travis Copeland's job. A man who needed to be needed more than most. As Judith remarked to her wondering niece, "The world is full of bizarre people, darl. Thea and Travis are a pair."

Secure in the love of her grandmother, Jewel found she was able to cope with the rest of her family. She and her father would never exactly hit it off, which might be a good thing, since—as everyone had noticed—Amelia tended to be insanely jealous. She simply couldn't abide not being the favored daughter. Jewel and Amelia were never going to be close, dashing Jewel's hopes, but the situation had improved considerably since Amelia had a new man in her life; Greg McCall had finally prevailed. These days, Jewel's relationship with Amelia was warily cordial.

What pleased Jewel most was the fact that Judith, who had withstood so much and put her own needs far down the list, had at long last found a soulmate. Her barrister friend, with a mind as sharp as her own. They were on the brink of tying the knot, and Jewel was thrilled for her aunt. If anyone deserved to be pampered and looked after, it was Judith, not her mother. Her aunt Judith had been her tower of strength. Judith finally was to have her reward.

"I've always had a pure heart, love. That's the reason," Judith told her, grinning.

Absolutely!

As for her? Jewel was so happy in her marriage that her radiance spilled over on everyone around her. Keefe was her husband, her most perfect lover, her closest, most intimate friend. And her colleague. She had moved very comfortably into the Copeland Connellan legal department, bringing her skills with her. Keefe told her many times he was proud of her. Her husband, who held her heart in his two hands. As she held his.

It was Keefe who had arranged this trip out to Mingaree, using the company plane. The plane would return for them when they were ready to go back to Brisbane. But for now it was glorious to revisit her desert home. To lay the ghosts, to pray at the simple grave of the young man who had loved her and raised her to age six. To cover that grave with a carpet of "snow," an exquisite desert bush with pure white flowers like frangipani. Her mother had assured her she'd cared deeply for Steven. According to Thea, they'd been happy until Travis Copeland had entered her life—apparently like a cyclone. At any rate, Thea had been swept away. After twenty years of denying it she'd finally admitted to her and Judith that she'd always known Jewel wasn't Steven's child.

"Just like that!" Judith jumped up to exclaim, after Thea had contributed that monumental bit of information. "You're such a pain in the ass, Thea." Judith shook her head wonderingly, while her sister smiled back as though Judith had paid her a compliment.

Ah well, her mother and Travis had paid for their sins—Jewel constantly had to remind herself that Travis was indeed her father—and they had nothing more to fear from judgmental society.

"It's time for forgiveness and reconciliation," Judith pointed out ironically.

Mingaree was the place to do it, Jewel felt. It was her territory. She'd remembered it in her dreams. Was there any sight so splendid as the great sweeping sand hills? They ran in continuous lines some quarter of a mile apart, calling to mind the great inland sea of prehistory. The highest dunes rose to one hundred feet and more, straightening out to half that height as they ran northward. Great masses of pure clean sand, blood-red in color, heaped and carved to perfection by the trade winds that blew incessantly all year round. Now at this wondrous time, the entire landscape—so savage in drought—was mantled with the exquisite beauty of the desert flora. Many of the plants were so delicate, one would've thought they couldn't possibly survive the blazing sun—yet they thrived in their trillions.

Heart uplifted, Jewel experienced a wave of euphoria. Life was so good! A little distance away, her husband was gathering a bouquet of yellow and white paper daisies from the fiery sand.

"What have you got there?" she called to him, starting to make a track through a fantastic yellow-and-white carpet, accented by fallen mulga branches that pointed skyward like wonderful abstract sculptures.

Keefe flashed her a loving smile. "I don't know yet. Maybe a garland for your head." Holding the pretty daisies in one hand, he put his other arm around his wife, drawing her to him and kissing her golden hair. "Isn't this a magic place?" He gave a sigh of great contentment, turning his face to the peacock-blue sky. In the short time they'd been on Mingaree, he had watched the desert work its miracles. His beautiful Jewel's wounded heart had healed completely. The truth about her childhood, her true parentage, had finally been revealed; the ghosts of so many painful memories were laid to rest.

Jewel, his wife. He loved her above all else.

She raised her lovely face for his kiss. "A miracle, darling," she agreed.

The Shannon Sisters

A Trilogy by C.J. Carmichael
**The stories of three sisters from Alberta whose
lives and loves are as rocky—and grand—as the
mountains they grew up in.**

A Second-Chance Proposal
A murder, a bride-to-be left at the altar, a reunion. Is
Cathleen Shannon willing to take a second chance on
the man involved in these?

A Convenient Proposal
Kelly Shannon feels guilty about what she's done,
and Mick Mizzoni feels that he's his brother's
keeper—a volatile situation, but maybe one
with a convenient way out!

A Lasting Proposal
Maureen Shannon doesn't want risks in her life
anymore. Not after everything she's lived through. But
Jake Hartman might be proposing a sure thing....

On sale starting February 2002

Available wherever Harlequin books are sold.

HARLEQUIN®
Makes any time special ®

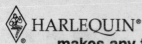

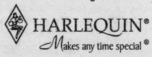

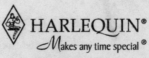